Flodden

Book 3 in the Tudor Warrior series.

By

Griff Hosker

Flodden

Published by Sword Books Ltd 2023

Copyright ©Griff Hosker First Edition

Dedication

To another new bairn come into the family, Sophia Craggs, welcome,
little one.

Contents

Historical characters

King Henry VII of England
Cardinal Wolsey
King Henry VIII of England
Queen Elizabeth (Woodville)
Jasper Tudor- Duke of Bedford and the uncle of King Henry VII
Margaret Beaufort- wife of the Earl of Derby and mother of King Henry VII
Margaret of York, the Dowager Duchess of Burgundy
Richard de la Pole- the last claimant to the Yorkist/Plantagenet crown
King Philip of Castile-Lord of the Netherlands and Duke of Burgundy
Sir Thomas Howard, - Earl of Surrey and later Duke of Norfolk
Sir Edmund Howard- His son
Sir Thomas Howard, Lord Admiral and the son of the Earl of Surrey
Lord Thomas Stanley- 1st Earl of Derby
Sir Edward Stanley, 1st Baron Monteagle-son of the 1st Earl of Derby
Sir Thomas Stanley, 2nd Earl of Derby- Son of the 1st Earl of Derby
King Louis XII of France
Sir Henry Clifford- Lord of Craven
King James IV of Scotland
Donald Dubh -Lord of the Isles
Lord Huntly- A Scottish noble
Lord Home- a Scottish Border lord
John 'Bastard' Heron of Ford- a Northumbrian knight
Sir Robert Kerr- a Scottish Border lord
Sir Marmaduke Constable – Sherriff of Yorkshire
Pope Leo X
Pope Julius II

Prologue

Ecclestone 1512

I am James of Ecclestone and no longer the wild child who had run away to join a company of billmen. I became a captain of billmen then a landowner. I served King Henry as I had served his father, the old King Henry. I had returned from my last efforts on behalf of the young king and his cardinal and I had buried my old friend Sir Edward. He had fought one battle too many and although his end was glorious it was not the end I would have chosen. He had allowed himself to become old and unfit. Both states were inevitable but Sir Edward had decided to serve the king and he died because of it. The former man at arms, elevated to the rank of knight had left his fortune to Sam, Stephen, Ned and to me. The king had given his manor of Hedingham to a new favourite but Sir Edward had been a successful warrior and he left a fortune. Added to my pay as a Captain of Billmen and my success as a farmer I was a rich man and, in a perfect world, I would have enjoyed the fruits of my labours and the good fortune which God had bestowed upon me. Soon I would have seen forty summers and that was when a man put away his billhook and spoke, instead, to old comrades in arms in the local inn. I knew that I was not destined for such a life. I had skills that the king and now the cardinal could use. I could speak French and Flemish. I could pass for a lord and, most important of all, I knew how to survive in a nest of vipers.

When I had returned it had been with the last of Sir Edward's men at arms, Ralf. He had asked if he could serve me and be trained by me. He had seen, when we had fought in the shadow of Ford Castle, that he still had much to learn. I liked him and we had room in my hall. I felt I owed Sir Edward something for, despite his end, he had been the one who had changed my fortune. Jane, my wife, was a kind soul and she enjoyed having the young warrior around. My sons thought well of him for he was not far from being a knight. A brave deed on the battlefield might result in a dubbing.

Flodden

Ralf was polite, hard-working and charming. Many of the young women in the village fluttered their eyes at him but he was also a gentleman. I was pleased that he had come to share my home.

I hoped for peace, and that seemed likely as the only prospect for war lay in France. King Henry, flattered by a pope who loved to plot, had been induced to make war on our old enemy France. There was talk of an army being mustered and sent over to Calais, now one of the last foreign territories that England possessed. I understood the lure, for victory against France could bring England new lands and the men who fought the French, treasure, land and gold. When we fought the Scots, we had little recompense. The Scottish warriors we had slain had yielded poor weapons and purses that were paltry compared with those we had taken when we had fought the French the last time. I just hoped that the constant threat of raids from Scotland would mean we were not mustered to travel to France.

So, having returned from action, Ralf and I settled into life in Ecclestone where we trained the men each Sunday and spent the rest of the time riding, farming and sparring with each other. Despite the fact that I was a billman my time with Perkin Warbeck had given me training in the sword and I was a good man with a blade. Indeed the blade I wielded was fit for a prince. My life was good and I was at peace.

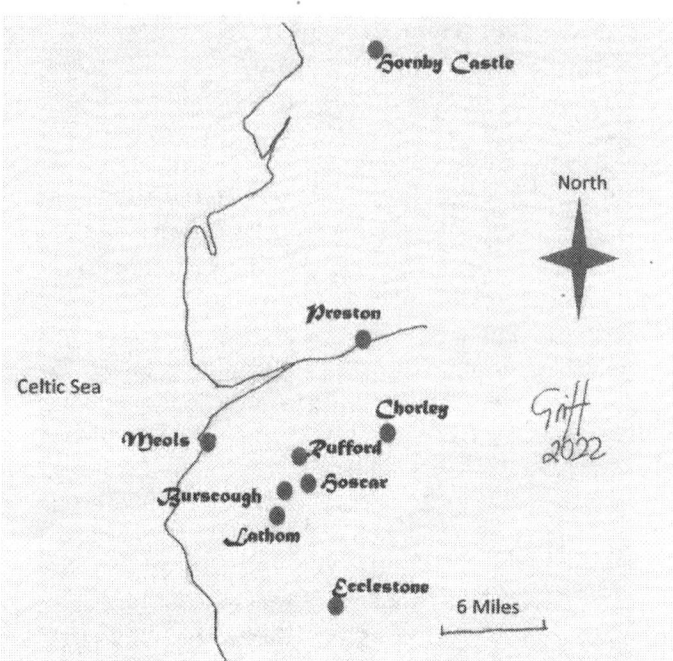

The manor of Lathom

Chapter 1

Lathom 1512

Each time I left my home in the fertile plains of Lancashire I never knew how long I would be away. The last adventure up by Ford Castle had been mercifully brief and it meant that I had not left my wife and children alone for long. I felt guilty when I did leave them. I had men I had hired who could fight and defend as well as farm but the raid from the brigands and pirates from Norway had been a warning. The nearest castles to us were Chester and Lancaster. There was not even a stronghold on the Ribble where my wife's family lived. We visited the hall at Clitheroe once or twice but it was a long journey and when my youngest children were born too difficult. I visited the home of the Lord of Lancashire, Lord Stanley more often. Lathom was a mansion but there were no walls and the garrison there was a small one. The days when lords of the manor had kept household knights, men at arms and archers were long gone. The wars between York and Lancaster had been viciously self-destructive and so many men had died in that conflict that there were fewer men left to defend England. Castles had been pulled down on the orders of Henry Tudor and moats were filled in.

I was aware, especially after the raid on Burscough, that there was still danger and I did my part and made a point of riding my horse around Ecclestone, including the outlying farms that were a couple of miles away, to let the people there know that someone would look in on them. I spoke to everyone. There were old people, men who had fought alongside my father and they lived alone. Not every child stayed in the village. Some took themselves to places where the employment was not agricultural. Some wanted to live in the towns that were expanding. It meant men and women were left to fend for themselves in their old age and I did not think that was right. With the greatest crop being sheep we needed fewer men to work the farms. England was beginning to change.

Flodden

When I rode my lands, I took James, my eldest son, with me. Walter sometimes came too, and when he did I walked. I could confidently have James on my horse behind me and he could even ride a horse himself but Walter was a lively boy. He was always safer when he was tethered to me by my hand. On those walks and rides, I came to know my sons. Both were clever boys and Jane had taught them their letters, numbers and prayers well. They would not be the wild child that their father had been. Even so, James was desperate to be a billman. He was a year or so shy of beginning his training when Ralf arrived. He was growing very quickly. When Ralf came his expectations changed for he liked the idea of becoming a man at arms rather than a billman like his father. Even though there was no war there might be the opportunity to be a knight. I had no such ambitions. Sir Edward had been used by the king once he was elevated to the peerage. Despite my skills and my service, I was mercifully overlooked by the king. I had been his spy but once my service was over then I was forgotten. It had been Sir Edward who had taken me to war the last time. I was happy to be an anonymous farmer living in the back of beyond.

"Can I be trained by Ralf, Father?"

I laughed. He had insulted me but James did not know that, "You know that Ralf came to me so that he would be a better man at arms. He is learning from me."

"But he is a man at arms."

I sighed, "If you wish those skills then I can teach you but you need to be proficient with a billhook first."

"Is not that the weapon of a common man?"

I shook my head for it was seen as a somewhat static and inglorious form of warfare by many. Men at arms, who were plated from head to foot and fought with expensive weapons, were seen as more heroic. "Once you learn to wield a billhook then a poleaxe, spear and other pole weapons are easier to use. A pole weapon keeps an enemy from being too close to you and fighting with your brothers in arms presents a solid wall that few can breach. When you use a sword, you are, perforce, working alone. The slightest mistake can cost you your life. Sir Edward discovered that up on the Tweed. He was the best man at arms I knew and became a good knight, yet because he did not keep up his training he died. You are still young. Spar with the pole and when you are big enough, I will let you use a billhook. You may watch me work with Ralf if that is your wish and learn that way." He was happy with the bone I threw him.

Ralf and I worked for an hour after breakfast and an hour before evening. The rest of the time he worked with my labourers for he was building up his muscles and wished to earn his keep. There was no contract between us and he could leave whenever he wished. He still had the horse given to him by Sir Edward and he had taken money from the men we had slain. He had sword skills but I had been taught by mercenaries who lived and died by their skills. I knew more tricks than he did and I had fought in more battles and skirmishes than he had. We used two old-fashioned swords I had taken from some battlefield or other. They were not the fashionable flexible blades men used these days but they were far better for training. Their extra weight also helped. Walter and James would sit on one of my walls and watch us as we sparred. Sometimes we used swords and daggers. That was a test not only of skill but also reactions. Poor Perkin Warbeck had not enjoyed such natural reactions. He was the man least suited to being a warrior.

By the time we entered my hall, in the evening, we had earned our ale and our food. Jane had taken to Ralf for he was younger than we were and had become the little brother she never had. She was constantly trying to get him married to one of the many young women in the village. He seemed naturally shy and fought against her efforts, in the most polite manner, of course. She would invite young women to our home where they would sew. Such activities had been going on since the time of William the Conqueror. They had probably started before that time when women would gather to sew, weave and talk. Jane was a clever woman and the talk in our parlour as they sewed also gave her information about their lives. She was not nosey but the talk told her who were the old people that needed help or which children were going hungry. I was not the lord of the manor but Jane was certainly the lady of the manor. Men talked too but our words, when we were gathered on Sunday after church, were about the practice of war. Whenever she had the young women around then she made a point of sending for Ralf to ask for his help. He might have to measure the place where a new wall hanging would go or stand and wear some garment that they had made. My wife hoped for a reaction from either one of the young women or Ralf. The young women did react but Ralf just took it all in good humour.

The weeks passed and I wondered when Ralf would tire of life on the farm. It was rumoured that men at arms, billmen and archers were being hired in the south for service in France. The pay was good. Not that Ralf was ready yet but a captain could earn four shillings a day. Even a light horseman such as Ralf could earn nine pence a day and eight pence for every twenty miles marched whilst on campaign. With food provided then a man could make a small fortune while he fought for his king and country. That was without the purses that could be lifted if you were victorious. My old comrade in arms, Sam, had been successful and now ran an inn close to Hedingham. He was a good example of success. I know that Ralf was tempted.

I had been at home for some time when I was summoned to the hall of the Earl of Derby. As soon as I spied the eagle's claw and the distinctive green and yellow livery of the Stanley family I knew what it meant. I realised, as I donned my finest garb and prepared White Star, my warhorse, that this would not be a social visit. The new earl did not hold me in the same high regard as his father had. I took with me Ralf who had become a sort of squire and James my eldest, as a page. Jane thought it a good idea as it was a sign of my importance. I was not lord of Ecclestone but the people for ten miles around regarded me as such. My efforts when we had sent the Viking raiders packing had made me something of a hero. Jane ensured that we were all appropriately dressed. She was not her mother but she had picked up on some of the values her mother, Mary de Clifton had. Mary aspired to be a great lady and while Jane did not, she was well aware of the differences between us and the great noble families of England. The Stanleys were the most important family in this part of the world.

When we reached the hall I discovered that it was not the Earl of Derby who had summoned me but his uncle, Sir Edward Stanley. While the 2nd Earl of Derby had little experience of warfare, Sir Edward did and after the Battle of Bosworth had been responsible for deterring the Scottish raiders who were intent on making mischief in the northern borders. He dismissed Ralf and James with an airy wave of his hand and he led me to a solar, a small chamber in the hall which faced south and had a pleasant aspect. It was the sort of room where he could speak privately and I was honoured to be admitted.

"Ecclestone, you are keeping well?"

"I am my lord, and yourself?"

He shook his head, "Once a man reaches fifty then his body becomes reluctant to obey even the simplest of commands." He poured us each a glass of something. I took it and sipped it. It was a fortified wine from Portugal. He seemed to be looking for a way to begin the conversation. "I was sorry to hear about Sir Edward. He was a good soldier. He died well?"

I nodded, "He had a sword in his hand and he fought bravely but I would have been happier if he had died in his bed in Hedingham."

"That is not the way warriors die." He shook his head. "Word has come to me that you acquitted yourself well." I shrugged. Whatever I said would be inappropriate. "It is because of that success and the manner in which you conducted yourself when my brother's lands were raided that I wish to use your undoubted skills. You are a captain of billmen but I would like to increase your responsibility." He hesitated, "I have been recently appointed as commissioner of array for Yorkshire and Westmoreland."

I nodded. I knew the title. It meant he was responsible for ensuring that the two counties would be ready for war should it come.

"Congratulations, my lord."

He snorted, "It is a poisoned chalice, Ecclestone. I have little power and if the Scots attack and are not defeated then I am blamed. It is a job for a scapegoat." He leaned forward, "You are a warrior and I trust you. Nothing that is said in here shall be repeated, do you understand?"

"Yes, my lord." In truth, I wished he would say nothing for I hated secrets.

"My nephew prefers London and the court. Lancashire is not as well defended as it should be. The raid on Burscough and the damage that was done was intolerable but my remit is further north. I will pay you, from our funds, to be captain of this part of Lancashire. I would have you ensure that the men are regularly trained. In this parchment," he tapped the document which lay on his desk, "are the numbers of men you command and your responsibility. It also gives you limited authority." That was not hard to do as I already met my own men each Sunday and it was not beyond the wit of man for me to visit each of the other manors and oversee their training. "I have instructed the steward to let the other captains know of your rank and their responsibilities." He gave me a thin smile, "You are to become my scapegoat."

I shifted uncomfortably in my chair, "Let me understand this properly, my lord, where does my responsibility lie?"

"The Ribble to the north and the Mersey to the south, Wigan and Bolton to the east."

"That is a large piece of land."

"And that is why you are to be paid four shillings a day." He took the parchment from a pile on the desk. "Here is your commission."

He handed it to me and I felt the weight of responsibility fall upon my shoulders.

"My lord, this is sudden. Is there something I should know?"

He smiled and this time it was a warmer one, "You are clever. There must be some noble blood in your veins. Aye, there is. With King Henry planning to take an army to France then the old alliance of Scotland and France may be rekindled. In any case, there are Border Reivers, families such as the Kerrs, Scotts, Pringles and Armstrongs who will seek to take advantage of what they perceive as English weakness in the borders. What we lack between here and the wall are castles. Barnard Castle, Durham, Lancaster, Stockton and Carlisle are the only places with garrisons."

"My lord, the men I lead will have to march on foot. The Ribble is half a day away."

"I did not say it would be easy." He relented a little, "Just be vigilant and respond to any danger and I will be satisfied."

With the parchment in my hand, we rode back to Ecclestone. "Ralf, I know that you have aspirations to be a leader. I have now come into an income that I need not and I would offer you employment, paid employment."

"I am curious, go on."

"I have been put in command of the men at arms, archers and billmen for this part of Lancashire. I confess that having perused the document there are only fifteen men at arms and ten of those are old men but I would have you as their captain. I will pay you one shilling a day. What say you?"

"I say that the day I chose to follow you was a most propitious one."

James looked at me with eager anticipation on his face, "And me, father, what about me?"

I sighed, "I shall need someone to hold my horse and help me dress. That shall be your task."

"And the pay?"

"Let us see if you can do it first but, if I am satisfied with your efforts then you shall be paid two pence a day but let us not get ahead of ourselves, eh?"

Jane took the news well. She saw it as advancement for me and saw no danger to either James or me. She was happy and that eased my mind. I was lucky in that I had good centenars who could train the archers and billmen of Ecclestone while the three of us spent each Sunday travelling up to twenty miles to oversee the training of the men who would be called upon to fight the Scots. As soon as I began my visits, I saw what Sir Edward had meant. There were good archers and good billmen but their training was more of a social rather than a martial event. I took the parchment with me and after flourishing it under the noses of some gentlemen who clearly thought that they outranked me, I began to whip the various companies into shape. It was painfully slow work. Luckily, I had Ralf with me and he rose to the challenge of making men at arms and spearmen become useful. I knew that in any battle it would be the billmen and the archers who would be the decisive force but we needed the handful of horsemen who might fight on horseback or on foot.

A month after we had begun our work and as we headed back to Ecclestone Ralf said, "You know, my lord, we need to have hobilars."

I nodded for he was right.

James asked, "What is a hobilar?"

I gestured for Ralf to explain while I put my mind to working out how to get such men.

"Hobilars, James, are men mounted not on war horses but smaller animals. They wear a helmet and a jakke, a leather or mail vest. They are armed with a short spear or latch and a sword."

"Latch?"

"Aye, a small crossbow that can be used from the back of a horse. The task of a hobilar is to find and hold an enemy until the archers and billmen can be brought close enough to defeat them."

While he had been talking the solution came to me, "The older men at arms are of little use, is that right, Ralf?"

"Most are older than you and many are older than Sir Edward."

"Then we use the younger ones as hobilars and we seek others who are young and have horses." Archers were trained from a young age. James was already too old to begin training and there were young men who grew up around horses. They could be trained as billmen but as we only needed twenty or so hobilars it would not be a great loss if I diverted some men for Ralf to lead. Hobilars were the eyes and ears of an army.

So we began to train horsemen too. My days were filled from dawn until dusk with running my land and training men. Sir Edward had more than doubled my workload. Surprisingly, we found six young men from within ten miles of Ecclestone who were good riders and wished to become mounted men. As a man at arms, a warrior needed a big horse that could carry a plated and mailed man. Ponies and smaller horses were more plentiful and cheaper. Indeed, we saved more horses from being turned into meat by creating my hobilars. We had no latches yet but I had enough skilled men to begin to manufacture them. Being small they did not require the drawing hook to pull them back and while they were not as accurate as a full crossbow, they were deadly from a range of twenty or so paces. The young men enjoyed being competitive and trying to outdo each other with their new weapons. I was impressed with them. I had seen crossbows, of course, but while they were accurate they were cumbersome and slow to load. My archers scorned crossbowmen as inferior warriors. The latches could be, well used, accurate up to fifty paces but, from the back of a horse that range shortened to twenty or thirty. They would be of little use against a plated man but their enemies were more likely to be similarly armoured men. Some months after my commission, we were improving and I was hopeful that, given time, we could be a formidable force. Then Sir Edward sprang a surprise. He sent a rider asking me to summon all the men I had trained to Lathom. He wished to inspect them. He gave us just ten days' notice and the three of us had to waste time we might have given to the farm to ride to distant manors to inform my companies of the orders. They came from a member of the Stanley family and so every man had to obey. They all lived on Stanley land. Sir Edward might not be the earl but every man depended upon the Stanley family in some shape or form. We all marched after visiting the church for the earliest service, to Lathom.

This would be the first time that we had all gathered together and I was nervous. I organised the men into their companies. Ralf had the easier task as he had the fewest men. Luckily the billmen and archers naturally formed up. There was some vying to be in the front rank and it was my company that won that battle. I smiled. Such competition was healthy. As I rode along the lines of billmen it gave me the opportunity to see the state of their weapons. There were many kinds of billhooks. Some favoured one with a longer spike and some a more curved hook but they were all sharp and, more importantly, all were the same length. When we went to war that would be vital as when we struck all the billhooks would strike as one. The archers had unstrung bows for none wanted their weapon weakened by leaving it strung when it would not be drawn.

It took until noon for the last men to arrive and I waited for his lordship. He had not made an appearance but he had clearly been watching for as the last men formed up, he emerged with half a dozen knights. I did not recognise them and guessed that they came from Yorkshire and Westmoreland. I dismounted for it would not do to be mounted in the presence of such scions of the nobility. They rode up and I bowed.

"Impressive, Ecclestone and I see that you have exceeded your orders and recruited hobilars."

"It seemed a useful activity, my lord. If it is the Scots we fight then hobilars are naturally well suited to border warfare."

He turned to the knights, "You see, gentlemen, why I have brought you here. James of Ecclestone has no title, not even that of a gentleman and yet he is a warrior and understands how to make war. I wanted you to see what could be done by men who are far from the border. You and your men will be the first to face the Scots. Are you as ready as these?"

The silence was eloquent.

"Would you like us to demonstrate our skills, my lord?"

"I would."

While the archers strung their bows, I had the billmen drill. Had I been remiss with my training it might have been a disaster but I had worked with them all and it went well. We marched in a block and none fell. We presented a solid line of bills. They even managed to make a charge that frightened the horses of the nobles and one knight was dumped unceremoniously on his backside. It brought a smile to Sir Edward's face and my men cheered.

The hobilars enjoyed charging at the billmen and feigning an attack. When my archers loosed their arrows at the marks set up by Sir Edward's retainers the nobles were even more impressed for the sky darkened with the flights and all hit the mark. It was a prodigious feat but my archers were proud of their skills. I had seen them watch their first arrow fly and hit the mark and then turn their heads to the side confident that every arrow would hit the same spot. I knew not how they did it but I knew that English archers were feared on any battlefield and they had no equal anywhere.

Sir Edward rode over to me as my archers unstrung their bows, "Well done, Ecclestone and you are ready but do not relent. I want these men to be as sharp as your billhooks and as keen as your hobilars."

We marched home happy knowing that our first test had been passed.

Flodden

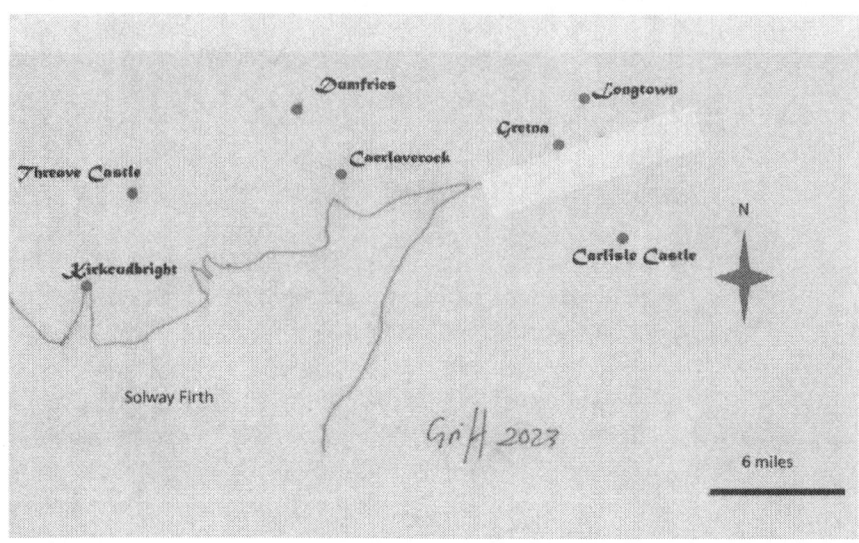

Chapter 2

Clifton 1512

We only saw Jane's family once a year. They lived less than twenty miles away but Jane's mother believed her daughter had married beneath her and, I think, found the grandchildren too rough and boisterous for her. Her father Roger did not but his wife ruled that roost. I liked Roger because he was a kind and gentle man. He was well-loved in Clifton, the nearby village, for he provided the work for them all. He had sheep and as they were lowland sheep needed less attention than highland ones. The result was that he was rich, far richer than any other farmer I knew. He did not have the faults of many rich men. He did not waste his money. Mary de Clifton, on the other hand, liked to spend money and she spent it to impress. I do not think that she really knew how rich her husband was. She was always carping on when they made their annual visit, at Christmas, about the shabby condition of their home. Jane expected her mother for her annual visit and so she was busy making our home and the guest quarters more presentable for her picky mother who always wanted everything to be done, just so. I had enlarged the stables for the horses Roger would be bringing and we had made the servant's quarters larger. The tiny house in which I had lived with my parents was now unrecognisable. Some of the land my father had used for crops like lettuce and cabbage had disappeared beneath the buildings we had erected. Of course, when I had lived there it had been just five of us who had crammed into the walls of the small house. I now owned and farmed almost half of the land in the village. It was not all the best land. I had, for instance, a small piece of land which bordered a pond and trees where we could grow little but I kept it because I knew that one day it would make a good plot for a small home. Perhaps when James married, he might wish to build there. One never knew what the future held and it was as well to be flexible in any plans that one made.

Flodden

It was a cold autumn morning and I was practising with Ralf on the piece of grazing we kept for the horses when we saw the rider galloping towards us. Riders, especially those who thrashed their horses were very rare. The last time one had ridden in so fast it had been Lord Stanley's steward and that had heralded war. We put down our weapons and walked towards him. He was not wearing the Stanley livery yet he came from the north. Perhaps there was trouble just south of the river. Was this a message to me as the Stanley captain? We had few such visitors on horseback and the only one I could think of who might send a rider to us was Roger de Clifton. I first wondered if Christmas had rushed up a little sooner than we had expected and that my in-laws were visiting earlier than was expected. Mary de Clifton yearned to be invited at Christmas to one of the great houses. Perhaps this year her wish had been fulfilled and she intended to visit with us before the real celebrations began. We headed for the cobbled yard that lay within my sturdy walls and solid double gates. I saw that the pony was lathered and the rider, a youth of perhaps fifteen looked shaken and more than that had a bloody bandage about his head. Someone had split his coxcomb. This was not a planned visit and something had happened to the north of us.

His words confirmed my fears, "Captain James, disaster and tragedy, the Scots have raided Clifton. They have burned the hall, killed men and taken hostages. My master and my mistress have been taken and my father lies dead."

It took me a moment to take all of that in.

Jane came to the door and said, "It is John, the bailiff's son, is it not?" The youth nodded, "What is the matter? Whence did you get that hurt?" He looked at me and I turned back to Jane. Her hand went to her mouth, "My parents?"

"Let us go indoors. Ralf, see to the animal."

I led my wife and the distraught messenger into my hall. I waved a servant over for wine and sat them both down by the fire in the room we called the parlour. It was where my wife sewed with her ladies. I waited until the youth had drunk some of the wine and then, with my arm around my wife's shoulders said, "Now then, John, begin at the beginning and tell us all." I had waited until his breathing was a little more regular.

My calm voice must have helped for he nodded and began, "It was yesternight, Captain, when we were about to dine. Scots suddenly attacked the hall without warning. They burst in both the front and back doors at the same time. They were well armed and we could not defend ourselves although some men tried. My father was killed and I was hit and knocked cold. When I came to the master and my lady were bound as were the other ladies in the house. They were guests of my mistress and were all gentlewomen from local villages. Six men lay dead. They must have thought that I was dead too for I was ignored and I just lay there. I heard their leader say that all were to be taken back to Threave Castle in Scotland and there held for ransom. The only man they had spared was Father Robert, the priest."

Ralf appeared at the door and I nodded for him to enter.

"The servants who had survived were all bound and Father Robert was sent to Lancaster Castle to demand a ransom of a thousand crowns. They left but not before setting fire to the hall."

Jane's eyes widened, "With you in it?"

"Aye, my lady, but they left too soon for I was able to rise and to loose their bonds and escape. The men of the village found weapons and ran after them but they had come by water. We saw the ship sailing down the Ribble. We saw the blood by the river where they had slaughtered animals before taking their carcasses on the ship. When we returned to the hall, it was burned to the ground and we saw that there were no animals grazing in the paddock."

"How did you get the horse?"

"It is mine, Captain. A gift from Master Roger and I keep it behind my father's cottage. I came here as soon as I could. I became lost else I would have reached here sooner. I know not the roads outside of Clifton." His head slumped as though exhaustion and the enormity of it all had struck him.

I said, "Jane, he needs food and his wound tended to." I knew that giving my wife something to do would occupy her mind and stop her fretting, albeit briefly, about her parents. It would allow me to think about what to do."

She nodded and put a comforting arm around his shoulders. "Come, John, let us go to the kitchen where I can tend to you."

Left alone with my man at arms, for I had not brought James into the house, I said to Ralf, "Why Clifton and why Roger?"

Ralf shook his head, "It is nothing to do with your marriage, Captain, nor our recent actions along the Tweed."

"Why do you say that?"

"Threave Castle is on the west coast and the families there have little connection with Sir Andrew. The Scottish are clannish and territorial. Does Mistress Jane's family have treasure?" He had yet to meet Roger and Mary de Clifton.

I nodded, "The manor is a rich one and as Master Roger has rarely been to war he has profited well. He is in the wool trade and known to be well off. More, the hall is undefended. There is neither ditch nor moat and he has, had, few warriors. That they came by ship makes sense for Clifton is isolated. The question is why Threave Castle?"

"Aye, for it is strange. It is a royal castle but this does not seem like the act of a king."

"Ralf, take my horse and ride to Lathom. Tell the steward there what has happened. Say that I intend to take men and find the hostages. All of them."

He nodded, "I will, Captain, but Clifton is north of the Ribble. Do you have jurisdiction?"

"I care not, Ralf. This is family and if I am chastised for my action then I can live with that. Do you think that Lancaster will pay a ransom?"

He shook his head. We both knew that Roger de Clifton was not important enough. I wondered, as Ralf left if this was the first act in a war. Were the Scots trying to provoke England into a war? They had struck at the heart of the land controlled by Sir Edward Stanley and seemed to me to be a deliberate choice of target. They must have scouted out the land and discovered just how rich and vulnerable Roger was. It was a provocative act and would also yield them great treasure. John's words implied that the Scottish had not lost a man. They would be celebrating all the way back to the Solway Firth. I thought back to my conversation with Sir Edward Stanley. He had been appointed to make the north defensible and yet an English family, deep in the heart of Lancashire had been attacked. Was it a message?

I went to the kitchen where my wife and her women fussed around the wounded youth. It was not a serious wound and had not needed stitches but I think it saved his life. Had he not been simply wounded he might have been killed along with the others. As I watched them with him, I began to plan. Threave Castle was less than one hundred miles away and lay north of the Solway Firth. I needed to know how many men we faced but John was still being tended to.

I planned while I sat in the kitchen. I had billmen that I could take but they would be slow and besides, they would be needed on the farms. The younger men, the hobilars, would be my best weapon. I would need horses and I started to work out the number I had available. The hobilars were keen to have some action and most of the hard work on the land was over; they could be spared. That gave me twenty men. Ralf and I made twenty-two but that would not be enough. I would need to call at Clifton on my way north and then Lancaster. If, as Ralf and I suspected, the ransom would not be paid then at least Sir Edward could furnish us with men. We did not have the animals to make a fast journey and it would take up to a week for us to reach the borders. I had not heard the terms of the ransom and they preyed on my mind. A ransom usually had penalties if payment was not forthcoming.

We left in the middle of the afternoon. James wanted to come but I dismissed his request. It would be hard enough for us without worrying about an untried youth. After his food and with his wound tended John looked to be in better shape and, after giving him a fresh pony, we rode hard for Clifton. We reached the village just after dark. I was just grateful that it had been untouched. It was clear that the raiders were just after my father-in-law's treasure.

The villagers made us welcome and, as my men made a camp, we gathered in the church where the headman and the priest added news. Robert, the priest, had returned and was happy to see that John had survived. "The Scots demanded the ransom by the end of the month, Captain." I was relieved as that gave us some time, not much, but enough to rescue Jane's parents. "Sir Edward does not think that the amount they demanded can be raised in time."

I knew that the priest was an honest man, "Father Robert, do you think that is true?"

The priest gave me a forthright answer. He shook his head, "The answer came before I mentioned the amount. I know, from talking with Sir Edward's people, that the knight does not like threats. Why did the Scots ask for ransom if they knew it might not be paid?"

I shook my head but I had my suspicions. This seemed more and more like provocation from the Scots. I knew that Roger kept his treasure in his hall and they must have taken that. They did not need a huge ransom, indeed, having taken the treasure the ransom was immaterial. It would have been much easier for them if they had simply left and not burdened themselves with hostages. They had another purpose. Were they trying to make England the aggressor and invade Scotland to rescue the hostages? I knew Sir Edward and that was unlikely. The innocent victims of this, my in-laws, could be the ones who paid the price for this political posturing. The choice of Roger and Mary was clear to me. Their home was undefended and they were rich. They had no connections with noble families. The only hope would be me, Ralf and my, as yet, untried hobilars.

"I will ride with my men tomorrow to Lancaster. Know you all that I intend to try to rescue Master Roger." That brought nods of approval from the men who were gathered in the church. "Is there some family who can take John in until we return?"

John shook his head, "Captain, they murdered my father and as my mother died some years ago, I am an orphan. Let me ride with you."

I hesitated and Ralf said, "If it was one of us, Captain James, then we would wish to do this and we need one to hold our horses."

"You have a weapon?"

"I can get one." He added enigmatically.

"And you know that this will be dangerous beyond words."

He nodded, "Aye, for the Scots if I get to use my steel on them."

The headman, Richard, said, "And I will come too, Captain, for I have a horse, a billhook and a sword. Master Roger was, is, the kindest of men and this village would not have prospered as it has under the hand of another. I know that you need speed else every man in the village would come but you have too few men to dismiss help." He looked to the door that John had just closed, "And I was John's father's best friend. We fought at Bosworth. This is personal. I will watch over the lad for my friend."

I nodded, "Very well. We leave at Lauds and I would be at Lancaster not long after dawn."

We ate and were given good ale. Richard and John sat together. I now had the identity of the captives. The ladies were gentle women whose husbands had died. They were not nobles but Mary de Clifton found their company agreeable and they often spent some days at the hall. They had just been unlucky in the timing of the raid.

It was dark when we rose and yet the villagers had breakfast ready for us. As we saddled our horses, I saw that John had a sword strapped to his baldric. He saw my look and said, "My father's. He fought at Bosworth and he buried this beneath the floor in our home. He kept it as a reminder of a bloody and dangerous time. I will put it to good use. If I am able I will have vengeance on the killers of my father and my friends."

We rode north along empty lanes and through villages that still slept. We crossed the Lune and reached the mighty castle at terces. I saw the standard flying from Adrian's Tower and knew that Sir Edward had not left. That disappointed me. At the very least he should have been

27

trying to raise the ransom and, if I was in command of these marches, I would have men ready to ride to recover the innocent. I had to remind myself that while I had rubbed shoulders with kings, princes, dukes and lords, I was just a captain of billmen and had neither power nor influence. What I would have done and what they would do were a world apart.

I left my men at the water trough and asked Ralf to find food for the next part of our journey. We had ridden twenty miles and before we slept, we would have another twenty to ride.

I was taken to Sir Edward who was busy in his hall. There were clerks and officials hurrying around. He looked up when I entered and stood, "Come, we need to speak." He led me to a quiet corner where cushions lay on the window seat that looked west to the sea. "I am sorry for what happened."

I nodded. He had every reason to be sorry, for while I had been watching south of the Ribble, Clifton lay to the north and was therefore his bailiwick. I wondered if my responsibility was seen as greater as I guarded Stanley lands.

He came to the point directly with no preamble, "You should know that the amount they demand is not available. I have sent a man to ask if it can be reduced to five hundred crowns."

I frowned, "My lord, a thousand crowns might be a huge amount for me but surely the crown, or even yourself, has more than that."

His face became stiff with indignation and his voice commanding, "What I have is no concern of yours, Captain. The Scots will accede to the request."

I shook my head, "No, they will not."

"And how do you know?"

"I have spent some time in the borders. Admittedly the eastern side but I think that I know the Scottish mind. When they took Roger de Clifton and his wife, they took the treasure of Clifton yet they still asked for a greater ransom than could be expected. They will hold out for the full amount. This is provocation and they wish you to make war on them." His eyes widened in surprise at my astute comments. "And you know that."

"You are clever. My brother recognised that fact and I know that both Cardinal Wolsey and the king know of you. Yes, it is provocation and I dare not, while the king prepares for this French war, to risk taking men north. Anything short of a major victory would be a disaster." He lowered his voice, "I know that you are clever and I will impart some intelligence that recently came into my possession. King James thinks that he is a great king but he is a king who has yet to win a battle. He is tempting England to make war and he has a full army while we have local levies. He has weaponsmiths making huge bombards to batter our castle walls. The civil war that rent this country apart has left us weaker than we might have been. I have seen the weaknesses in Yorkshire and Westmoreland. Men like Sir William of Wilton and Sir Marmaduke Constable are great captains but they have not the men to take on a Scottish army that has not had to fight a major war in living memory."

"Thank you for that information. I intend to rescue my in-laws."

His mouth gaped, briefly, like a fish's, "You? With how many men?"

"I have twenty-four but perhaps you have some or the constable at Carlisle..."

He seemed to ignore my request and shook his head, "That is a tiny number and doomed to failure."

I smiled, "Yet you like the idea, my lord, as it is a gesture that might assuage those in the Ribble Valley who feel that they were let down by the men to whom they pay taxes."

He nodded but his look told me he was not happy with my tone, "You are clever. The men here in Lancaster are not the men you need. Sir Richard, the constable of Carlisle, however, has local men he could loan you. If you are determined to do this, I will put quill to parchment and ask for his help."

"It is family, my lord, and I am determined."

"Very well, then there are some things you need to know. Threave Castle is not only a royal castle, it has also withstood sieges. It has a position in a loop of the Dee with just a causeway or a ferry as the only way to reach it. The man who has taken your family is Sir John Maxwell although I do not believe that he will be at Threave. He seeks power at the court of King James and this act will ensure he is given more power if the plan succeeds. You cannot assault the castle, you must use stealth and cunning." He smiled, "From what my brother told me, you possess those character traits in abundance. I know not how you will do this but if anyone can succeed it will be you. Sir Richard can give you better information about the castle than can I." He stood and waved over a servant, "Take Captain James and feed him and his men. Find them six spare horses." It was a crumb he was throwing at us but I would gratefully take the six horses. We would need them and more for the hostages when we rescued them. In my mind I had decided that, come what may, I would bring home Roger and Mary safely. I knew not how I would do it but we would succeed, no matter what the cost.

I went with the servant to the hall they used for dining and he organised the food. My men were fetched. Ralf said as we ate the bread, cheese and ham, "Well, do we get help?"

"We have six spare horses and the promise of men from Carlisle but Sir Edward will not lift a finger himself. I think that this has been a warning for him and he prepares for a war which will come but he will not allow this insult to be the start of it. We are on our own."

The rest helped and we headed the twenty miles to Kendal. There was no castle there but there was a small monastery and I used some of my own coins to pay for food and beds. The roads around Kendal were the worst I had ever known as the land was boggy and the roads ill-made. When we left the monks advised us to use high ground until we reached Ambleside, from there the road was better. They were proved right although it was intimidating to ride through the narrow steep-sided valleys and I was just glad that the Scots did not hold this part of England. It was a barrier through which men could not pass easily and it explained why they had used the sea and also why Scottish raids were largely confined to the central part of England to the north and the east. All that Sir Edward needed to do was to send men to block the road close by Helvellyn and no army could pass south.

We reached Carlisle after dark and had we not had the letter from Sir Edward we would not have been admitted. Carlisle Castle was a bastion. The men of the garrison were wary of strangers. The Scots had used many cunning ploys over the years to gain access to the fortress. It had been a castle since the time of the Romans and I knew that it had, in the reign of the second King Henry, changed hands a number of times. Thankfully, since then, the English Royal family had realised the importance of the defence and it had not fallen. Even William Wallace and Sir Andrew Murray had not managed to wrest it from English hands.

Sir Richard Willoughby was a wily old campaigner. He and his wife and sons were from Westmoreland and they knew the land well. Lady Anne was appalled when she heard of the kidnap. Sir Edward had failed to warn the constable of the danger.

"One of his men rode through here yesterday but he did not say whence he was going. He was the messenger?"

"I am guessing so."

"So, Captain James, you wish to try to rescue the hostages from Threave Castle. How many are there?"

"We know that there are Sir Roger and his wife and four or five ladies. I could not discover the exact number as those serving in the hall were slain. The kitchen staff fled when they heard the commotion. There could be as many as eight people to rescue."

He shook his head, "You have set yourself a task fit for Hercules, my friend, but I understand your urgency. It is your wife's family that has driven you to this."

"Husband, we must do all that we can. We cannot allow English women to be prisoners of these barbarians."

Sir Richard sighed. Only Ralf and I were dining with the knight and his family and the cosy atmosphere invited intimacy. He nodded, "I can let you have ten men. They are local men and know the paths well. They can get you to Threave Castle but then…" he spread his arms, "I know not how you will manage their rescue."

"The castle, my lord, could you describe it?"

"The curtain wall was destroyed when one of the former owners rebelled against the king. It was not repaired but as the keep remains that is a moot point."

"Then there are other buildings that still remain?"

"Of course, there are stables, a warrior hall, a chapel, and bread ovens."

"So while the hostages would be in the keep and a watch kept from the top, there are no towers or walls to keep us out."

I saw the glimmer of a smile on the knight's face, "I can see that you have a sharp mind. You would still have the problem of getting into the keep itself."

"The castle has a good aspect? Sir Edward said it was in a piece of water."

He shook his head, "It stands proud of the land and is surrounded, not by a lake but the river. The river is not deep. There are woods nearby and, of course, it is close to the estuary and the sea. Kirkcudbright is just eight miles away."

His eldest son, also called Richard and a squire, said, "There is a beach closer, just six miles away."

"Thank you." I picked up a duck bone to pick the meat from it. It was a way of thinking.

Sir Richard said, "You have a plan?"

"I do, Sir Richard, but it needs the help of the people of Carlisle." I used the bone I had just picked clean. "Here is Threave Castle." I put my napkin on the table, "And here is the firth. We watch the keep from the trees and I will take a handful of my men to the keep and gain entry."

Richard the squire said, "How?"

"There are always ways and means. They will feel secure at Threave Castle and while they might fear an army, they will not think that a handful of fools would try to enter for as they are many miles north of the border then those fools, slowed by hostages, would be doomed to be caught."

Sir Richard said, "But the chief fool has a way to avoid that?"

"This beach your son speaks of could be our salvation. If a ship was moored there then the hostages could be taken off and brought here."

"But not the rescuers and their horses."

"No, my lord, the rescuers would be leading the men of Threave west to chase them. It would be your men that would escort the hostages to safety. My men and I would make such a noise that they would follow us. We can ride hard but hostages cannot."

Sir Richard raised his goblet, "A fine plan; it may not succeed but it seems to me the only one that might. Tomorrow I will have the men brought to you and they can offer their insight. Leave the ship to me." He laughed, "This will give Maxwell a bloody nose."

"You know the knight, my lord?"

"He is arrogant and cunning. On the odd times that I have met him all that he can speak of is the Battle of Stirling Bridge or Bannockburn. All the defeats of the Scots are never mentioned. He is a deluded man if he thinks the Scots are superior to the English on the battlefield. You and your men rest this night for you have a mighty task ahead of you." He leaned forward, "And a word of advice, steer well clear of Caerlaverock Castle. It is a mighty bastion surrounded by water and with a good view of the land around. Sir John has a large garrison and they are mounted on good horses."

Chapter 3

Carlisle Castle 1512

The leader of the hobilars provided by Sir Richard showed my own men their shortcomings. These men had been hobilars for years and their skills were well honed. They were real border horsemen and their array of weapons was formidable. There was less uniformity than amongst my men and their horses were sturdier. Their leader, Arkham, was a north countryman who had served the castle since he had been a boy of fourteen. I liked him as soon as I met him for he was a warrior and understood how to make war on this northern frontier. He knew border raids and he knew the Scots. I explained what I needed and he nodded, "My men and I can get you there unseen and we can get your hostages safely to the firth but what I cannot do is get you inside the keep and it seems to me, Captain James, that such an act is impossible."

I smiled. I could never tell him how I had managed to infiltrate the rebels who sought to usurp King Henry IVth. Instead, I said, "And I do not yet. So long as we can stay hidden and examine the castle then I can find a weakness. Every castle has a weakness. It is just a case of finding it." He shrugged, patently not believing me. I was curious, "How can you guarantee to get the hostages to safety?"

"You have brought six spare horses and we will take more so that the ladies can ride double if needs be. They may not be riders and we do not want a horse to falter because of the extra weight. If your plan works then you will draw off any pursuit and we should have an easy time getting back to Carlisle."

"You will not board the ship?"

"I will judge that when we reach the sea. It might take too long for we have horses. Do not worry. We know the land and we can avoid the places where the Scots might look for us. It is you who will have the problem. There will be a hue and cry and they will follow you. If they think you have their hostages then they will hunt you down relentlessly." He was clearly a horseman and knew the strengths and weaknesses of animals. "It is forty-odd miles to Threave. If we leave now, we can reach the woods after dark and that will give you the morrow to spy this weakness of which you speak. I will go to my men."

I gathered my own men around me and told them my plan, "Now as Captain Arkham has pointed out this is not only perilous but possibly impossible. Any who wish to stay here until we return has my blessing. I want no man's death on my conscience." I looked pointedly at John.

Ralf looked around the men and said, "Captain, while you were in conference we spoke of this task and, yes, it is impossible but that does not mean we should not attempt it. There are English gentle women who are prisoners and that is not right. We may be common men but that does not mean we cannot behave like gentlemen. We are decided."

"Then let us mount. We are now in the hands of the hobilars of Carlisle. Watch them and learn,"

As we left to cross the river by the ferry, I saw differences between the Carlisle men and mine. None wore mail but their jakkes were studded with metal. They also all wore a sallet helmet. They had short spears attached to their saddles and swords in their belts. The biggest difference lay in their mounts. Their horses were bigger than the pony-like horses used by my men. I would need to address that for as soon as we landed their larger mounts covered the ground far faster than we did and our horses struggled to keep up. The forty miles home would be a difficult ride. We had the Esk to cross too and that meant a ford. Had we not been with Arkham we might have struggled to find it and I made a note of its location. Coming back we would be alone.

There was a rider on the ferry wearing Stanley livery and I spoke to him as he left the wooden vessel. "Sir, you have come from Scotland?"

"Aye, and what is it to you?"

"I am Captain James of Ecclestone and I believe you are the messenger sent by Sir Edward to ask Sir John Maxwell to reduce the ransom."

He looked relieved and smiled, "I am but I fear my news is not good. The earl refuses to reduce the amount although he has given an extra week for Sir Edward to raise the payment." He was suddenly aware of the armed men waiting with me, "You plan to rescue them?"

"We do. Did you see them?"

"I did not go to Threave. I was accosted close to Dumfries and taken to Caerlaverock where I met with Sir John Maxwell. He has many men, Captain James."

I nodded, "That is to be expected. Ride hard and tell Sir Edward. Mayhap your news may prompt him to some martial activity." I knew it would not.

It took two journeys for us to cross the river. While we waited on the north bank Arkham spoke to me. He pointed to the southwest, "There lie the two villages of Graitney and Gretna. Neither has a castle nor a garrison but they are beholden to the Maxwell clan and if we go near to them then a message will be sent. It adds another five miles to our journey but we will head further north and cross the river at the ford that lies close to Longtown."

There were hills to the north but we kept to trails and tracks that wound through the forest and did not sap too much energy from our horses. I paid close attention to every twist and turn. I needed to find this route when we returned from our quest. Arkham stopped frequently to let the horses graze, give them water but, more importantly, to give him time to look for signs of the Scots. We were in Scotland but he was looking for evidence of warriors: animal dung, the marks of boots and evidence of campfires. He seemed satisfied when he found none.

I rode next to him and asked him why he was looking this close to Carlisle for the crossing that led to the castle lay five miles to the south and east of us. "Simple, Captain, this excursion is interesting but our main function is being aware of where the Scots are and what they are doing. While we escort you, we will watch for danger so that we can be one step ahead of the Scots. We are the border warriors and we take our task seriously."

I could see, with men like Arkham, why this side of England was relatively secure while the east had to endure far more cross-border raids. Here the river was a more solid barrier than the Tweed which I had crossed many times. The only way across the river we had just crossed was by ferry or a twenty odd mile detour to the east where the ground rose and the wall began.

As we rode, I studied the land and secured it in my memory. We would be riding back through this land and not only alone but pursued. I looked for memorable signs on the trail, I looked for deserted buildings and suitable hedges. I looked for places we could ambush pursuers. There were many and that made me glad that we were led by such a skilled border warrior. That he knew where the Scots dwelt was clear for we avoided any settlements. The castle of Caerlaverock was the biggest obstacle we had to negotiate. It dominated the entrance to the land of Dumfries and was the Clan Maxwell's fortress. We detoured five miles to ensure that we would not be seen. We then had to avoid the uncertain town of Dumfries. Once we had passed those two barriers we closed in on our destination.

We had to pass around the water called Carlingwark Loch before we entered the small wood. By judicious changing of our horses, we managed to get to the wood Arkham sought just after dark. It would be a cold and cheerless camp but not a man complained. While the horses were tended to I went with Ralf and Arkham to a place where we could observe the castle without being seen. He had already told me that the castle lay on an island in a loop of the River Dee. It explained why the site for the castle had been chosen. Arkham had told me that the river was but sixty paces wide and could easily be forded. It looked intimidatingly huge but I saw there the castle's defences had been reduced in recent civil disorder. If an attacker wished to take the castle then they would just need to bring up bombards and they could blast the keep with impunity from across the river. The keep stood apart from the other buildings. I saw a warrior hall, small buildings, and a bread oven. There was also a granary. In addition, close to the river on the side furthest from the castle there looked to be a workshop and foundry. They were making weapons. I saw the smoke billowing and the occasional flash of flames as the bellows were operated. The doors to the outside buildings opened and closed regularly and I saw people moving around. They were mainly men and that made sense. The keep had what looked like gates for a stable and a wooden staircase that ascended to a door. It meant that the castle could not be attacked by means of a ram. The keep and the now demolished outer curtain had been built on a higher piece of ground. It was a natural mound surrounded by uneven ground. There were many places where a man could remain hidden if he approached the keep cautiously. The natural defence against an attack by an army was the water.

We were patient and watched for an hour or so. The sun set in the west and darkness descended. When the keep door opened and a man came out, illuminated by the light, I stared intently at him. They left the door open and the spilt light lit him as he headed down the slope to the warrior hall. He had an apron covering a belly that suggested he liked both food and ale. I took him for a cook. He walked down the stairs and headed for the warrior hall. I saw that he was carrying, in two hands, a large pot which steamed. His hands were covered in a cloth. It was clearly heavy as well as hot and he struggled to carry it without spilling. Now that it was darker, I could hear the noise of conversation in the building. After kicking on the door to gain entrance, he entered what I took to be a warrior hall. The noise from the inside became louder. He was in for some time and when he came out, he had no cauldron. He then went back to the castle and re-entered. We waited and watched until a second figure came out carrying a large jug. It was clearly ale. This time he made the journey to the warrior hall far more quickly. Then he went to the bread ovens. What I had not seen was the baker who was there, in the shadows. When the second man left, laden with loaves, the baker carried more loaves to the warrior hall. This time, when the man entered the castle, he did not return and, after waiting a short time and seeing no further movement, we left.

"Arkham, have you ever been in the castle?"

He shook his head, "No, but I know what the interior is like. The stables are at the base of the tower. The ground floor, where the gate lies, is a guard room. Above that is the hall where the lord would dine and above that is his sleeping chamber. The top floor will have a fighting platform and I am guessing that there will be men there at night." He stopped and turned, peering across the open ground to the keep, He rubbed his beard. "They would see little at night. I cannot see their faces but they may be eating. It could be that they do not keep watch at night. With the door to the keep locked and barred, they would be safe from a surprise attack. They have more men in the warrior hall than I expected. That is their security." We continued to our camp.

"Do they have garderobes?"

"I am guessing that they do. This is a royal castle and I can't see the king of Scotland dropping his breeks for all the world to see his backside hanging out."

We all laughed at the image.

I had worked out most of what Arkham had said myself but it was good to have it confirmed. I had served in Hedingham and knew that men on night watch, especially if there was no war, spent more time asleep than watching. The height of the keep made it a very secure place. Men could not climb it and slit their throats. We reached our camp and John rose to bring Ralf and me a coistrel of ale each, "Then, Arkham, I have a plan. While we eat, I will tell you and Ralf about it. Look for flaws and suggestions to improve it."

"First, I will set sentries. They will be my men. Yours have journeyed further and," he smiled, "seem to me to be new to this."

"They are."

After he left us, Ralf said, "I cannot see how this can be achieved. We need to get across the river. Secondly, there is but one entrance and if there is a guard room then the battle would wake those in the warrior hall. Thirdly, we might be able to ford the river but how will the hostages get away?"

"Tomorrow, we need to find out exact numbers but my plan does not rely on brute force but cunning."

Arkham returned and, after filling his coistrel with ale and taking some bread and cheese, sat. "Tell me your plan."

"First, we must get across the river. We either swim our horses across or, if you think it judicious, we cross by the causeway. We wait outside the keep, just three of us. When the man with the cauldron emerges, we take him. We bring the rest of the men over and enter the castle. They will be expecting the cauldron man to return and when the door opens will not be anxious. We overpower the guards and rescue the prisoners."

Arkham swallowed and drank some ale, "And those in the warrior hall and the baker?"

"As I have just said to Ralf, we need to know numbers but two men could overpower the baker and we would have men waiting at the door to the warrior hall. If we are quick to rescue the hostages then we should be able to escape before they know anything."

Ralf asked, "And inside the hall?"

I sighed for this was the most dangerous part of the plan, "I am counting on the fact that the only way in or out of the castle will be through the gate and guard room. I am depending on all the men being there."

"What about men on the fighting platform, sentries, Captain?"

"Ralf, did you see any sentries?"

"I did not look."

Arkham smiled, "I watched. The sentries were not there until just before we left to return here. They were eating." I nodded, "I see a glimmer of hope then. Let me add my thoughts. My men will deal with the baker and the warrior hall. You will need to have at least six men with the horses that the hostages will ride and guard the rest of your horses."

"I was thinking ten."

"Even better. That, however, leaves you with the bare minimum necessary to get the job done."

"I know and that is why we must count the men tomorrow. Numbers will ease my mind."

I slept well but that was through exhaustion. It had been a hard ride but the presence of such men as Arkham made me secure in the knowledge that we would not be attacked at night. I rose before dawn. Arkham was asleep and I went to speak to his lieutenant who was in command of the other sentry. "How goes the night, Thurston?"

"Quiet, captain. They have women in the warrior hall for I heard the sound of squealing and some commotion. Then it went quiet. Dawn will be upon us soon." He nodded to the north, "There is a priory there and they have bells to summon their priests to prayer. It marks the time."

I made water and then went to break my fast. As the sun came up so men came to life. I walked back to the edge of the wood and squatted close to the base of a large tree. The weeds and tares had sprouted there, encouraged no doubt by the light of the sun and I had some shelter. I had long ago learned how to be still. When I was satisfied that I was unobserved I took my knife and cut a stout twig the length of my arm. I stripped the foliage from it. I would use it as a tally stick.

The river looked wide and I wondered if my plan was feasible. I had not counted on such a wide one. However, I spied hope when I saw the two boats tied up on the castle side of the river. We might be able to cross the causeway but the hostages were a different matter. As I watched, the door to the warrior hall opened and men came out, in ones and twos, to make water and empty their bowels. They did so some twenty feet from the building. I took that to be the place they used as a privy. I made a mark on my twig each time I saw a different man. As I watched, light gradually lit the keep, I saw that there were just two sentries on the fighting platform. Their faces were close together which told me they were not keeping a close watch on the land. They were clearly confident that they were safe. Once again, the door to the keep opened and the cook emerged again, struggling with the cauldron. I saw him more clearly in the daylight and realised that he was not a young man. He walked down to the door and this time, as there was no noise, I heard his words. They were heavily accented but after my time at Ford and Etal, I was able to make them out.

"Open the door before this porridge goes cold. There are others who wish to eat, too." As on the previous night he was inside for a short while and when he emerged he carried what I took to be the cauldron he had taken the previous night.

As he headed back to the keep, I saw that while there was a tendril of smoke from the bread oven it was unattended. Even as I watched I saw the baker emerge from the warrior hall and head for the bread oven. He rekindled the embers and I saw the flames lick into life. I was getting a picture of the pattern of life here. The man who headed back to the warrior hall was not the cook, but a youth. The previous night had been too dark to determine if the same man had done the journey. Now, in the cold light of dawn, I saw that there were two, a cook and his assistant. The young man carried the ale. I wondered why they did not make the journey together. There had to be a reason but it evaded me. I saw other men emerge from the hall and head for the workshop. Soon smoke was billowing from it and then we heard the sound of banging. It confirmed that they were making weapons. That explained the boats. They would need to bring the iron across the river and boats were safer than horses or men. A boat could not slip.

Ralf and Arkham joined me and found places where we were hidden from sight. The river and the castle were more than a hundred paces from us but, as I had watched, I had seen that the sentries kept their eyes to the south, where the road lay, and not the east, where we were hidden. We said not a word and none of us moved. I was hoping for a sight of my wife's parents and the ladies but all that we saw were men emerging from the hall to go to the warrior hall. Horses were fetched out from the subterranean stable and taken to a pen I had not seen before. There were just eight horses and they grazed happily on the grass in the pen and the dried grasses the men threw there. Two of the men watched them.

I took the stout twig and, as I identified different men, made more marks on it. Thurston was right, there were women in the hall and three of them came out. They headed for a small wooden hut some way from the other buildings and I took it to be the privy. I made different marks on the twig to identify the women. By prime, I had counted at least fourteen men and three women. I added the cook and his assistant. Annoyingly the hostages did not emerge and it confirmed that there was a privy or garderobes in the keep. That knowledge meant that there could be another ten men unaccounted for. I worked out that the keep had to have garderobes for the hostages had not been brought out to use the privies which lay close to the warrior hall.

"I need to make water, will you keep watch on the castle?" They nodded and I handed the stout twig to Ralf. When I had made water, I returned.

Arkham rose, "You do not need me here for I can see that you know your business. I will go and take some rest while I can. You should do the same, James of Ecclestone. Tired men make mistakes."

He was right and I decided to wait until a short while after the priory bell sounded sext before Ralf and I would take our rest. We were rewarded just before noon when six riders approached the castle from the road that led from the south. Leaving three men at what looked like a recently made causeway the other three headed up to the castle. One looked to have flecks of grey in his hair and his beard. The other two were younger. The three who had ridden the best horses and were wearing the finest clothes were the ones taken across the causeway and when they headed towards the keep, I knew who were the nobles. As they left their horses on the bank of the river then I knew that they would not be staying long. I decided then that it would be foolish to risk the horses making a noise on the causeway. We would cross on foot and avoid the water by using the stones that rose above the water. Horses would not do that. I would try to capture the horses that were stabled in the keep too.

I studied the livery of the men waiting with the horses. They each bore a shield upon their back and I saw that it had a double-headed bird. When I had spoken to Sir Richard. he had described the livery of the Maxwell clan and that was what I spied. It was confirmation of the identity of the lord who had taken my in-laws as hostages. I did not now if it would be Lord Maxwell but they were from the clan and they rode warhorses. They had to be knights.

We watched until, in the middle of the afternoon, the nobles left and were taken back to their horses. They headed north and east and we returned to the camp. I guessed that they had come from Caerlaverock the day after the visit of Sir Edward's man and that they were keeping their guards informed.

Thurston was just rising, having enjoyed a daytime sleep. "Thurston, where is the nearest residence of the Maxwell family?" I wondered if there was some stronghold nearer to us. If there was then that could create a problem.

He pointed to the east, "Caerlaverock Castle. As the crow flies is it less than eighteen miles but as the crossing is well to the north, where we crossed yesterday, then the journey is nearer to twenty-eight miles. Why, Captain?"

"I have just seen three nobles visit the castle."

"Then that will be either Sir John Maxwell or his son Robert."

"He had grey in his hair."

"Sir John then."

"Tell Arkham, when he wakes, that I have modified my plan and we had better have two men watching the castle."

"Aye, Captain, you rest. This will be a long night and tomorrow will be the longest day."

Chapter 4

Threave Castle 1512

I did not sleep well but I rested and when I woke, it was getting close to dusk. I saw Ralf speaking with Arkham. Arkham nodded as I approached them.

"I think that we use the causeway and pick our way across. We would be harder to see and we could be quieter. If we have men close to the river with horses then they can cross with the mounts when the commotion begins. I intend to use surprise. We have to take out as many men as we can in our initial attack. We need superiority of numbers and that means being ruthless."

Arkham nodded, "These men have already put themselves beyond the law and God, Captain James. They have kidnapped people and brought them here. Your relatives are not border folk. We guard against such attacks. My men and I will slay any in our path for you cannot risk a wounded snake biting. My men and I will take care of those in the warrior hall."

After eating I gathered my men around me and explained what we would be doing. "John, I want you, Ned, William, and Harold to hold the horses. I know that I am asking much of you for there will be many horses. You need to keep them as close to the causeway as you can and, to be quiet." They nodded, obviously disappointed not to be crossing the Dee with us but they were the youngest and I wanted them to survive. I looked at the rest of my young warriors. "I will go with Richard and Ralf. We will secure the cook. The rest of you should cross the causeway and shelter where you can see us but not be seen from the top of the fighting platform. You need to keep a good watch and then race to us when you see us enter the keep. By the time you reach us, I will be at the top of the stairs. Edgar and Walter, I want you two to follow the three of us closely. Your first task is to bind and gag the cook. Then go to the stables and listen for any noise. If you hear noise then open the stable doors. Take the horses to the river for it will mean that the attack has begun but do not open the door to the stable if all is quiet. When you have the horses then drive them towards the river."

"And if we hear no noise?"

"Then God smiles upon us and we will escape easily but let us prepare for the worst, eh?" They nodded. "Once inside we slay everyone who bars our way. Those of you with latches have them loaded and ready. We need to kill silently but I doubt that they will all go quietly into the night. Ralf and I will get up the stairs for we will need to eliminate the sentries and any guards who watch over the hostages. The aim is to save the hostages. They will be taken to the horses first. Richard, your task is to stay with them and mount them on horses. Leofric, you will help Richard and we all try to get safely to the horses. We will try to take any wounded men back but I can promise nothing. Richard and John, while we make our escape to the east you will go with Arkham and his men. Your task is to watch over and guard the hostages. They know you and your presence will ease their minds," I looked all of them in the eyes as my head turned around to each of them, "Once again, I offer you the chance of safety. Any who wish to do so may stay with the horses."

No one said anything and I took that to mean they accepted the risk.

"As for the warrior hall and bread oven." I nodded to Arkham who was speaking with his men. "The men of Carlisle will deal with them and they will take the hostages to the ship that will be waiting in the firth. We do not hide when we leave. We want them to follow us and until we pass Dumfries then we are at risk for we will be the human bait that draws on these dogs of war. If word reaches the Maxwells at Caerlaverock then they can bar our progress back to Carlisle. This will not be easy. Now prepare and remember, these Scots showed no mercy at Clifton. We show them none."

As soon as the sun set, we headed down to the river. We approached the castle from the side that did not face the causeway and worked our way around using the undergrowth for cover. When we had watched I had seen that the ground around the roughly made causeway was surrounded by reeds and weeds. We could use them to disguise our movements. This time it was me who led. I watched the top of the keep as we crept closer but saw no faces. I could hear the noise from the warrior hall and all appeared to be going well. I saw the posts at the river where they had tethered the ferry used before the causeway had been built. I knew that the stone was recently laid for there was no weed on the rocks they had used and no order to their arrangement. It explained why the nobles had not risked riding across it. They had not risked a dousing. It was after I had crossed the causeway with half of my men that my plans began to unravel. I saw the cook heading down to the hall. He was early. I took an instant decision. The sentries would be eating and so, waving to Richard and Ralf I raced up to the keep. I hoped that, as we kept close to the river, we would not be seen by the baker or the cook and that, as it would take the cook time to deliver his food, we could ambush him by the steps. I tried to remember how long it had taken the night before but could not. We reached the corner of the keep and there was no sound of alarm.

We waited and listened in the darkness of the keep's shadow. I heard the huffing and puffing of a man labouring and, peering around the corner of the keep, I saw the cook trudging up the slight slope to the keep. As soon as he stepped onto the first step I raced around behind him and, putting my hand around his mouth, I gripped his arms and dragged him back to the others. Ralf had made a sap from a leather bag filled with sand and he smacked the man hard on the head. Edgar and Walter were right behind us and they grabbed the man. They would not be part of my attack. I waved and the rest of my men rose from cover and hurried to the steps. I had no idea if they creaked or not and so I ascended first. When they did not, I waved the others up. The platform close to the door could only accommodate six of us and the rest waited on the steps. I drew my sword and dagger. Richard and Ralf did the same. The other three had loaded latches.

I took a deep breath and nodded to Richard, who, holding his dagger and sword in his left hand, opened the door. I rushed in and took in that eight men were seated at a table. Another was descending the stairs from the floor above. The wooden stairs clung precariously to the wall. The cook's assistant stood with the jug of ale ready. In two strides I was across the guardroom and I lunged at the man seated there and my sword entered his neck. He gurgled his life away as blood spurted from a wound. Richard and Ralf stabbed their opponents in the back and Ralf even had time to hit and stun the cook's assistant with the pommel of his sword. He fell to the ground, his jug clattering and spilling ale to flood across the floor. The stunned silence ended with that and the cries of the guards who, shouting the alarm, reached for weapons. Even as the rest rose four bolts from latches hit them and I ran for the stairs. The man who had been descending drew his sword and dagger. He was torn between coming for me and returning to the hostages. The delay enabled me to reach the stairs and make his decision for him. There he held the advantage for I could not swing my sword for fear of hitting the wall. He swung his heavier sword at my head and I blocked it with my dagger. Before he could stab me with his dagger, as I was below him I rammed my sword up under his chin. The tip emerged from his skull and I threw his body to the floor of the guardroom. I heard a bell tolling from the top floor. The alarm had been given and everyone within ten miles would hear it. Men would be riding to their aid whilst others would be riding to Caerlaverock Castle. Men make plans but there are always flaws in every plan. I prayed that my mistakes would not cost any of my men their lives.

As I burst into the room that would have been the lord of the manor's bedroom, I saw Janes' parents and three ladies cowering in the corner. Two men, well-armed and with breastplates came towards me. Until Ralf and Richard joined me, I was alone. I took the offensive and ran at the nearest warrior. I made no attempt to swing at his breastplate for it would avail me nothing. Instead, I slashed at his unprotected leg with my sword and was rewarded with blood spurting as the razor-sharp edge tore through his breeks and his flesh. I did not finish him off but ran at the next warrior and this time lunged with my sword at his throat. He blocked it but stepped back and I slashed my dagger perilously close to his face. He reeled once more. This time he tumbled. One of the ladies shouted, "Behind you!"

I turned as the wounded man raised his sword to end my life. Richard and Ralf were now in the room but the two sentries from the fighting platform had descended and would occupy my companions. I had two men to fight. I made a cross of my sword and dagger to block his sword for it was a bigger and heavier sword than mine and he was using it two handed. Before he could swing again, I brought my knee hard between his legs. It is a foul blow but I had never known any man to ignore the pain. As his face came down, I smashed the hilts of my sword and dagger against his face. I knew that the man who had tripped would be rising and I turned. I had no need to worry. Roger de Clifton had smashed a pot over his head. The man was not dead but out of the fight. I whipped around just as the wounded man rose. Mindful of my orders to my men I stabbed him in the throat and he died. I looked up as the body of the first of the sentries tumbled down the stairs. The other ran back up the stairs and I heard the bolt slide across the hatch. He would survive and be able to tell Sir John Maxell of the attack.

"Quickly, we have to flee." Roger nodded, "Is this all?"

As he passed me, he nodded, "Two others were killed trying to escape as we boarded the ship and a third fell from the ship and drowned."

I nodded. I had been right and the men deserved no mercy.

My men had killed all the guards and we appeared to have been lucky. I saw Edgar and Walter with five horses driven from the stable. Another three had escaped them and were galloping away. Their hooves clattered loudly on the causeway. Richard had obeyed me and he shepherded the hostages with Leofric. I looked to the warrior hall and saw Arkham and men hurrying towards us. They were helping two obviously wounded men.

Flodden

Ralf and I stood with swords drawn until all had crossed the causeway. There were men banging on the barred door to the warrior hall. They would soon escape and follow. Arkham and his men mounted and did so before Richard, John and Leofric had managed to help the hostages into their saddles. I heard Arkham shout, "Ride." He headed his men and the hostages to the east to give the illusion that they were heading for Carlisle. We mounted our horses. We could have left immediately but I wanted to be sure that the ones in the castle knew which way we had gone. I saw the white face from the top of the keep. He was the man who had fled Richard and Ralf and he was watching us whilst tolling the bell. We were four hundred paces behind the Carlisle hobilars when they disappeared into the trees. We rode more slowly than they had. As we entered the trees the tolling ceased. I did not see the trail they took to head south but when we emerged from the forest the road ahead was empty. Richard, as I had commanded and John, had gone with the hostages. I saw some dung on the road south and I rode my horse to walk in it. Ralf, seeing what I had done, emulated me. With just five miles to ride the hostages would be safely at the river before any Maxwell man could follow them. We were a different story.

I reined in and looked at my men, "Are any of you hurt?"

Edgar said, "A scratch but it has stopped bleeding."

Nodding I said, "Now begins the game of cat and mouse. They know whence we are heading." I nodded at the ground, our animals had obligingly left steaming piles of dung. "Now we have to ride as quickly as we can and get beyond Dumfries before the hue and cry begins." The dung and our hoofprints would mark our trail. Thanks to my horse and Ralf's, I could not see the trail left by Arkham and his men. Our horses, when we had stopped, had milled around and obscured all the other hoofprints.

Arkham had led us well when we had come west and I retraced our steps to the east. I rode forty paces ahead of Ned and Ralf brought up the rear. Whenever I held up my hand Ned stopped the others and I was able to investigate any danger that we found. My reasoning was that one man who was seen would not arouse as much suspicion as a column of men and none of us wore livery. My cloak was a plain one with a cowl and hood. Dumfries was the one town Arkham had assiduously avoided on our travels. The River Nith had no bridges until Dumfries. There was no castle there for the town had often rebelled against the Scottish rulers and that meant they were not even allowed walls. That lack of defence, however, made them more vigilant and so we headed north and west to bypass the town. It was now daylight and country folk were up early and working, especially at this time of year with short days and long nights. Despite our care, we were seen as we turned to head north along the greenway. A farmer who had been tending to his hawthorn hedge heard our hooves and looked up. He peered over and saw my line of men. We could have killed him but all of us worked the land and while the hostage takers had been fair game a farmer going about his business was not. We rode harder. He would report if he was asked that we were heading north.

The carrot was out of the ground and we could do nothing about it. As soon as we came to some woods with a small river running through it, where we could rest, change horses and I could speak with Ralf, we stopped. I ensured that we were deep enough inside to be hidden and that there was water for the horses. We had a couple of spares and we would change the riders who rode the weakest of the others. We had covered twenty miles but we were still in the heart of the land of the Maxwell family.

"Edgar, have the wound tended to. The rest of you make water, eat and see that your horses are watered." Ralf and I stood apart. "My fear, Ralf is that the men we left could recapture the three stray horses and ride directly to Caerlaverock Castle."

"But it is across the River Nith."

I nodded, "But if this was us would we not risk a dousing to get a message to our master?" He saw that what I said made sense and nodded. "We change our plans. They will send men here and that farmer will speak to others. Maxwell will not know that the hostages are safely on a ship and will assume that the women will slow us down. He will set a net between here and Carlisle. We will head further east before we turn south. Remember those villages we need to avoid, Graitney and Gretna? Maxwell can easily reach them before us by using the road and they are part of his clan. We will have to travel even further north and east than we might have wished and then head for the ford. We may have to spend another night in Scotland."

There was an outburst of laughter from the men and Ralf smiled, "They are in good spirits, captain. If nothing else this adventure has made them better warriors and they have learned much at the expense of the Maxwells. They acquitted themselves well in the castle."

"Aye, they did." The training with the latches had paid off and in killing those in the keep they had avoided having to use uncertain sword skills.

We had to avoid roads and now that we were within a few miles of Caerlaverock Castle we had to use whatever cover we could. I rode as a scout. I daresay that there were some of the men I led who could be scouts but this was not the time to test them. I knew that I could do so and these young men had followed me. I owed it to them to bring them all home safely. Not using the roads meant I used the sun as my compass. I erred on the side of caution and always went further north whenever I saw people in the distance.

I spied the village ahead as the sun began to set behind us. There was a wood further up the road just a mile or so from the village, I saw its shadows and I chose that as our stop for the night. It was not perfect but who knew where we would find another copse that would afford us shelter? Night carries sound and I knew that we had to get into the wood and away from the village quickly and quietly. The sun had set when I saw the hunter's trail that led into the trees and I dismounted and led my men along it. The horses, despite the changes we had made, were exhausted and needed water. As soon as I found the small stream, I decided that would be our camp for the night. "We camp here. Water your horses and see if there is some grazing."

Edgar said, "Captain, when we took the horses I also took some oats. I thought we could eat them but my horse is so weary that perhaps we should feed them instead."

"Well done, Edgar. It was remiss of me not to have brought grain for them. Share what you have equitably. For us, this will be a cold camp."

Ned said, "I managed to grab some food from the castle, captain. The bread was already a day old and will be stale but even stale bread is better than nothing."

Others had some food in their bags and we shared it all. No one was full but then again, none were hungry. More importantly, the men I led, my hobilars, were becoming brothers in arms and the lessons they were learning were not just military ones. They were learning to look after one another and that, as I had learned, was of more use. I organised the watches so that each of us lost just two hours of sleep. Had the horses not been as tired I might have left before dawn but the animals were our lifeline and needed to be husbanded. While I watched I used my whetstone to sharpen my sword. I was not arrogant enough to think that I would not need it. We would have to use our weapons before we reached Carlisle. We left after the sun had risen and headed west towards the distant Esk. I used the same method as the day before and we veered north whenever we saw people. The result was that we found the Esk well north of the ford. Had I known my men better then I might have risked swimming the river but this was not the time to be reckless. We headed south and I looked for the ford.

The river was lined with trees and shrubs. The brambles were to be avoided but other than that I risked riding through thin climbers and avoiding tree roots. It was good that I did for my cautious approach made me stop to study an easy way through the tumble and tangle of a blackberry bush and it was then that I spied the ambush at the ford. Ahead of me, hidden on this side of the river were Maxwell's men. They were using the same vegetation as I was to hide themselves and they were all watching to the west. The road came that way and I saw that they had crossbows at the ready. I held up my hand but did not turn around. I counted all those that I

could see. There were at least fourteen men and I guessed
that there would be more on the other side. Some wore the
Maxwell livery.

I turned White Star slowly around and walked back to
Ned. Although the sound of the Esk would drown out my
words I did not want to risk a raised voice alerting the Scots.
I whispered to him, "There is an ambush ahead. Tell each
man to pass my words along." He nodded. "Have them load
their latches. I want Ralf up here with me and then the men
with the spare horses. I want the spares tethered to the horse
holders' mounts. When I raise my sword, we gallop at the
men at the ford. Ralf and I will try to prevent pursuit but the
rest of you cross the river and head for Carlisle. Now tell
Edgar."

It took some time for the message to be passed but that
was no bad thing as it gave the horses a brief rest. Ralf rode
next to me and we both drew our swords. The men's latches
all had a lanyard so that after they had used them, they could
simply drop them. It was then that they would draw their
swords. As soon as they were all ready, I nodded and led the
men through the trees to the hunter's trail that bordered the
river. Here it was wide enough for two men and there were
no entanglements. We could not risk trying to break through
the undergrowth. We walked down the trail and the bubbling
river, allied to the turf of the trail drowned any noise we
might make as hooves struck turf and not stone. We were
riding in pairs and as soon as I spied, just thirty paces from
us, the first crossbowman, I raised my sword and dug my
heels into White Star's sides. Ralf and I had the biggest and
the best horses. As soon as I dug my heels in, my warhorse
leapt.

In a few strides, we reached the Scots and it was only
when we were three paces from them that the Scottish
warrior realised his danger. He turned and saw death slice
down at him. I leaned to the other side and struck the next
Scot in the side of the head. His halberd fell to the ground. I
rode at the four crossbowmen who were levelling their
weapons or trying to load a bolt. Ralf and I, along with our
horses, eliminated the danger by smashing through them and

slashing with our swords. Having reached the ford I reined in. I looked, not behind but ahead and saw the Scots from the other side of the ambush rushing towards us. A man cannot run and loose a crossbow at the same time. Suddenly, from behind me came a flurry of bolts as my men loosed their latches. Some Scots fell and others took cover. We had a chance.

"Across the ford. Ralf, with me."

I had fought in enough battles to know that a horseman riding at a man on foot always had the advantage for horses seem to be bigger and more threatening than they actually are. The crossbows all snapped at the same time. One came close to my shoulder but missed. Their bolts having been loosed the men dropped their now useless weapons and attempted to draw their swords. I whirled White Star around and swung my sword in an arc. The men reeled and tried to get away from both the blade and the horse's hooves. I heard a cry from behind me. It was Ned, "We are across, captain!"

I wheeled my horse and headed for the river, following Ralf's horse. To my horror, I saw a bolt sticking from Ralf's leg and blood was pouring from it. His hands were trying to stem the flow and so I grabbed his horse's reins and headed for the ford.

"Hang on Ralf."

My hobilars had all reloaded their latches and, as we splashed across the ford, they raised them. As soon as our horses made the other side there was a collective crack as the latches were released. The range was too far for most of them but the six eager Scots who had waded to the middle were all struck. Only one looked to be a damaging wound but it was enough to make the others fall back to their side of the ford.

We were too close to them to stop and I led Ralf's horse to the road south. I knew from our journey north that we were less than ten miles from Carlisle but I did not think that Ralf would last that long. We also had a river to cross and the ferry would probably be on the other side. I took my hat and passed it to him. "Press that against the wound. We will stop as soon as I think that we are safe."

"Do not worry about me, captain." His words sounded slurred and although he obeyed me I knew that he was losing blood and that would weaken him.

Without turning around I shouted, "Ned, take Walter and see if they are following us but take no risks."

"Aye, captain."

I knew that Ralf could not hang on if we rode fast and so I slowed us a little. We passed through a hamlet and I was tempted to stop but we were too close to our enemies and I knew not the allegiance of the people who lived there. Life in the borders was parlous and men were flexible in their loyalty. The land became a little flatter and more open. I heard a cry from behind, "They are not following, Captain James."

I reined in and Edgar and I helped the wounded man at arms to the ground. There was a great deal of blood and I knew that once I pulled out the bolt there would be even more. I used my dagger to cut away the cloth from Ralf's breeks. "Edgar fetch vinegar and honey." I looked up, "Davy, give Ralf some ale to drink."

Ned and Walter reined in and said, "They are still on the far side of the ford. We hurt them, Captain James."

"Was Ralf our only casualty?"

"Edward has a cut to his leg and Dick was struck in the cheek."

"See to their wounds and keep watch in case they do decide to follow."

I had a cloth wound around my neck and I took it off and laid it on the ground. "Edgar, when I pull the bolt then wipe the wound with vinegar. I will tie a cloth around the upper leg to stop the flow of blood and you can smear honey into the wound."

"Aye, captain."

The awe in his voice told me that he had never seen this done before. It was another mark of the inexperience of my men. I took hold of the bolt. The saddle had arrested its progress and I prayed that it was not barbed.

"Brace Ralf. This will hurt." In one firm movement, I pulled the bolt out and I saw that it was a simple one, without barbs. Even so, Ralf's back arched. I tied the cloth tightly above the wound and although I was spattered and splashed with blood the flow soon lessened. The honey having been applied, I made sure that the cloth was still tied tightly. I leaned next to Ralf's head and spoke in his ear, "Ralf, there are healers in Carlisle. If we hurry, we may be able to save the leg."

"I am game, captain."

"Let us mount." It took four of us to help him to his saddle. I put the reins in his hands and said, "When I tell you I want you to untie your cloth and then tighten it again."

"Aye, captain, I did not know you were a doctor."

"In war, Ralf, you soon learn to deal with wounds. It is only the great and the good who are healed on the battlefield."

I used the distance we travelled to measure the times I told Ralf to loosen his bandage. In all, we did it four times and when I saw the river ahead, I almost cheered. The constable must have been watching for us as the gates opened and horsemen came out. The ferrymen had already seen us and were punting across as the riders approached.

"We have three wounded men. Take them and their horses first."

We walked the men and their horses onto the ferry and I had Davy and Ned go with them to ensure that they did not fall into the river.

"Did we do well, captain?"

I turned and saw Edgar and the rest looking at me, "You did far better than anyone could have hoped. You have all become warriors. I was honoured to lead you." The joy on their faces humbled me.

It took three crossings for us all to be ferried and I rode with Arkham who had ridden forth to join us. "The hostages?"

"All safe and grateful to you. The ladies were all most concerned about you and your men. When you did not arrive back yesterday then they feared the worst."

"How did you get back so quickly?"

He shrugged, "The captain of the boat had enough room for the horses and as there was no pursuit, we were able to load them. It was you who had the harder journey. We have been watching for you all day."

I nodded, "We had to travel further north than expected and they were waiting in ambush. They have learned that Englishmen have teeth."

We rode through the gates and into the inner bailey. My wife's parents and their ladies were all waiting for us. As we dismounted Mary de Clifton gave a scream and fainted. One of the other ladies said, "Captain, are you wounded too?"

I looked down and saw the blood on my jack. I laughed, "It looks like I have been slaughtering pigs but it is just blood from my man at arms. I must go to him and see him. I will speak with you later."

Leaving Roger to tend to his wife I followed Arkham to the infirmary. The healer was in the process of stitching the leg and Ralf's eyes were closed. He looked up at me, "You applied the bandage?" I nodded. "Then you have not only saved the man's leg but his life too."

"And for that I thank God. I have buried enough of my brothers in arms."

Chapter 5

Ecclestone 1512

Once I had satisfied myself that Ralf would live, I joined those we had rescued. The most remarkable change was in Mary de Clifton. She had never really approved of me for I had no title. Roger de Clifton did not care for such things. Her abduction and our rescue of her changed her completely. She had fainted when she saw my bloodied clothes for she had feared that I had been hurt. There would have been a time when her reaction would have been to turn away with a look of disgust on her face. She gushed over me and I confess that I found it uncomfortable. I wanted no praise for they were family and I was doing what any family member would do for another. That I had involved others meant that if any praise was due it was owed to my men. We also spoke of the future. Roger had not seen the devastation to his land and on their way home Richard had told his master that the hall had been almost completely destroyed and would need rebuilding.

Roger looked downcast, "And they have my fortune too. I am impoverished. What shall we do, James?"

Richard spoke, "They did not get all your coin, master. They found that which was in your hall but that was but half of it. You remember that you buried the other half under the floor of your bailiff's home? That still stands."

Roger said, "How did you know the treasure was buried there? Only John knew that."

Richard smiled, "John of Clifton and I were in the same company of billmen. We had no secrets and he wanted another to know of the treasure in case anything happened to him. He was not a young man although I think he thought to die in his bed and not have his life snatched away by a Scottish sword."

"I do not mind your knowing, Richard, but I was curious. Still, even half of my fortune does not help. The hall would cost that to rebuild and the men who tend the land would need to be hired."

Richard's face fell, "If you do not restore the estate, master, then where will the villagers find employment? We all depend upon the estate in one form or another."

I rubbed my chin, "It seems to me, Roger, that you need not worry about the hall, at least not for a while. At Ecclestone, we have more than enough room for you both. Jane has prepared your quarters for the Christmas visit and you shall be comfortable there. You have grandchildren to see and Richard here strikes me as a man who would make a good replacement for John. You know he has your best interests at heart and when your business begins to make money again then you can put your mind to rebuilding the hall."

Richard nodded eagerly, "I would be more than happy to do as the captain suggests if it meets with your approval."

I saw the relief flood on Roger's face. He was not a warrior and the ordeal had shaken him to his core, "I am touched by your concern and if you would have us then Mary and I would happily live with you. For my part, I regret the times away from the grandchildren."

Mary began to weep, "And that is my fault. I can see now that I was cursed by the sin of pride. I did not see the goodness within you, James. and I am sorry. If you can forgive an old lady…"

"There is nothing to forgive." I turned to the ladies, "And if you are without homes…"

It was only then that I noticed they were all of an age with my wife's mother. Alice, the spokeswoman of them, shook her head, "We all have families, Captain James. It was just bad luck that we were visiting at Clifton. We tried to plead with the Scots that we were not worth ransoming but they cared not. I, for one, will never leave my home again. I lost my husband in the wars and thought my son and his family were not important. I now see that being a farmer is as noble as any profession. Get us back to the Ribble, Captain James, and we are in your debt."

I turned to look at John who had been quiet, "And in all this, John, you have been silent. You have lost your family too."

Richard said, "There is always a home for you with me, John. I would be as a father to you."

The young man shook his head, "Clifton will always be a bad memory for me, Master Richard. I am sorry but I would see the scars of the buildings, the blood might be cleansed but I would still see it. The grave of my father and that night would be forever in my head and a visible reminder of all that was lost. I would not sleep."

Roger nodded, "I can understand that. In truth, I am loath to return. I will give you some of my treasure so that you may have a new life."

He shook his head again, "I would like to become a warrior. When I saw the captain and his men taking on those brigands, I felt helpless. I could not do as they did and yet some of his men are little older than me." He looked at me, "Captain, I would do as Ralf does and work for you whilst becoming a warrior."

My heart sank for I liked the boy and Ralf's close encounter with death made me more than a little afraid. Ralf was a warrior already. In John, I would be taking on the moulding of unformed clay. "What I will do, John, is take you back to Ecclestone and I will find you employment. Like your father and Richard here I will have you train with my billmen, but as for becoming a warrior...I am hoping that King Henry will bring peace to this land and that we will not be needed to go to war."

Roger said, "That is a kind offer, James, but until the Scots and other predators are tamed then nowhere, not even Ecclestone, will be safe. When we were prisoners, we heard disturbing words from our gaolers. The Scottish lord, Maxwell, who visited with us shortly before you rescued us, boasted that soon the Scottish lands stolen, he said, by the English, would be returned to them once more." He looked at his wife who was deep in conversation with Alice and lowered his voice, "It was also clear to me that they had no intention of letting us leave no matter how much ransom was paid. I think that we were the bait to make Sir Edward come north." He shrugged, "The Scottish lord miscalculated for my wife and I were not important enough."

Perhaps he was right and war was coming whether we wanted it or not.

We could not leave Carlisle for a week as the healers were concerned that their work on Ralf's leg would be undone. Ralf told us to leave him but I was having none of it. We would all travel back together. We used the time to pay the castle carpenter to build a wagon and we used the captured horses to pull it. The ladies were not riders. I knew that it would slow us down but that could not be helped. We left with Richard driving the wagon in which resided my wife's parents, Ralf and the three ladies. We left early for it was many miles to Kendal. Once again, I had to use my own coins to pay for the food and the beds. We reached Lancaster in the early evening of the next day. I had sent Ned ahead to tell the castle of our imminent arrival. The least that Sir Edward could do was to accommodate us and it was the lord himself who greeted us. He was effusive in his attention to the hostages. I thought it was cynical for he could have paid the full ransom had he wanted to. My men were given palliasses in the warrior hall while I was given a chamber in the keep. While the hostages were settling in Sir Edward sent for me. Once more I was taken to his solar.

"You did well, captain, and I am impressed. Tell me all." He poured wine and I gave him an account of the rescue and the ambush. When I finished, he nodded, "I confess, Captain James, that this attack has shaken me to the core. When I was given the task of organising Yorkshire and Westmoreland, I thought it an easy diversion but I see now that it is not. The Scots were trying to provoke war. Those who have dealings with King James tell me that he has a belligerent attitude towards England and wishes the return of Northumberland to Scotland."

I laughed for when I had spoken with Gerald of Etal, I had learned much about Northumberland, "It has never been Scottish, my lord. During the time of Stephen and Matilda, they briefly stole it but once the second King Henry attained the throne then they lost any claim to it that they might have thought that they had."

"Robert the Bruce has much to answer for. His candle burned brightly for a while and made the Scots have aspirations beyond their martial abilities. King James wishes to rekindle those aspirations. You and your men will be needed sooner rather than later. However, for the moment you are to be congratulated."

He raised his goblet to me. I acknowledged it and asked, as innocently as I could, "And the horses, my lord?"

"Horses?"

"Aye, the horses you gave us. Do you wish them returned?"

He laughed, "Of course not. Call it payment for services rendered."

I was pleased for it meant I could now train more hobilars. If either John or my son James did not have the body for a billman then they could become hobilars. The rescue had shown me the value of such warriors."

The old Mary de Clifton resurfaced that night for we dined with Sir Edward, his nobles and their wives and she beamed at the splendour of the castle. However, when she saw the attention that I was given I think she realised that I was more important than she had first thought.

The next day we headed back to Clifton. The ladies lived closer to the coast at Freckleton and Richard promised that he would see them home. They would spend the night with him in his home. The sight of the burnt-out buildings proved too much for Mary, who broke down and wept. I sent the wagon to the village while we retrieved Roger's treasure. It would not do to risk the chance of thieves discovering it.

The goodbyes of the ladies were tearful. Roger grew impatient with the four of them, "Come wife, we have many miles to go and I am anxious to see our daughter and the grandbairns. Remember, she knows not if her husband lives or died trying to rescue us."

We headed back across the Ribble and took the road to Ecclestone. It was getting on for dark when we neared Parr and I sent Ned to warn my wife that we were returning. It meant that the whole village turned out to greet us. The men I had led all lived within two miles of Ecclestone and none knew if any of my hobilars had been hurt. The joy when they spied that we were whole was unbounded. If any did notice that Ralf was not riding that was to be understood. He had no family. Understandably Jane gave her whole attention to her parents as did my daughters. My two sons, however, looked for Ralf.

"Father, where is Ralf? He was not…"

I heard the catch in James' voice as did Ralf who pulled himself from the bottom of the wagon, "No, James, I was not killed but I owe my life to your father."

Riding in the wagon had made the journey home easier for Ralf but getting in and out was harder. He shuffled to the rear where Ned and Edward, after opening it, helped him to the ground. We had fashioned two crutches and he put them under his arms.

It was then that Jane saw him, "Husband, why do you not help poor Ralf."

Ralf grinned, "I can manage, my lady, but I fear that I will not be racing through the hall for a while."

She shook her head and spoke to my assembled hobilars, "And we are all outside getting cold. I thank you men for rescuing my parents. I am in your debt and if you ever need aught, I beg you just to ask."

They all gave a slight bow and Edgar said, "My lady, it was an honour and we would do so again." He turned to me, "Practice on Sunday, Captain James?"

It was my turn to grin, "Of course, you have much to show the other men of the levy," I waved over John, "And wife, we have another guest."

She saw John for the first time and her face lit up, "Why John, you are most welcome."

I caught Jane's eye, "John has no one in the world and asked to stay with us."

She hugged him and said, "Of course. For tonight I will make you a bed with James and Walter. Tomorrow I shall rearrange the sleeping arrangements. You are all more than welcome." Despite the extra work their presence created, I knew that Jane meant every word. She was the kindest soul I had ever known and I knew I had been lucky to find her.

We went inside as Ned and the others took the horses from the wagon and stabled ours. They were all horsemen and the care of our animals came above all else. The extra horses meant we would have to build new stables.

James placed a chair by the fire for Ralf while Walter hurried off to find us some ale. She took her parents up the stairs to the bedchamber we had always kept for guests. The only ones who had used it had been Jane's parents and now it would be theirs for the foreseeable future. Clifton would take a year or more to be rebuilt and the work could not begin until the spring at the earliest. As they headed up the stairs I heard Mary moan, "And I have worn these clothes since I was taken. All my fine dresses were destroyed." I did not hear Jane's reply but knew that my practical wife would find more clothes for her mother.

As Ralf and I sat with my sons by the fire Ralf said, "Captain, you know wounds better than I. Will this make me a cripple?"

I shook my head, "It was a clean wound and the healer at Carlisle found no hidden injury when he sewed it. The wound has not been hot to the touch, has it?" He shook his head. "Then when we remove the stitches, you can begin to walk about. The more you walk the quicker you will heal." The healer had said to leave the stitches in for a fortnight. The nearest doctor to Ecclestone was at Windle and it would be me who removed them. I had done so before. We were self-reliant in the village. The women of Ecclestone were the midwives and could handle minor ailments and injuries. I was the one who knew how to tend to war injuries. My father had been the same.

The table, when we ate, was full. John was seated between James and Ralf and I knew that my son would make the daunting experience easy for the son of the bailiff. The meal we ate was simple but when we said Grace before we ate the words had more meaning. We all knew that God had aided us. We could not have done what we had without his help. Jane sat between her parents and fussed over them but each time she looked across at me and caught my eye I saw the gratitude in hers. We all retired early. These were the first stairs that Ralf had encountered since his wound and it took James, John and me to help him to his chamber. James and Walter along with John, helped him, despite the protestations of the man at arms, to bed. It showed me how close my boys were to Ralf.

I waited, alone in our bed until Jane had ensured that all our guests were comfortable. She undressed and snuggled next to me. She looked up and, putting her hand behind my head, pulled it down to give me a long and passionate kiss, "I always knew that I had the best of husbands but what you did for my parents went above and beyond what was to be expected of any man."

I kissed her and we put our heads on the pillow, "It was family."

She shook her head, "My father told me what you had to do and the risks you took. Poor Ralf is visible evidence of what might have happened."

"But it did not and that, my love, is why we practise each Sunday. We never know when we will be called to war. I fear that the Scots have belligerence in their hearts and that there will be war once more. King Henry casts his eye towards France and the Pope. He seeks land there and when he takes the best of our soldiers east then the plague of Scots will descend from the north. Our journey north taught me that there are too few defences between the Scots and this fertile land of Lancashire. In the east, there are castles and defences but here in the west we are vulnerable."

She sighed, "Why do they wish to make war?"

"Their land is poor and ours is rich. Your father showed that by making a fortune from sheep. The wool he sells travels beyond England's shores. Husbandry is a skilled trade and we have it in abundance. It is why, unlike your father, I have good defences here in Ecclestone. If an enemy was foolish enough to try to do what they did at Clifton, then they would pay a bloody price."

She squeezed me tightly, "And I appreciate it. Now come closer so that I can show you my full appreciation."

The next morning I could not keep the smile from my face. I was home and despite the crowded nature of my hall, it was harmonious. John and I helped Ralf down the stairs. James had wanted to help but I sent him to help his mother and the cook prepare breakfast. Until Jane could reorganise the household then everyone would have to pitch in.

When we reached the bottom of the stairs Ralf said, "And this will be the last time I am helped up and down the stairs. I will give myself plenty of time this evening to ascend the stairs by myself. There is no rush. You are right, Captain, the more I use my leg the stronger it will become."

We went to the table which was already being filled with a variety of food. We had our own bread oven and it had been the smell of fresh bread wafting up the stairs that had woken me. We cured our own ham and it was ready to be sliced. A pot of steaming porridge also stood on the table along with honey and jam made from the summer and autumn fruits. The bread was not manchet. We did have wheat bread but not for breakfast. It was not Carter's bread made with darker flour but was raveled, wholesome bread but with a coarser texture than manchet. I wondered what Mary de Clifton would make of the plainer fare.

She and her husband rose late. This had been their first night in a decent bed for some time and their late rising was understandable. Mary had been changed by her experience. We had eaten the bread that she had endured at Threave and it was Carter's bread made with oats and barley. Wholesome enough but chewier than raveled and certainly not what Mary was used to. She beamed when she saw the table, "A feast for breakfast, you are spoiling us, Jane." I was relieved and knew that the normally highly critical Mary had died at Clifton and was now reborn. The kidnapping had exorcised the demons from within her.

After I had enjoyed the best breakfast in a long time, I rose, "Come, James, John and Walter, I have been absent from my land and I need to show John our people."

Walter grew visibly at his inclusion. The truth was I had missed my family and I would enjoy walking the village with the three of them. We wrapped cloaks around us because the cold weather was coming. It was James who found one for John. Like my father-in-law, the attack had left him as a pauper. I was lucky that I had coins I could use to good effect. If we had more time we could have robbed the dead at Threave but we had not had time. I knew that the treasure taken by the Maxwells would be filling their coffers at Caerlaverock.

The village always rose early and men were already tending their fields. This was the time of year when all was gathered in for winter. Nothing was wasted. It was a lucky bird that found a windfall apple. Most were picked and crushed to make cider. The mash that was left would feed the fields. The berry bushes had been stripped and any fruit that looked like it was going over would be made into jam. Trees were being trimmed to make kindling and provide firewood for the winter as well as encouraging healthier growth in the spring. Children had been in the woods to gather the nuts before the squirrels could store them. When the migrating wildfowl landed to rest, men would trap them and take nature's bounty. We wasted nothing. Farmers spoke to me as I passed through. The questions and requests I had been given were nothing to do with the rescue, they were to do with farming. My pair of oxen were in great demand. They made the ploughing for the winter crops much easier and fertilised their fields. Some men charged but I did not. I knew that the village would all benefit and my oxen would ensure that people did not starve. There were also questions about borrowing my bull, ram and my boar to fertilise their flocks and herds. My absence, while I was on the raid, had delayed what was a necessary part of our year. At the end of the season, we would be slaughtering the old animals who were not worth keeping over the winter. Then, when all the meat had been used and the bones boiled to make potage and stock, we would burn the bones at the bone fire along with other rubbish that could be used on the fields. The burnt bones would be spread in every field in the village and our farms would all be more fertile.

John knew much of this already but Clifton had been a different sort of enterprise and his father had largely been involved in the raising of sheep, the harvesting of their wool and their protection over winter. We were a more varied farming community. I think he was pleased to be involved. We returned to my hall at noon for food. It would be simple fare: bread, cheese and pickles. My wife sat with me as I ate, "Husband, we need more servants." Her mother and father were no longer young and both rested in the room we called the parlour. "I need more help in the kitchen and both my mother and father need a body servant." She shrugged, "They are used to such things. You and I need them not but…"

"Whatever you need, you take. Do not forget my extra pay is there waiting to be used. You have the keys and the purse strings. Whatever coins we have, wife, are for you to use. We will not argue about such inconsequential matters."

She looked relieved, "And I will need money for material. We can make the clothes but my mother will need finer ones."

I knew that Roger would need all of his money for the rebuilding of Clifton, "Whatever you need."

James begged permission to be allowed to spar in the afternoon with John and Walter. Normally I would have been with them but Roger came to ask me for advice. I nodded my agreement, "But James, if Walter returns with a bloody coxcomb, then you will be punished. You are the elder and responsible no matter how wild is your little brother."

"I know, father, and I will be mindful."

"And I will watch over them too, captain."

"Thank you, John."

Roger and I wrapped up to walk in the village. I think he wanted privacy and to be able to speak openly to me. "I want to say, once more, James, that I can never repay you for what you did."

"There is no need."

"There is for I cannot see Clifton being rebuilt any time soon and we will need your charity."

"It is not charity for you are family and I do not mind. I know Mary once had a low opinion of me but I am well off, Roger, and my lands are profitable. I am paid by Sir Edward Stanley and my success on the battlefield brings me coins.

Do not worry if you never rebuild Clifton. We are happy to be your hosts."

He looked relieved. "Do not misunderstand me, James, I want the estate rebuilding but that is different from creating a fine manor. Before the weather changes too much, I would have you escort me back to Clifton so that I can speak with Richard and provide him with the funds that he will need."

"Whenever you are ready, we shall go back."

He asked for and received advice about how he should proceed. He knew sheep and wool making but it was clear that John's father, John, had been the one who managed the estate. I had been forced to learn such skills when my father died and Roger had never had to. By the time we returned to my hall, he was satisfied that he had a plan in his mind. It was a start and allowed me to forget war for a while.

I knew that Roger was keen to speak to his people and we rode north, at the start of November to speak to Richard and to provide the funds needed to pay the workers on the estate. They all farmed a strip of land but that only gave them food for the summer and autumn. Soon it would be the short days when men tightened their belts and the old and sick starved and died. James and John came with us and we left before dawn. It would not do to ask the villagers to accommodate us. Roger gave Richard permission to cull as many of the older animals as he saw fit. The meat would see them through the worst of winter. He provided funds so that in spring Richard could buy more animals. The Scots had taken the horses and cows, as well as the oxen and the bull when they had raided. The horses had been retained but the others slaughtered for their meat. Roger would have to start afresh. I think that Richard relished the challenge. It was as though the death of John of Clifton had somehow energised his friend. As we left, I was confident that Clifton would be prosperous once more but this time better protected. I doubted that the Scots would risk a raid a second time but if they did then the village would be prepared.

Chapter 6

Ecclestone Christmas 1512

At the end of the year, as we celebrated Christmas and the good things in our lives, I received two pieces of news that I kept to myself. I did not want to spoil the happy atmosphere in my hall. Ecclestone, since I had begun to farm there, had prospered and of the four villages which were close mine had become the most vibrant and important. One sign of its increased prosperity was that the inn, at the end of the village close by the church, the Griffin, now enjoyed more folk who passed through. Since the end of the divisive civil war, King Henry had made the whole land prosperous. I had heard rumours that one way he had done this was to put copper in the coins but whatever he had done it had worked. I only drank there on Sunday, with my centenars after practice, but I often rode to pass it on my rides to Knowsley. Ned, having married following our return from Threave, had inherited a small farm in the tiny village of Knowsley and I often visited.

As I passed the inn I was hailed, "Captain James, is that you?"

I did not recognise the voice nor, at first, the man but I had been taught to be courteous and I rode White Star over to him. He was swathed in a cloak and with scarves wrapped around him. He and his companion had just dismounted from their horses. "You have the advantage of me, sir." He unswathed his scarf and I recognised him immediately, "John of Hedingham, what brings you this far north?" John had been one of the billmen who had served Sir Edward although he had long given that up.

I dismounted and clasped his arm. He said, "Business." He turned to his companions, "Stable our horses and go within." He smiled, "Our old friend, Sam, used the money left to him by Sir Edward to become a merchant and he and I became partners. We buy sheepskins and turn them into wool. Being as close as we are to the river, we can sell them across the channel where they fetch higher prices."

"Surely the sheep of Suffolk are closer."

He nodded, "They are but, in the north, beyond Lancaster, you have a sheep called a Herdwick and while the wool is coarser than other sheep it has the ability to keep out water. Sailors heading across the seas to the New World prize garments made from such wool. Sam is a clever man, as you well know, and he has seen an opportunity. Will you come and have an ale with us?"

"I must first visit with a friend in Knowsley but I will call in on the way back."

"We will be here. We heard this inn was a good one and we will leave early in the morning and hope to be north of the Ribble by evening."

I had done the journey and knew that he had chosen the wrong time to make the journey. Snow had not yet come in this part of the world but once in Westmoreland and Cumberland, his horses could expect to have to wade through drifts. Ned had good news when I visited with him for his wife, Rosemary, was with child. Ned had been paid, as we all had, by the county for our services at Threave and he had used the coins wisely. I did not stay long but left a gold crown to help with the child. Ned was one of my men and the bond was a tight one.

I dismounted at The Griffin and left White Star with the ostler, Matthew. He was one of my hobilars and would look after White Star well. John and his two companions were seated at a table and had just finished their meal when I entered. John introduced the two men and I instantly forgot their names for John looked as though he had news to impart.

"You remember, Stephen?"

"Of course." Stephen, Sam and I were inseparable when we had served as Sir Edward's billmen.

"He has been made captain of five hundred and has been commissioned to go with King Henry to France next year."

"So King Henry finally goes to war. The rumours have abounded for some time."

"He does. As he is now paying for the men then he must intend to fight. Emperor Maximilian has now joined the papal alliance and France could rue its decision to oppose the pope. There was a sea battle off Brest at the end of summer and, although we won, Sir Edward Howard was killed. King James has renewed the alliance with France. It will not be long before war comes to the borders. Already there is unrest."

The news disturbed me but I recognised the cunning of Sam and I nodded, "You hope to use the unrest to get your wool at lower prices."

He nodded and his broad grin told me that I had hit the mark, "The price for salted meat will rise and the farmers may well be willing to kill off some of their animals early to take advantage of the high price of salted meat and to be less of a target for raiding Scots. They cannot steal dead animals, can they?"

"A clever piece of business if it works. I take it you will be up around Carlisle and Hexham?"

He nodded and drank some of the ale before him, "We will and then we will cross to the west and take a ship from Newcastle back to Hedingham. We hope to have our skins with us and be home for Christmas but if not, we will still have a good New Year."

I drank a pot of ale with them and we spoke of Sam and Stephen. "Give my old friends my best wishes. Tell Stephen," I shook my head, "if he is the captain of five hundred then I need tell him nothing. I wish him well."

I walked White Star the half a mile back to my hall. As I had not been asked to the muster then I would not be going to France but if King Henry was taking the best of his army to fight the French, then who would be watching the northern borders? Our rescue had shown me that the defence of the north was thinly spread. When I rode from Ecclestone to Lathom I passed many farms and each one teemed with men working them. We produced crops in this fertile part of England that needed many men to labour. The raising of sheep on open fells needed only a couple of shepherds. When war came it would be the men of Lancashire and Cheshire who would be called upon to stem the attacks and fields and animals would be untended. There was little point in bringing it up before Christmas but I knew that I would have to ensure that as much work was done before the call for the muster came. War was generally fought in the summer months. Spring was the time for sowing and Autumn the time for harvesting. Summer meant long days spent with an eye on the weather. I began to plan the crops we would sow. I needed crops that could be harvested in October or could be picked by women. I smiled, as I stabled White Star. When I had been King Henry's spy, living in the court of Burgundy such thoughts would have been far from my head.

Ralf's injury had improved. He still limped a little but he no longer winced when he walked. The wound had been a chastening experience not only for him but the rest of the men who had come with us. Ralf's breeks had not been any defence against the bolt. While Ralf would be able to use plate armour when he led my hobilars his men would need protection. We had knee-length leather boots made for them. I used my own treasure to pay for them but as they were made by my tanner in the village it cost me little and the extra protection was worth it. The leather jack that they wore was also lengthened so that two pieces of leather, rather like a man at arms fauld, covered their thighs. It did not impair their movement and Ralf was happier knowing that they were better protected. Not all of my hobilars had helmets but my travails and battles had resulted in a collection of various helmets. A visit to Lathom also resulted in the steward finding old swords, spears and helmets gathered after the Viking raid. Considered too old-fashioned for most professional soldiers, my warriors for the working day welcomed them.

While I was there, I learned that Earl Stanley would be joining the king in France and he would not be returning to Lathom in the foreseeable future. Sir Edward would be the one commanding the levy from Lathom. For that reason, the steward was happy for me to ransack the armoury. Weapons and armour had changed in the last years. The swords and mail that had gone to war at Bosworth were now considered out of date. Lighter swords with basket hilts were becoming more popular. Helmets were now changing too. I cared not for even an old pot helmet, or old fashioned sallet could protect my billmen and hobilars. I knew who our enemy would be, the Scots, and that they were wild fighters. We might have more skill but my men's heads needed protection and the helmets would guarantee that. The result was that, as Christmas approached and we drilled on the green, my men looked more like the company of billmen that Stephen led at Hedingham and less like the levy that they were.

The last practice was the Sunday before Christmas and my archers, hobilars and billmen paraded before Ralf and me. John rode with the hobilars and James, standing close to Ralf and I, looked enviously at the young man who had become part of our family. Despite the rain which pelted down, the sixty men of Ecclestone looked as professional a force as I had seen at the various battles I had been involved with.

"Men, I shall not see you for a fortnight while we enjoy the celebration of the birth of Christ but you have all earned a break from parading and practising in such conditions. I will not keep you longer. Go and enjoy an ale at the inn. I have put money behind the bar so that you may all have a drink on me."

They cheered and we parted. As they left and the four of us headed back to my hall, I hoped that my father, looking down from heaven, would be proud of me and what I had achieved. I had almost ruined my life but something had changed me and made me into what I hoped was a better leader.

We celebrated Christmas well. We slaughtered three geese and one of the old sows who had stopped giving birth and we all dined in my hall. We filled the table. John had long since stopped feeling uncomfortable in the presence of those he saw as his betters. That was down to my children. Jane had brought them up well and they did not see themselves as any better or worse than anyone else. Ralf, too, was happy to be part of my family.

After Grace and as we tucked into the food which made the table groan, Roger, seated next to me said, "You are lucky, James, or perhaps made better decisions than I did. The Christmases my wife and I enjoyed, before you came into the family, were quiet and boring." He leaned closer to me and spoke conspiratorially, "Mary liked to invite those she thought important, priests, lawyers and the like. Their conversations were dull beyond words." He spread his arm around, "this is the kind of Christmas a man should enjoy. I fear that such celebrations will make me loath to leave and return to Clifton. Even a rebuilt hall will seem lifeless with just we two within."

"And you need not leave, Roger. You are no longer a young man. Richard cares for the estate and having fought alongside him I know that he will run your estate as well as any. Build your hall but do not feel as though you have to leave here. Your grandchildren and your daughter enjoy your company as much as you do theirs."

"Then you have put my mind at rest."

It was after the feast that we gave gifts to one another. Most were homemade but I gave James, John and Walter, daggers which I had collected over the years. Jane's eyes told me that she did not totally approve but she said nothing. The boys had carved bone and their sisters were given combs for their hair as were my wife and their grandmother. To me, they gave a finely made scabbard for my sword. It must have taken them weeks to do. The best present, however, came from Jane. When the gifts had been exchanged, she smiled and took my hand, "And there is one more gift to give on this day when we celebrate the birth of Christ. I am with child. There will be another in this hall come the summer."

Better news could not be conceived, everyone cheered and it made the day even better. We drank more than was usual and we were all merry and happy. I worked out that the baby had been conceived on the day I had returned from Threave. It was meant to be. I cared not if it would be a boy or girl. So long as it was born healthy with the required number of limbs and eyes then I would be happy.

The news changed us all. Mary would be on hand to witness a child being born and my other four children were now old enough to realise the changes that a baby would make in a household. It also had an effect on Ralf. I knew that his wound not only made him think about his mortality but also about the mark he would leave on this earth. I had once been like Ralf, young and single with none to worry about. Now I had children and I hoped that they would have children so that the line that Jane and I had begun would continue. He started to think about his own family. He was an orphan and had neither brothers nor sisters.

When the first snow came and he and I walked my fields to ensure that there were no animals left without shelter he spoke to me. "Captain, how did you meet Mistress Jane?" I told him. "And how did you know that you and she were meant for each other?"

I stopped and looked at him. I had never thought about that, "A good question, Ralf, and I had not thought about it before." I rubbed my chin and said, "I liked Jane and found that I wanted to be with her more than with others. If that does not sound romantic then I am sorry. I was not brought up with tales of heroic lovers. We were just comfortable with one another."

He nodded, "You know Elizabeth, the tanner's daughter?"

"Aye, she is a comely girl with a wicked sense of humour."

He laughed, "I know that to my cost. When I visited with him to arrange for the boots to be made, she took great pleasure in sending me past the place they soaked the hides."

I laughed. The tanner used urine to make the hides pliable and he had the vats around the back of the house for the stink was awful. Elizabeth had deliberately made him endure the smell. I said nothing.

"Rather than being offended, I liked her spirit. I enjoy being with her for she makes me smile."

"Have you said anything to her or her father?"

He shook his head, "I have nothing to offer a young maid, Captain James."

"You have, you have the stipend I give you and if you wish for land and a home then we have enough men to build you one." I waved a hand at the snow, "Now, of course, is not the time but…"

"She might not even want me. She is the prettiest girl in the village and I know that there are others who have more to offer."

I nodded, "Ralf, you are one of the bravest men I know. Up the Tweed and the Till, you fought as bravely as any. On the Esk, you stood alone with me and faced a warband of Scots. Are you truly intimidated by this young maid? What is the worst that could happen?"

"I could have a broken heart which is harder to mend than a bolt from a crossbow."

"Aye, you are right there but a heart can heal and at least you will know. The longer you delay the more likely it is that another suitor will strike."

"I have not said that I wish to be a suitor."

I laughed, "Yes you have. Think about what I have said and if it is just a roof over your head that you worry about then do not. We can remedy that quickly but you need to decide if this is what you wish and if this is the woman with whom you will spend the rest of your life."

That evening I told Jane what Ralf had said, "If Elizabeth played such a trick on Ralf, then it was to attract his attention. You men do not understand women. Ralf is an attractive young man. Other women in the village look at him with admiring eyes." She shook her head at my expression of wonder, "You do not think that when we sew in my parlour we talk of cross stitching and yarn do you?"

The next day I watched Jane as she found the time to speak alone with Ralf. I did not interfere but smiled when I saw him blushing. When he joined me to practise, along with James and John I knew he had something to say to me. After we had finished sparring and while James and John put away the weapons he said, "Mistress Jane has spoken to me and her advice was sage but how do I proceed, Captain James?"

"You have two targets in this campaign, Ralf, Tom the Tanner and Elizabeth. Which one do you think you should approach first?"

"That is clear, Elizabeth for if she does not return my affection then I need not risk the wrath of Tom."

"Then you have your answer."

It was a week later that he plucked up the courage to speak to Elizabeth and my wife was quite right, she had been waiting for an approach. He then spoke to Tom to ask his permission to court his daughter. I think Ralf was taken aback by the fulsome welcome he received. The courting began and Jane and I knew it would just be a matter of time before they wed.

It was interesting to look at the courtship with detachment. One day James would find a bride and Eliza, my eldest, would be courted by a young man. I wondered how I would react to their potential partners. Ralf was courteous, even shy and it was Elizabeth who was the more forceful of the two. Jane knew the girl well and told me that it was a good thing. "Every marriage needs two who have differences. I know that I am quieter than you, my sweet, yet our marriage is harmonious is it not?"

I had not thought of that but she was right. "I did not think I was the louder."

She laughed, "It all depends on what you speak of. I am not criticising. I think it was one of the reasons mother took against you. She thought you were brash and loud. You are not and she has learned the errors of her ways but Ralf and Elizabeth fit well. He might be the sharp sword but she is the pretty and well-made scabbard that will protect him."

I was a lucky man and I knew it.

Chapter 7

Lancaster Castle 1513

The wedding was arranged for Easter. It was a propitious time. The fields had been sown and new animals were being born daily. Ralf was so popular that every man in the village had pitched in to build them a home. The land I gave him was a pleasant corner bounded by a small copse and a pond. It was not suitable for farming but his income from me would provide enough for him and Elizabeth to be comfortable. Roger gave him ten crowns. His fortune had also grown over the winter and the wool sold by Richard had yielded great profits. As he had not begun work on the new hall, he had money to spare. It was his way of thanking the man at arms for his efforts at Threave. The whole village celebrated and, unusually for Easter, the weather was benign and the celebrations spilt out onto the green. It was a perfect way for the couple to begin a life together. They looked made for each other and John and Betty looked happy that their only child had married so well.

The dark clouds appeared just a week after the wedding. I was summoned to Lancaster by Sir Edward and I knew what that meant. War.

I did not take Ralf for he and his new bride were busily setting up home. I took John and James. James because he wanted to be a warrior and John because he always looked after James. He had become a sort of big brother. James had grown over the winter and was now approaching John's height. He was able to ride a horse rather than a pony. We did not ride armed for war but we went prepared. We had woollen hats upon our heads and cloaks wrapped around us. We all carried swords and daggers but I thought it unlikely that we would need to draw them. I also had the other two pack as I did, spare breeks. The Roman Roads we used were cobbled but the minor roads were constructed of compacted clay and soil. After a benign Easter, we had endured three days of rain that, while welcomed by the farmers, made the roads muddy and slippery. We would be filthy when we reached Lancaster Castle and I did not wish us to appear like beggars at the feast.

For James, it was an adventure and he pictured himself, I am sure, going to war with a sword and cloak. For John and me, it was something to be endured.

The first thing I noticed when I reached the castle was the increased number of men wearing the Stanley livery, the yellow and green with the eagle claw was a very distinctive one. Most were new men and until I was recognised, we were viewed with suspicion. When the steward was fetched, he had our horses stabled and we were taken to a small chamber. There was one bed and two paillasses. It might not be the adventure that James hoped it would be. We changed into clean breeks and took advantage of the jug of water, bowl and clean towels to freshen up.

"You need to know that you may well be used as servants. The squires of nobles act as such and if you are asked to serve at the table you should do so."

"But do we get to eat, father?"

I laughed, James was a typical growing youth and was never full, "Of course, but it will be in the kitchen and you will be eating that which those at the tables have not eaten." James' face fell. "Do not worry, there will be plenty of it. Be kind to the cook and who knows what treats may come your way."

It was a martial gathering. I saw, next to Sir Edward, the Earl of Surrey, Sir Thomas Howard. The earl's two sons, Thomas and Edmund were there too. I was seated at the low end of the table with the other commoners. As I had expected my son and John were given the task of serving at table. They brought food to the commoners at the end of the table. They both looked as though they regarded the task as an honourable one and carried their platters proudly. I was seated with the gentlemen of Lancashire and Westmoreland. I enjoyed their conversations for these were warriors who would fight to protect the land in which they lived and not for the hope of enrichment. They knew, better than any, the dangers of a Scottish invasion and it was clear that all knew the Scots intended to raid. Most were keen to return to their homes to prepare their defences. Lancaster, Craven and the Forest of Bowland might be many miles from the border but the Scots could move swiftly when they chose. They had all heard of my rescue of Roger and Mary. They knew of Sir John Maxwell and feared him.

"The raid on Clifton was a warning, Captain James. I serve Lord Clifford in Craven and we have been on a war footing all winter. The Scots do not normally raid in winter but neither do they sail up the Ribble to boldly kidnap gentle women." George of Clitheroe was a good soldier. I had known him when I was a younger man. The presence of George and the other gentleman farmers filled me with confidence. These were not the preening courtiers who worried more about fashionable armour. These were the yeomen of England who were solid and reliable.

That I was noticed was clear. Sir Edward actually pointed to me at one point and I saw the Earl of Surrey peering myopically at me. He was an old soldier. One of those seated close to me, when he saw the earl's interest, told me that the Earl Marshal was over seventy years of age. He had fought at Bosworth on the losing side and languished in the tower for three years. He had regained his lands and won the confidence of the king. I wondered at his presence. When the feast ended the nobles at the top table retired and we were left in the hall. It was clear that I was not to be summoned to speak with Sir Edward until the morrow. Left with men like myself I discovered the reason for the feast. They had all arrived earlier in the day and been honoured by a speech from the earl who told them to be ready to heed the call for the muster. The others would all be departing the next day which begged the question, why was I there and why had I not been summoned earlier to hear the date of the muster for myself?

John and James were bubbling with excitement when they returned to our bedchamber. They had rubbed shoulders with the squires of the earl and his sons as well as the other assembled knights. The cooks had, indeed, rewarded their diligence for the two boys had not tried to avoid work as some of the nobler squires did. They had enjoyed all sorts of delicacies including marchpane. It was as though they had died and gone to heaven. I had not consumed as much wine as most of the other gentlemen and I was not woken by my bladder. I enjoyed a good night of rest and rose before James or John. I descended to the hall and was one of the first to arrive and enjoy the breakfast of freshly baked bread and the leftovers from the previous night. When the earl rose then the cooks would fetch out more appropriate delicacies but I did not mind the leftovers.

Sir Edward was an early riser and he joined me. I had been summoned away from my family and I could see no reason for it and I was blunt when I spoke with Sir Edward. "Thank you for the feast last evening but as I was not summoned early enough to hear what the others heard I am at a loss as to my inclusion."

He smiled, "That is because it was not necessary for you heard the earl's inspiring words. Even if the Scots struck more quickly than we expected, a raid through Westmoreland, Lancashire and across the Ribble could not happen. My family's lands will be safe, Ecclestone will be safe, but the earl needs to speak with you. He will join us soon, for breakfast, and then we will retire to my solar, away from prying eyes and ears that might hear what we wish to keep secret."

My heart sank. I now had a clear suspicion about my inclusion in this obvious conspiracy.

When I was alone with Sir Edward and Sir Thomas, my fears were confirmed. The earl might have had white hair but he had a mind as sharp as the dagger I kept in my boot. "Sir Edward has told me of your past, James of Ecclestone, and had I not heard rumours before I would have thought them fantastical," I said nothing. "I am to command the army that will meet with the foolish King James when he obeys the request from the French queen to attack England." He shook his head, "I would have been happier to be with the king and lead his armies in France but ..." he waved a hand as though the words were in the air before him and he was flitting them away like flies. "I shall do my duty and use every means in my power to thwart the Scottish plans. It goes without saying that all that is spoken in this solar is of a secret nature and that if it is divulged then you will lose your head." He said it in such a matter-of-fact tone that he might have been commenting on the state of the weather.

Sir Edward leaned over, "But you should know, James, that there will be a reward in this for you." They were dangling bait before me, "My nephew has agreed that you should be rewarded for services to your country and to our family in particular by being given the manor of Ecclestone. The title of lord of the manor will accompany that gift."

I said nothing but nodded and smiled. The title would be just that, a title and it would not increase my wealth. If anything it would give me more responsibilities but Jane and her parents would like it. I wondered what would be the price for such a reward.

The earl smiled a cold smile, "As I well know, James of Ecclestone, no gift comes without a price and King Henry would have you as his spy once more." My face showed my surprise. The earl nodded, "The cardinal and the king spoke with me and it was they told me of your clandestine deeds. You did not think that you would be forgotten, did you?"

I felt as though a door had slammed shut. I would, once again, have to lie and deceive others for my country. I would be forced to leave my family and leave them bereft of news. I briefly thought about refusal but realised that it would be seen as treachery and, at best, I would be incarcerated in the Tower, at worst I would lose my head.

The earl leaned back in his seat, "I will order the muster in July and it will be in Newcastle. Men will need time to reach the north for men will be coming from Yorkshire, Lancashire as well as Westmoreland. I will move to Pontefract at the start of August. England will need her men working in the fields for as long as possible. You will begin your service before the others do. You are commanded to go to Scotland in the middle of May. Sir Edward has the plan." He reached over and drank some wine, "Wolsey has concocted this plan." He spat the words out and it confirmed what I had heard, the earl and the cardinal did not get on. "That greasy man is good at such things and I daresay it will be a competent one. I prefer to be more open but…" He replaced the goblet and wiped his mouth with his napkin. "You are to let me know as soon as the Scots muster and prepare to move south. That is why you will be travelling north earlier. You will be King Henry's spy in Scotland. At the first sign of danger to England, you will first ride to Newcastle and tell Lord Dacre, the lord of the West March and then get word to me." He rose and I did too. He waved me to my seat, "You shall stay and speak with Sir Edward. I must begin my ride back to my estates in the south. Remember, you tell no one what you are about. You, of all people, know that. The fewer who know of your mission the better it is for you."

He left us. I sat and looked at Sir Edward. To be fair to the noble, he looked uncomfortable and when he spoke his words confirmed that, "I know that it is asking much of you, James but you are singularly well qualified to carry out the task. You are to play the part of a Flemish knight who seeks to serve King James. There are many such mercenaries flocking to Scotland in the hope of financial reward. The plate and the sword you own came from the court of Burgundy and you can speak both Flemish and French."

I shook my head, "It has been some time since I spoke those languages, my lord, and I am rusty."

"I know I am teaching my grandmother to suck eggs but it seems to me you could play a dour, silent and resentful knight. The cardinal suggested that you say you come from Touraine and lost your lands to the English."

I shook my head, "That would be a risk as I know not if there might be another mercenary who knows that area."

Sir Edward smiled, "You see, you have natural skills."

"What of the men I lead? Who will train them and take them to muster?"

"Your man, Ralf?" I nodded, "Is he a good leader?"

"He is."

"Then he can lead your men. I will pay him as a captain from this moment on." He picked a purse up from his desk and handed it to me. "Here is a purse filled with French, Burgundian, and Flemish coins. It will add colour to your story. Once you leave here then you will be on your own. Until you rejoin us for the battle, wherever that might be, you will have disappeared. I know that Sir Thomas advised you to tell no one but I suspect you will need to concoct a story for your family. All I will say is, be circumspect." He sat back, assuming the matter was settled, "Your title and deeds will await my nephew's signature. That will be when the battle is fought and won."

I stood and then asked, "And the title, is it hereditary?"

He nodded, "When the king returns and we have defeated this Scottish threat, it will be confirmed." Once more they were using the lure of the title, which I now knew I could pass on to my children, to ensure that I did my job.

As I left it was clear what that meant. If I failed or if we lost then I would have nothing. I realised that in the event it would not matter for if we lost then I would, in all likelihood, be dead.

My son and John were too full of their time in the castle to notice that I was silent and withdrawn as we headed along the long road back to Ecclestone. I began to plan as I rode. I could not use White Star. Sir John Maxwell or his men might well remember it. Similarly, I would have to change my appearance. That would be easy. I would trim my rough beard and make it more like the beards which were worn on the continent. It would be well-trimmed and oiled. It would add to the story. I still had some clothes I had worn when I had served with Perkin Warbeck. I had grown since then but my wife could use her skills to make them fit once more. The hat, boots and cloak would all still fit and their age might make my story more believable. By the time I reached home, I had decided on an identity. I made up both a name and a place I had been born. The cardinal's choice was his. I would be the only one who knew my story. If challenged I would reveal that I had committed a crime under my real name and had to change it. I had learned that covering a story with layers helped to confuse. I would become an onion. My revealed lies would make my story more convincing. I would, however, have to avoid King James. I had been of some service to him but that had been in the guise of an Englishman. It had been some years earlier but it would be foolish to risk an encounter. I doubted that a Flemish mercenary would be accorded an interview with the king. While I stabled my horse, I made a mental list of the Scottish nobles who might know me. Lord Home, Huntley and Maxwell, all knew me. I decided that I would visit with Gerald of Etal. I could not tell him my task although I knew him well enough to know that he would guess the truth but he might well be able to suggest a place to start. I just needed a minor lord from the borders who would be summoned to fight. Once I had ingratiated myself into their manor I would know exactly when the Scots would strike. I intended to leave for Newcastle the moment I had useful intelligence.

I walked into my house and was greeted with smiles and a warm welcome. I smiled back. I would tell my wife that evening when we lay together.

She had been suspicious by my quiet, depressed demeanour and was not surprised when I told her all, "You are to be a spy …again?"

I kissed her, "I fear so, my love, and it is likely that I will miss the birth of our unborn child."

She hugged me tightly, "I pray that you do not miss the life of your child. And you can tell no one?"

"I am not even supposed to tell you. I have a story ready. I was summoned by Sir Edward as he wishes me to go to Yorkshire and train the billmen there."

"James will want to come."

"I know, but I shall tell him that he is needed to help Ralf. In truth, Ralf will need some help. You cannot tell your parents."

"I know, for they would worry. This is not right, my love. You have served the Tudor family enough."

"And I am now trapped by that service. I know too much to be allowed to live if I refused. The manor of Ecclestone when it was given to me became my chains and millstone. I have stepped along this path and we cannot go back and change it, can we?"

She was silent for a while, "And this may continue long after our new child is born."

"It could but the good side is that James and Walter will never need to do as I have done and they will inherit the title and the manor. You shall be Lady Jane."

She snorted, "And you know what I think of titles."

I laughed, "I know but I was looking for the silver lining to this cloud."

"This cloud has no lining. It is storm filled and threatens us all for without you we have nothing."

She began to weep and I pulled her closer, "I shall do all that is in my power to survive. I am tougher than you know."

"Perhaps but I think you are like the cat who has nine lives. One day you shall use your last one and I pray that it is not now."

I tried out the story on the family at breakfast and they seemed to believe it although James wanted to know why he could not come with me. He accepted the explanation that Ralf would need him. When I visited with Ralf and Elizabeth, I knew that it would be harder. Ralf was delighted that he would be paid as a captain and did not mind that he would have to lead the men of Ecclestone when war came, however, he could not swallow my fiction.

"Come outside, Captain James, and I will show you the improvements we have made." Once outside he shook his head, "Your words may fool others, captain, but not me. What has Sir Edward conjured for you this time?" I looked at him askance and he shook his head, "Come, Captain James, we are brothers in arms and saved each other's lives. If you cannot trust me then…"

I sighed for he was right. I told him and found that it was a relief. When I had finished, he said, "You tread a tricky path, Captain James, for you are known." I told him of my plan for my beard and he nodded, "A good idea but you should change your hair too. Have it cut in the continental style."

"Aye, but it shall have to be done on the night before I leave when all the family are abed and I will leave before dawn. The change might fill them with suspicion."

We talked of other ideas and I was pleased that I had spoken with him. "When do you leave?"

"I have a little over three weeks. There is much to prepare and most of it will be in secret. You and I will need to spend as much time together as we can for you will have to organise the muster and the march north yourself."

He nodded, "And a thought has just occurred. If you trim your beard a little more each day then you will have little work to do on the night before you leave and remember that the lighter skin where the beard grew will be a sign."

He was, as ever, right and I would have to spend as much time in the sun without a hat as I could. The next three weeks would be hard.

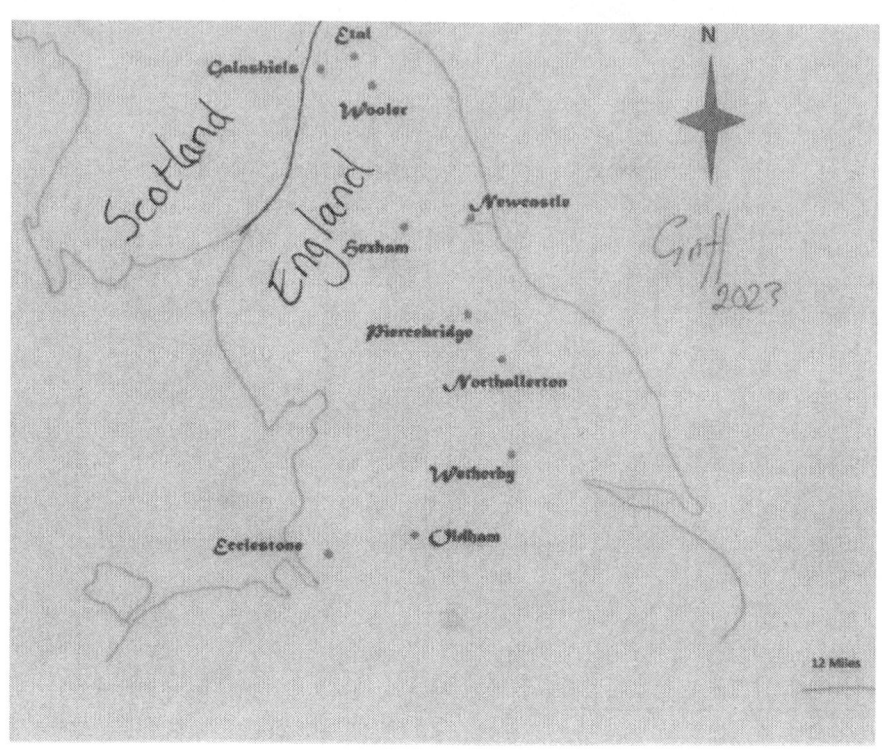

Chapter 8

Etal 1513

The night before I left my wife and I retired early. They all knew I was leaving early and it was seen as a sensible act. I had said my goodbyes already. My clothes were packed and Jane shaved me so that I had a trimmed moustache and a beard just around my mouth. She oiled it and that made it look darker. She took out her scissors and trimmed my unkempt locks. We had a mirror and when I looked in it, I saw another man. Of course, it could have been the candlelight. That night we cuddled. We had spoken every night since I had divulged my secret and now was the time for tenderness. I put my hand on the growing bump and felt my unborn child. It was comforting to know that if I died part of me would live on in my children.

I found that I could not sleep and rose while she still slept. I slipped down to the kitchen and ate the food that had been left out for me. The horse I would ride, Lion, was in his own stall. I had bought him just a week earlier at the Ormskirk market. He was not a young horse but I knew as soon as I saw him walk that he had what I needed, heart. He would add to the illusion of a warrior fallen on hard times but still using his old horse. We had almost ten days to get used to one another for it would be a long journey up to the borders. I would not risk the west coast because that was Maxwell's land and there were men now who would remember me. They might know my name but they had seen me fight and I might be known. I would also take old Dan, my sumpter. I realised as I headed to the stables, that I was playing the same part I had when I had been the bodyguard of the Queen of Scotland. I strapped my bag on his saddle and walked him to my gate. I had the hood of my cloak up and Will, the night watchman, did not see my hair and beard.

"Good luck, Captain James, and you teach those men from Yorkshire the right way to fight."

"I will."

I smiled as I headed to the road that would take me not north but east. I was adding thirty odd miles to my journey and making it more unpleasant but by heading for Oldham and the high moors and thence to Leeds, I would be travelling roads I had never used. I was known in Craven and Clitheroe. Indeed I had dined with many of the lords there, Yorkshire and the West Riding were unknown to me. It would give me the chance to practise my Flemish and the foreign accent I would adopt. My greatest fear was that I would meet a Flemish soldier. I had a plan if that happened but I hoped I would not need to use it.

I knew that I had thirty miles to travel. It gave me the chance to get to know my new horse. I used my new accent to speak to him and I quickly found that he was a good horse. The man I had bought him from said he was ten years old. I had him older than that but his age mattered not. I would not be using him for war. He was part of my disguise. When we met other travellers, I used my foreign accent to greet them. It made them suspicious and discouraged conversation. The English were always wary of foreigners and I played upon that. I found an inn that took travellers, just on the outskirts of Oldham. The merchants who used the road frequented it. When heading east it meant you had the whole day to get over Saddleworth Moor. I had been told that it was a bleak place and travellers might have to endure snow even in May.

The innkeeper was a miserable man and I was not greeted warmly. He made a great deal more money from merchants who travelled with a larger number of horses. He made money from the horses in his stables, greater quantities of food and ale consumed and more beds filled. The room he gave me was little more than a box with a paillasse and yet I was charged the same rate as if I had been given a bed. I was being robbed and I was surly with him. The ostler, in contrast, was a genial fellow. He was as thin as a rake and yet he had all the good humour of a trencherman with a beer belly. It was he who gave me sound advice.

"It is seventeen miles to Huddersfield but that can feel like twice the distance for the road climbs and drops, twists and turns and if clouds come down then you can lose your way." He grinned, "It is nothing like Flanders." I cocked an eye, "I rode there many years since, flat country with nary a hill. I like the mountains. Good luck, sir."

I gave him a coin and thought that he was misinformed about mountains. I would be travelling through the high country but Westmoreland and Cumberland were the places that could boast of having mountains. He was right in that the road did twist and turn but I saw few peaks. I also saw few other travellers and that suited me. I wanted isolation and the road over Saddleworth Moor gave that to me.

Once again Huddersfield had inns for the same reason there were inns in Oldham. This time the host was more genial and also curious as well as intrigued about my presence. I tried out my story that I was a soldier of fortune seeking employment. Had that been the truth then the innkeeper had a dozen men who would hire me and all lived within ten miles of Huddersfield. "The word is, sir, that there will be a war and lords are hiring men rather than sending their sons to war. You can name your own price." I feigned an answer that I hoped to meet fellow mercenaries further north and he seemed to accept that answer.

That was the story of my journey north. Innkeepers and travellers all told me of the threat from the north and the scarcity of mercenaries. Sir Edward's meeting and Sir Thomas' words had certainly been effective. This part of the country was now on a war footing. I headed not for Leeds but Wetherby and Bramham. I saw signs for the Pontefract Road when I was close to Cleckheaton. The earl would soon be heading there to establish his northern headquarters. I was now more familiar with both my new horse and my story. I still stayed close-mouthed but if pushed I was able to tell my story with ease and it sounded truer every time I tried it. Northallerton and Piercebridge saw people being more suspicious of me than hitherto as I was now getting closer to the border. At Hexham, I found no inn and had to pay for a bed in the abbey there. That proved to be my hardest test as the monks in the abbey were well-read and knew some of the history and geography of Flanders and Northern France. My

dour and uncommunicative character helped me. Once I left
Hexham and headed for the Tweed then I knew I was in a
land where I would be known. I would have to sleep rough
and find some way to contact Gerald of Etal. That would be
harder said than done. There was a market in Hexham and I
bought as much food as I could and ensured I had both
waterskins and a full ale skin. I bought a bag of oats for Lion
and Dan and then I disappeared across the Roman Wall into
the real borderlands. I avoided roads and people.

Had anyone been watching me then they might have been
suspicious for the last ten miles to Etal were amongst the
slowest I had endured. I kept stopping to see if I was being
followed and chose trails and paths that did not pass through
villages and hamlets. I counted on Gerald following his
normal routine. I had learned it the last time I had been on
the Tweed. Every morning, after he had breakfasted, he
would set his men to their duties and then ride his horse
through the woods and lanes close to Etal. He was simply
looking for signs of strangers. I had not hidden my signs and
I was praying that he would find them and then seek me out
or I would see him. It meant I had one night alone in the
woods close to the place where we had fought off Sir
Andrew and his ambushers.

I found a small clearing with flat ground and a little grass
where Lion and Dan could graze although after they had
watered in the river, I fed them both some oats for the
grazing would be poor. I ate a cold supper of bread, ham and
cheese washed down with ale. I made a bed of my horse
blankets and wrapped myself in my cloak. I did not sleep
well for it had been many years since I had slept on the
ground. As I rose, in the dark, to make water I reflected that I
had not done so since before I had first joined Perkin
Warbeck. Then I shook my head, I was becoming forgetful. I
had slept on the ground close to Threave Castle but then I
had not been alone. Arkham and his men had watched. Here
I was one man. I watered Lion and Dan at the river and then
led them back to the camp I had made and ate another cold
meal. I was getting too old for this.

I tethered both animals and then retraced my steps, masking the hoofprints. There was a stand of willow trees with overhanging branches and I climbed one on the trail side and squatted on the thickest overhanging branch. With full leaves, it offered me a disguise of foliage. I waited. If Gerald did not come on this day, I would have to endure another night in the woods. I heard an approaching horse as it clip-clopped along the trail. There were enough stones for hooves to scrape along to ensure that I heard the animal. When it was just ten paces from me it whinnied having smelled Lion and Dan.

"Good girl." I recognised Gerald's voice. I saw him dismount and lead the horse along the path. His head was down as he was looking for sign. He knelt down and chuckled, "Well, someone is keen to hide their presence but they have to get up early in the day to catch me out."

I dropped to the ground and landed beside him. "Hello, Gerald of Etal." His dagger was out and at my throat in a flash. Holding my hands up I said, "Is that any way to greet an old comrade?"

The scowl turned to a smile and, sheathing his dagger he grinned, "You have changed, James of Ecclestone but perhaps that is deliberate. What brings you here and in disguise?"

"Come with me and I will explain all." I led him to my camp. He took out his coistrel and we shared some ale. I told him my mission.

He nodded, "There is war afoot and I fear that this time the castles along the Tweed may well fall and suffer the fate of Twesilhaugh for I have heard rumours of huge bombards and cannons being gathered in Edinburgh." He emptied his coistrel. "You say you are sent to spy on the Scots and need a Scottish master?" I nodded and having refilled his coistrel, replaced the stopper in the ale skin. "Many men will remember you but there is one who comes to mind who was not part of the fight we had the last time. David Pringle and his sons live at Smailholm which is close to Galashiels. It is a fine hall. He is a loyal Scot and is keen to fight against we English. If truth be told I think he has aspirations to be Lord of Norham. He would have that pretty jewel. You may find he is willing to hire a sword." He rubbed his chin. "There are other lords in Galashiels and they too might be willing to hire a mercenary. It will be dangerous, James."

"I know but all I need to do is discover when they muster and where. Do they intend to attack along the Tweed or further west at Carlisle?"

"I might be able to find that out."

I shook my head, "Might is not a word that the king and the cardinal understand."

I told him of the kidnap of my in-laws and he nodded, "Sir John Maxwell is an ambitious man. I hear he murdered Lord Robert Crichton of Sanquhar and got away with it. He would favour an attack in the west but who knows? My feeling is that they will attack here in the east for this is land they feel is theirs."

"What is my best approach?"

"The village is small but there is a green and, as I recall from a raid we made when I was younger, an alewife sells ale to travellers. If you were a mercenary then you would be heading up to Edinburgh. If you cross the river here and head due west, you can avoid those places you might be known until you strike the road that goes north from Hawick and Selkirk. The road there runs parallel to the one that passes through the Jedburgh Road. When you cross that one then be careful. That is the land that followed Sir Andrew. He may be dead but who knows if there was one who saw you and lives there still?"

I clasped his arm and then began to saddle Lion. "If they come for Norham and Etal, what will you do, old friend?"

"Hold out as long as we can but if the Scots muster before the English, then we are doomed. Both castles are old and not meant to suffer an assault by bombards. I will warn his lordship. If he has any sense he will flee to Newcastle or Bamburgh but he is stubborn."

I mounted my horse. "And when I learn any news I will pass this way, as myself, of course, and give it to you."

"God speed."

I headed back towards the ford I had used before. I had a tough twenty-five miles to go but once I reached the Selkirk Road, I knew I could make better time. I followed the hunters' trails that crossed this heavily forested land and kept going due west. When I reached the Jedburgh Road, I waited in the trees until I was sure that there was no traffic on the road and then crossed. I knew I did not have far to go. One advantage of my route was that I passed plenty of water and Lion was not overly fatigued. When I reached the Selkirk Road, I spurred on Lion for I knew that Galashiels lay just a couple of miles up the road and I was anxious to reach there before dark. Dan was a solid sumpter. He complained about the speed but he kept up with my new horse. I needed to reach the town in daylight. Arriving after dark would arouse suspicion.

I was lucky in that I met, just a mile or so from my destination, a couple of travellers also heading to Galashiels. It was a merchant and his servant. They were heading for Edinburgh and that fitted in with my plans. They turned when they heard my horses for they were moving a little more slowly than I was. Had there been more than one rider then they might have been alarmed but I saw smiles when they realised that I was alone. I knew that travellers liked company.

"Hail friend."

The man had a Scottish accent but one that was not as strong as I might meet further north. He was a borderer. As soon as I replied he knew I was not Scottish, "I am Charles of Wervik."

The man nodded, "A foreigner, eh? I am Robert Kerr and this is my servant, Angus. What brings you here?"

I had slowed to the same gait as the two men and I patted my sword, "Sword for hire."

He nodded, seemingly satisfied, "Ah, you have heard the pleas of the Queen of France. She wants us to fight a war against the English. There will be plenty of work although the army is yet to be mustered."

I affected a disappointed expression, "I thought that the king would strike as quickly as he could. When I landed, I saw the vast camps of the men preparing to sail to France."

"Why did you not stay in Flanders and fight the English there?"

I tested my story with the two men and tapped my nose, "Let us say I fell out with a certain French lord whose wife found me more attractive than he." I shrugged, "A pig would have been preferable to him."

They both laughed and Robert Kerr said, "Your English is good, for a foreigner."

"When you live in Flanders it helps to speak many languages." I used some French and German to make my point and they nodded.

"To us, English is a foreign language." He pointed ahead, "We are close to our destination. We have come just as the market is ending."

I could not have picked a better time. With the market packing up and traders heading home I could blend in a little easier. Robert Kerr pointed to a substantial building which looked busy, "Angus and I have a room arranged there. You may be able to sleep in the stable. I know the owner and might be able to arrange it. If you come to fight for our country then the least we can do is to give you a bed, albeit rough, for the night."

I dismounted to make it easier to follow the two men and we wound our way past farmers and other traders loading their horses, carts and small wagons. We entered the gate into the courtyard of what was clearly an inn. Gerald had not mentioned an inn. Robert said, to the ostler, "We have a room for the night but my friend here has not. Stable his horses with ours."

I gave a half bow, "I thank you, sir."

He shrugged, "We usually have more horses and a couple more will not be added to my bill." As the ostler and the servant led the horses away I saw that there were four good horses in the stable already. The interior of the inn was packed and loud. It was hard to hear Robert. The merchant put his mouth next to my ear. "Ten years ago this was just a small building but Annie Melrose brews good ale and she married an old soldier with money. She has done well."

I saw the woman pouring ale from a jug. She spied Robert and handed the jug to a youth and, wiping her hands on her apron, made her way over to us, "Robert Kerr, welcome. I have your room ready but where is Angus? I do not recognise this man." There was suspicion in her voice.

"Angus is tending to the horses. He will join us shortly and this is a soldier we met on the road."

"I am Charles of Wervik, a Flemish sword for hire. Could I pay to sleep in your stable and for a meal and ale?"

She beamed, "Of course, I never turn away a coin." She looked around, "The room will empty a little soon. Most of these were here for the market and when his lordship leaves then there will be a table. I will keep a tally," she picked up the wooden board and made a mark with a piece of charcoal next to another mark which must have identified me. "Eoin, two ales."

She was right and by the time the ale came half the room had emptied and Robert and I were able to sit at a table so that when Angus arrived, we had room to breathe. It was then I saw the four men with good swords. One was clearly a knight and was much older. He had to be the father. I saw Annie lean in and speak to him and then point over at me. The knight detached himself and came over to us. Robert and Angus stood and bowed. I did so a heartbeat later.

"Good evening, my lord."

"Good evening, Robert." He looked at me, "I am Sir David Pringle, the lord of the manor and you, I do not know." It was an interrogation.

"I am a sword for hire, my lord, come from Flanders. I am passing through and on my way to Edinburgh to seek work."

"A mercenary, eh?"

"I am."

"And are you any good? It seems to me that if you were you would have employment already."

I shrugged and said, "I believe I am good but I am here because..." I smiled, "There were problems of a romantic nature in Flanders which made it more convenient for me to seek an employer abroad."

He seemed satisfied, "On the morrow ask Annie for directions to my hall at Smailholm. I would speak with you there. Perhaps, if you are good enough, I might hire you."

He waved to his three companions and they departed. There were just the three of us left.

Robert leaned over, "Sir David is the most important man in these parts. He has money and you may just have fallen on your feet for if he hired you then you would save a journey to Edinburgh."

The food came and it was good and wholesome. As we ate, I learned much. Robert hated the English but, from his words, it was clear that much of that hatred came from envy. The English were seen as richer than their northern neighbours. In addition, the attitude of the English royal family to the Scots annoyed them. Robert was annoyed that the English saw themselves as superior. I nodded my agreement at the appropriate moments but, playing the part I had created, I listened more than I spoke.

After the meal, I paid with my Flemish coins. Annie bit them to make sure that they were worth the price of the meal and, after bidding goodnight to Robert and Angus, I headed for the stable. The ostler had already gone for his meal and I made a bed in the hayloft and then fed Lion and Dan. I had made a start but I knew that when I spoke with Sir David I would be interrogated more thoroughly.

The next morning I paid for a simple breakfast of oatcakes and honey. Annie was more than happy to give me directions. It seemed that her prosperity depended upon the lord of the manor and she would do all that she could to continue to enjoy his favour. I learned that the Sottish knight had five sons. The elder three had been with him in the inn the previous night. Armed with the information I rode the few miles to the hall of the Pringle family. It was a place to be defended. There was a small square keep and a hall just twenty paces from it. The stables, kitchens and bakehouse were also well away from the keep so that they could not be used to fire the building. The keep itself was small and I guessed it was a refuge, more like a pele tower, and only to be used when men raided. Having said that there were a pair of sentries on the top and their shouts as I approached warned the men that I was coming. There were a dozen men, the knight and his sons included and they were sparring with spears and swords. I guessed they were preparing for the war that was to come. I reined in and dismounted. The knight waved over a man to take Lion and Dan.

"So, warrior of Flanders, you are come to take my money?"

I shook my head, "I am in Scotland to be paid gold to fight your enemies, my lord. So far, I know not what rate you might be willing to pay."

One of his sons, I later learned it was his eldest, Davy, snorted, "Arrogant! Send him hence, father, we do not need his kind. There are Scotsmen aplenty who will fight the English for no pay."

I gave a bow and took the reins from the man with my horses, "Then I will bid you farewell and be on my way. I have many miles to go to reach Edinburgh."

Sir David snapped, firmly, "Davy, hold your tongue. I decide who we need." He nodded to the man who took my reins again. "My son is quite right, we can hire Scottish spears and blades at a tenth of the rate you would charge but," he glared at his son, "they are rough clay. When the English come to fight us, they will bring professional soldiers. Men like you. I would have you teach them how to fight and win."

"I could do that if the price was right."

He grinned, "Before I part with my money, I would see what I am paying for. Caleb." A huge warrior stepped forward. "Caleb is the captain of my men and even I cannot defeat him, not often anyway. Fight him and I will see how long he takes to defeat you."

I took off my cloak and hung it on Lion's back while I studied the man I was to fight. He had a sword favoured by the Scots, a claidheamh-mòr. It was a weapon that was longer by a handspan than my sword and had a broader blade. It usually required two hands to use but I saw that

Caleb handled it easily in one. Usually, the wielder of such a weapon would have a small buckler that would protect his left hand and allow him to use two hands on the sword. The sword was so long that it could be used against a man with a pole weapon. I nodded and went to Lion. I would not use my best sword. I had a second that was as long as my gift from Perkin Warbeck but was heavier. If I was to exchange blows, I would not risk my best sword. I also drew my dagger.

Sir David shook his head, "Just the sword." I sheathed it. "First blood wins."

I stood balanced and Caleb did the same.

Davy shouted, "Kill the bastard, Caleb, and there is a crown in it for you."

"Davy!" I could see that Davy and his father clashed and that there was tension in the family.

I saw Caleb nod. He studied me and my stance and I knew what he intended. He held the sword above his head in two hands. It was the best way to use such a weapon as it meant he could strike for the head and end the contest quickly or he could swing at either side and make me parry the blow. Each time he struck it would weaken both me and my sword. He would wear me down. The two advantages I had were my nimbleness and the lightness of my weapon. I was used to wielding a billhook for hours and my shoulders were strong.

He signalled his intent quickly. He would earn the money and split me in two. He brought the sword down and I simply stepped to the side. I could have ended the contest then and slashed him across his bare arm but I wanted the knight to see my worth and did not want to make an enemy of Caleb. Instead, I used the flat of my sword to smack into the back of his left hand. It hurt him and I saw his eyes widen. As I moved away, for he raised the sword again, I saw the knight watching carefully. He knew what I had done. Caleb next tried a wide arcing swing to take my neck but I simply stepped away. He reversed the swing in case I tried to hurt his hands again. I did not. He then tried something unusual, he lunged at my face with the tip of the long sword. Normally a warrior would step back but as I had faced billhooks and spears coming at me, I merely moved my head and the unwieldy blade slid over my shoulder. The knight's sons thought that he had hurt me for they cheered but when I brought the hilt of my sword up to hit his already weakened left hand the cheers ended. He was now wary of me. I guessed that he had used all the tricks he had and now had to go back to the only way he knew how to beat me, he would batter me into submission. I saw his eyes flicker behind me and sensed, rather than saw, that there were men behind me who would bar any retreat. When he came at me, I used my sword to deflect the end of his sword and then danced to the side. I saw that Davy and three others had formed a wall.

"Come on, Caleb, finish him. He has not laid a blow on you yet."

"Aye, Master Davy." He swung again and having no one behind me this time I danced out of the way and then went on the offensive. I lunged at his middle and he struggled to bring his own sword back around. I kept moving and punched his left hand with my left hand. His hand was already hurting and the blow was well-struck. I knew how to use my fists. He reeled and I stepped forward punching at his face with the hilt of my sword. He must have tired more than he had expected for his sword was slow to rise and when the hilt hit him his nose erupted in blood as I broke his nose.

Sir David said, simply, "First blood. The contest is over."

Caleb put his hand to his nose and wiped away the blood, he smiled and said quietly and without any anger, "You could have had me any time you chose."

I said nothing but held out my right hand, "A good contest."

Davy shouted, "My turn now." I smiled as Caleb's eyes rolled.

Sir David said, "Go and cool yourself off." I saw the anger in the young man's eyes. Sir David came over to me and I sheathed my sword in the scabbard on Lion. "You were never under pressure there. You were taught well."

"I was taught by the best."

"I would hire you to train my men and when we go to war to fight alongside me."

"When do we go to war?"

"The muster will be at Burgh Muir but the date has yet to be set. I would think July or August."

"And the pay?"

"A shilling a week, food and lodging until we go to the muster and then two shillings a week."

I shook my head, "Then if that is your best offer, I will leave."

"It is a fair offer."

"When I was in London, I was offered captain's pay. Two shillings a day."

His eyes narrowed, "Then why did you not take it?"

"Simple, I have fought the English too many times to fight for them and I did not want to find an old enemy who would slit my throat as I slept. I do not expect two shillings a day for you are only Scotsmen." The jibe struck home and I saw it in his face, "But at least a shilling a day while we train and two shillings a day while we are on campaign and for that I will lead your men." I saw him hesitate. "You know that there are nobles like Lord Home and Lord Maxwell who would pay me two shillings a day now. If my price is too high then I will bid you farewell."

He nodded, "Very well." He smiled, "You drive a hard bargain but when we take Northumberland, I will be given a good estate and be a much richer man. You will be an investment." He waved over Caleb. The bleeding had stopped but he was covered in blood. "Take Charles to the stables and then show him where he sleeps. He will fight with us."

Caleb grinned, "Aye, my lord." I led Lion and he continued to speak, "I can beat any man around here every day of the week and twice on Sunday but you could have had me in the first pass. Why did you not?"

"Sir David said that you were the best, what better way to see what is needed of me. You have courage but your sword leaves you well open to an attack from someone with a quicker blade."

"Aye, I know but we usually fight with the pike. It keeps the English horse from us and when they are beaten then the sword is a fierce weapon." He looked at my horse, "Do you not have a pole weapon?"

"I can use one and I daresay I can pick one up while I am here but if Sir David wishes me to lead his men, then I will have to use the pike."

He grinned, "I look forward to that. It takes a strong man to wield one."

I spent the rest of the day with Caleb while he showed me around the estate. The training over, the rest of the men went to work on the land while the knight's sons retired indoors. Sir David did not and I kept seeing him as he oversaw the work on the manor.

As we headed back, he said, "Davy is a good lad but he is a little arrogant and, if I am honest, something of a bully. He is stronger and more skilled than his brothers and takes pleasure from hurting them."

"And Sir David does not prevent it?"

"He thinks it will make better men of them but I do not think he approves."

It was late in the afternoon and men were returning to the hall to wash up and eat. Caleb and I had just been to the stables to look at the horses when we met up again with Sir David, "Well, Charles, what are your thoughts?"

"Your men are tough and strong but they need better jakkes. The English billhooks will tear through the leather. You need metal to strengthen them."

"That is what I have said many times, my lord."

"I know, Caleb, and you may well be right, both of you, but we do not have the time. I have helmets ready for the men." The Scottish knight looked at me, "You have a helmet?"

"Aye and plate. They are on the sumpter."

"We have all my men on Sunday but tomorrow you can work with my sons. They are keen but they are rough." He smiled, "You will have your work cut out with Davy for he hates you already."

I feigned innocence, "Me, my lord, after I saved him a whole crown?"

He grunted, "You have my permission to work them hard but I do not want them cut, understand?"

"I understand, my lord. I hope they do too."

Chapter 9

Smailholm near to Galashiels 1513

Sir David's other sons were not cut from the same cloth as the elder boy. James was the second and, at seventeen, had potential. He knew how to balance himself and he was a cautious fighter. William was the third and was just fourteen. I could see that both he and the other brother had the most to learn and were raw clay. The youngest was Malcolm and he was thirteen. There was another, Robert, but he was just five years old and merely watched. I had decided that I had to make it look as though I was earning my pay. I needed to stay with the family until the muster and then I could leave.

The hall had an armoury and rather than damaging one of my own weapons I took a serviceable sword from it. I wore a leather cap and my jack. His men would need to work on their spear skills but the sons of a noble would fight with a sword or a pole weapon such as an axe, war hammer, or poleaxe. I decided to begin with the sword.

Davy set the tone as soon as he arrived. He was both belligerent and aggressive. He swaggered as he walked up to me, "This will be a waste of time for there is nothing that you can teach me."

I had to tackle this head on and I nodded, "Then prove it to me. Have a bout with me now and show me that you need no tuition." I waved a hand, "Then you can enjoy watching me teach your brothers and the men who will follow you into battle against the English.

This time I drew my dagger. Davy also had a longer sword than me but not a mighty one like Caleb. He also drew his dagger. He pointedly walked over to the grindstone and had one of the men put an edge to it. He intended to hurt me. When he was satisfied with its sharpness, he boldly walked up to me and confidently swung his sword at my head.

I easily blocked it with my dagger and as he tried to gut me with his dagger I brought up my sword to prevent it from striking. I spoke calmly. My words were directed over my shoulder at his siblings, "Now an attack like this is easily defeated and leaves the attacker open to this." I hooked my right leg around his left and pushed. He sprawled on the ground and my sword pricked his neck. "And there you have a dead man."

The men in the yard all stopped working to look at the bully lying on the ground and smiled. Davy's three brothers were hooting with laughter and jeering at him. I could see that it maddened him and he rose.

"Now let us try something else, eh?" My calm words enraged him and he charged at me. He was a big man and he intended to bowl me over. I simply sidestepped him and left a trailing leg. I smacked his rump with my sword as he fell. He struck the water trough with his head. Sheathing my sword and dagger I went over to him to help him to his feet. His sword had fallen beneath the trough and I took his right hand to pull him upright. Although still stunned as soon as he realised what I was doing he stabbed at my face with his dagger. Had he connected I might have lost an eye or my life but I had been expecting something like this and holding his left arm up with my stronger one I elbowed him in the gut and winded him. As he doubled over, I said, in a calm manner, "And even without a weapon you can still overcome a wild and reckless warrior. You should always remain cold when fighting. Hot blood does no one any good."

"That is enough, Davy."

I realised then that Caleb must have gone for his lordship as the boy's father was watching. Caleb was grinning and Sir David shook his head, "A fine lesson, Charles of Wervik and I thank you for showing such restraint." He and Caleb hauled Davy away. The winding had left the young man bereft of words but I knew that I had made my enemy even more desirous of vengeance.

Turning and drawing my sword and dagger I said, "Now let us see what we have learned."

Caleb returned so that we could pair up and the lesson went well. I just did it the way I had been taught in Mechelen with the mercenaries. The boys all improved, even after that first lesson, but I felt like a fraud. I was deceiving them and they seemed like John and James back in Ecclestone. They were eager young men who wanted to learn and I was not what I seemed. Men like the cardinal could never understand such thoughts. For them, the ends justified the means.

Davy was kept from me. I was never sure if it was a joint decision or just Sir David's. Until the practice with the men, I just worked with the other three and they improved steadily. For me what was worse was that they seemed to like me. My deception was working but it was hurting me. When the practice came for the men with pikes, the sons I was training and their father also joined us. Even lords fought in the schiltron. They might carry their sword or war hammer over their backs for when they discarded the pike, but the formidable formation was the one every Scotsman knew.

I found the pike unwieldy compared with a billhook but I was easily able to use one. It was all a case of finding the point of balance. I just used the drills I employed at Ecclestone when working with my billmen. I even improved them. By showing them the point of balance they had more stability and I hoped that would not come back to haunt me. I taught them rhymes to keep in step and commands to help them strike as one. I made it a game and they enjoyed it. James and Davy each carried a pike. The presence of their father prevented Davy from being foolish. Although William and Malcolm drilled with the others they used a spear and if they went to war they would be at the rear of the formation and armed with a spear. By the end of the second week and as June approached, I had them drilling well and Sir David and Caleb were pleased. My fear that I was making them too good disappeared when, after we had eaten well, Caleb and I were talking.

"You have made a real difference, and the men respond better to you than to me."

"I am sorry. I did not wish to do that. I would not replace you. I am a warrior for this war and that is all."

He shook his head, "I know my limitations and that I am too loud and rough. I shout wildly and that does not help. You are calm and the games you have used have improved them already. By the time we are mustered, we will be the

finest body of pikemen in the army. When Sir David and you
lead them, we will show these Englishmen that we now have
a weapon to rival their longbow." He put a mighty mitt
around my shoulder, "And with your clever mind at the fore
then my wildness will be curbed, eh, Charles?"

It was then I knew that without me to give their orders
they would revert to being wild men. Davy had just been one
example of the men we would face when we fought them.

"And when will we muster?"

Caleb shrugged, "Sir David and his sons travel next week
to Edinburgh. They will have a better idea then. Perhaps he
might wish you to go with them."

That was the last thing I wanted but the question never
arose mainly, I think, because Davy objected. It suited me
because in Edinburgh I was known. I had saved the life of
King James and trimmed beard or not I would be identified.
A visit to Edinburgh and the king's court was an important
event and all the family went, including Lady Pringle and the
infant son. I had an easier time mainly because Davy was not
there but also because I had little work to do after the first
hour of the day. I took to riding in the countryside. I was not
sure how useful the intelligence I gathered would be but I
needed to be occupied and spying out the land helped. It also
brought me into contact with many men who lived and
worked close by. Once it was established that I was working
for the lord then I was accepted. I watched men work in their
fields and saw just how hardy they were. They were also
strong and it explained how they could wield a pike five
paces long. I rode the land as far as the Tweed and found
other paths and trails I could use. I was not seen as
suspicious and each day saw me gain more information and
intelligence. I began to devise my plan to escape. I knew it
would not be easy and I had to work out how best to achieve
it. If I was caught then all my work would be in vain and the
earl would be blind.

The family returned at the start of the second week in
July. The date of the muster was the twenty-fourth of July
and it meant I could leave. The muster was to be held at the
Burgh Muir south of Edinburgh and confirmed that the first

target would be the east coast and Newcastle. I had time to escape and still get word to Lord Dacre and the Earl of Surrey. I knew it would be tricky to leave for while there was no wall around the keep and the hall there was a guard kept on the top of the keep and anyone leaving at night would be noticed. If I tried to leave during the day then I would not be able to take my plate. I had to plan carefully.

I noticed that Davy watched me closely when he returned. We rarely came into contact with each other and when, as I groomed Lion, he entered the stable I was suspicious. "So, mercenary, you are still here. I am surprised for you have been paid your wages in advance and I thought you would have left us already."

He was trying to anger me and I remained calm, "I have yet to do that which I promised your father, Master Davy and fight for you against the English."

He nodded and smiled, "Ah, yes, the skilful swordsman who bested Caleb Long Sword. You know I heard of another such skilful swordsman when I was in Edinburgh. It was a warrior who served King James and was the queen's bodyguard. He sounded much like you."

My blood ran cold, "As this is the first time I have served in Scotland, that is unlikely." I held a pail of water for Lion to drink. "There are many men as skilled as I am in both Flanders and France. We were all taught the same way probably by the same men."

"Perhaps but I shall watch you carefully until the muster. Then we shall see."

After he had gone, I realised that he knew nothing for definite but he was suspicious and that would make my escape even more perilous. There must have been talk about the queen's English bodyguard and from that moment I was on my guard. I kept a bag of food in the stables and ensured that my water skin was always full. I kept both Lion and Dan well fed although I feared that I might have to leave Dan and my plate if I had to flee quickly. In the event, it was a raid by the family of John Heron that gave me an opportunity to escape. A few days before we were to be mustered a rider came in and said that English riders were raiding Jedburgh.

Sir David ordered us mailed and armed and he led his sons, Caleb, me, and another four riders to head for Jedburgh. I donned my plate. It was the first time I had worn it and as I rode from the stable, I saw the knight's sons, Davy excepted, look at me with unveiled admiration.

Sir David said, "Your plate puts mine to shame, Charles. How did you acquire it?"

"War is my trade, my lord, and I bought the best I could in Burgundy. Whilst it cost me gold it protects me well."

Sir David nodded, "I thought I recognised the workmanship. When we return from chasing these bandits back across the border, we will talk a little more about your life. For the present, we have many miles to ride."

He was right for it was sixteen miles to Jedburgh but my mind was planning my escape as the raided town lay close to the border. I had ridden close to the town when I had been scouting out an escape route. We rode hard and reached the town by noon. I saw the two smoking buildings that showed the town had been attacked. While the horses were watered Sir David spoke with the men who had witnessed the attack. The Heron family at Ford were irresponsible and 'The Bastard' had almost caused a war before. I stood close to Sir David as he was told of the raid and it became clear to me that the heads of the family had not sanctioned this raid. The word was that forty or so young men on ponies had raided the town in an attempt to cause mischief. They had burned a couple of buildings and taken some objects from the church before they had been chased off. It was clearly an unsanctioned raid. There was no talk of men at arms, just young men, border horsemen.

"They left just two hours since and Sir Robert followed them with eight men."

"Then he shall need my help. Which road did they take?"

The wounded man pointed north, "The road to Norham."

"It looks like they are headed home. We have the chance to catch them." We crossed Jed Water and followed the road. My spirits lifted for this was my chance to escape. We were heading in the right direction and I just had to choose my moment well.

The men of Ford had known they were being followed and we found where they had ambushed Sir Robert and his men. The Scottish knight was not wounded but four of his men were and two lay dead. He was angry and he jabbed a finger to the north. "They are just an hour ahead of us. They lay in wait and used their bows to great effect. We have the chance to catch them."

This time the two Scottish knights rode at the fore and I was relegated to the rear. Every step we rode took me closer to Etal. I knew that I should be riding due east when I escaped but I had promised Gerald a warning. This raid was not sanctioned but its effect would ripple through the land. It would add fuel to the Scottish anger. The foolish young men of Ford might not have thought that they were starting a war but that might be the result of the raid. The road and the land dipped towards the Tweed. We passed open, harvested fields but we also passed places where we could be ambushed and Sir David rode cautiously through the wooded sections.

He waved me forward at one point, "Charles, take Donald and ride ahead. I would not be ambushed. Donald is clever and you are plated."

It was a mile and a half from the village of Eckford. The villagers had reported the men galloping through a little earlier and Sir David and Sir Robert were worried that there might be another ambush. What was the point of hiring a sword if you did not use him?"

I did not gallop along the road even though Donald was keen to do so. We walked our horses and my eyes scanned the ground for signs of an ambush. My cloak was wrapped tightly about me. It was just my practice. It meant that light did not shine off my breastplate. It saved my life as half a dozen arrows flew from the eaves of the trees. One clanked off my helmet and two hit my breastplate. Poor Donald had no such protection and an arrow slammed into his chest and threw him to the ground. I shouted, "Ambush! Murder! Ambush!"

Sir David had a horn and when I heard it sound, I knew that they were coming. Before more arrows could be sent after me, I took to the trees. I heard an English voice shout, "Jack, Will, get him. He wears plate!"

Glancing over my shoulder I saw two men detach themselves from the trees and gallop after me. I saw that they rode hardy ponies but their ponies had suffered a hard two days. Lion had only ridden thirty miles. They had ridden twice that far. I headed north and east. That would take them by surprise as they would have expected me to ride back to the Scots who were hurtling along the road. I jinked Lion to the right and when I reached a fork in the trail I slowed, knowing they would think I was looping back to Scotland. I watched, under my arm, as they also took the right fork and as soon as they were committed, I took Lion through a gap in the trees and left the trail. I headed north. It was only then that I spurred him and he responded well. He leapt forward. When I heard the sounds of pursuit fading, I knew that my sudden and unexpected move in the thick forest had fooled them. I kept riding hard until I reached the trail I had left and then I walked Lion. It was partly to give him a rest and, at the same time, to allow me to listen. There was silence. The raiders of Ford had done me a favour although I was sorry about Donald. I liked him. I hoped that he had not died but the wound would mean that he would not be able to attend the muster.

Dismounting I led Lion along the path until I reached a road. I was still in Scotland. Ford, Etal and Norham were the border and I needed to disappear. I kept walking until I saw a village and I led Lion around it only mounting him on the far side. I came to a fork and took the north-eastern side knowing that, at some time I would cross the border and that every step took me closer to Gerald of Etal.

The journey was a nerve-wracking one. The raiders would be heading along the main road that led across the border but I did not know if they would be caught or would do as I had done and leave the road. I had to skirt every village and as darkness fell, I knew that I had to find shelter. I was beyond where I had scouted and not yet in the land I knew. I had no map in my head but as Lion's head drooped, I knew that the wood I saw ahead would have to be my bed for the night. I had passed just one lonely farm a mile or so before it and I risked entering the trees. I found no water but I did discover a clearing. The trails I had used were barely that and I gambled that few men would use the wood and none at night.

I used my helmet for a pail and after filling it from my waterskin let Lion drink first. His need was greater than mine. The oat bag was still attached to my saddle and I allowed him to greedily gobble more than I normally fed him. That done I tethered him and saw to myself. I drank and ate the ham. Poor Dan would now be a Scottish horse and my blanket and spare clothes lay in Galashiels but, thus far, I had managed an escape. After removing my plate I made a rough bed and slept. I know not what woke me. It was probably a fox come to investigate the smell of ham lying in the hessian sack close to my head but it was still dark and my hand went to my sword. I listened but there were no sounds of danger. I made water and donned my plate. I ate more of the ham and drank. I filled my helmet again and Lion drank too.

After saddling Lion I walked back towards the road I had left and headed towards England. I did not push Lion, he was an old horse and afoot I would be easy game for men seeking me. There were signs on the road and at each place where there was a crossroad, there was a signpost. In that way, I knew I was still heading for Etal and Ford and that I had walked three miles. It was still dark when I heard scurrying noises ahead. I drew my sword and dismounted. Leading Lion by his reins I walked along the road. I was greeted by a grisly sight. The raiders, or some of them at least, had been caught. There were three headless and naked bodies and the heads were stuck on spears at the side of the road. The naked bodies showed that they had been mutilated after death. The scurrying had to have been carrion and had there been any left alive close by then I would have been greeted by an arrow. I did not touch the bodies but mounted Lion and continued on. It was only later I realised that the fight had not taken place where I found the bodies. It was the border and the Scots were sending a message to the English.

115

When dawn broke, I found myself close to Ford and Etal Castle. For obvious reasons I avoided Ford Castle and I reached the village of Etal at terces. As luck would have it Gerald of Etal was walking the walls when I reached the barred gates. He looked down and immediately ordered the gates to be opened. Once inside I expected to be whisked to see the lord of the manor but Gerald shook his head as he led me to the great hall. "His lordship took his family to safety once I told him that war might be coming." He saw the look on my face and shook his head, "I said nothing about you."

"It was a wise decision for his lordship to leave, Gerald, for the muster is on the twenty-fourth of July and in the last couple of days, men from Ford have raided Jedburgh. War will come here soon and the Earl of Surrey has yet to muster." He nodded and waved over a servant to bring food and ale. "What will you do?"

He smiled as we sat at the table in the empty hall, "With twenty men and not a cannon in the castle? Wait until they cross the border and then head for safety in Norham. Ford and Etal cannot be held against any kind of assault."

It was depressing news. The border would not stop the Scots.

Chapter 10

Newcastle August 1513 the Ill Raid

Poor Lion was exhausted by his exertions and I spent three days at Etal for it was a mighty ride back to Newcastle and I was not sure what the mood along the border would be like. Gerald rode to Norham to tell the constable about the raid and the muster. He claimed he had discovered it and my identity remained a secret. The constable sent word both to Lord Dacre and the Bishop of Durham. Knowing that I had done the first part meant I could rest my horse before heading back to Newcastle. The constable also began to lay in supplies of powder for his guns. I bade farewell to Gerald not knowing if I would ever see him again. We were warriors and the arm clasp was enough.

It took me two days to reach Lord Dacre and he appreciated the finer details I was able to give him, for having lived with the Pringle family and seen the men train I believed I had a better idea of how they would fight. The constable's message had just been to tell the Lord of the Marches that the Scots were mustering. I was able to put some meat on the bones of the message. I told him of the raid which had facilitated my escape. He shook his head, "The men of Ford are like their master, 'The Bastard'. They are good warriors but wild and reckless men. They are like gunpowder and unpredictable. I have also sent a message to the Earl of Surrey. He will know that you have done your duty."

I brightened, "Then I can return to my home?"

He shook his head, "The earl was quite adamant that once you reached me you should stay here. You will not be needed to bring your men north and they will already be on the road." He smiled, "He has a high opinion of you Captain James and from what I can gather so has Cardinal Wolsey."

Once more I had done too good a job and I would be tied to the north until this war, which had not even started yet, was over. I did, however, like Baron Dacre. He was older than I was and must have fought at Bosworth Field when he was barely John's age. He was now Warden of the Western Marches and that meant he commanded the border. His lands lay close to the western end of the Roman wall but he knew where he and his border horsemen needed to be. He had brought them all to the east. He told me that he had left Arkham the Carlisle Borderers in Carlisle. It would not do to leave that particular stable door open. He was a knight and rode plated but the men he led were like my hobilars and the men led by Arkham of Carlisle.

He was also a considerate leader and understood how hard had been my journey, "You may rest today but tomorrow I want you to ride with Sir William Bulmer of Brancepath and Wilton. He is leaving with his men on the morrow as our advanced warning of the Scots. He has mounted archers and hobilars. We have few men as good but your local and more recent knowledge may prove useful. He and his men will range north of here to ensure that those who are at risk can move to a fortified place."

"How many men does he lead?"

"More than five hundred. They are not all his men. He leads as many mounted archers as we could manage to muster."

I was a farmer and knew that the idea, while it should be applauded, was flawed, "My lord, it is harvest time and farmers will not leave their fields."

"I know, Ecclestone, but if we can save the women and the children…"

I was given a bed in the warrior hall of the castle. I sought the weaponsmith and had him polish off the scratches made by the arrows on both my breastplate and helmet. It cost me but a couple of pennies to do so and my plate and helmet were restored to their former glory.

I dined with Lord Dacre and Sir William that night. I discovered that Sir William's lands were further south than Brancepath and he hailed from Wilton in Yorkshire. He had fought under the Earl of Surrey in the Scottish campaign sixteen years earlier. He was a doughty old soldier and I liked him, from the moment I met him.

"I know that you are a hard-riding soldier, captain, and that is what we shall need. We have a large area to cover and I do not intend to be merely a shepherd. We shall be a sheepdog and when the Scottish wolves come to take our sheep, they will find us snapping at their heels."

The men who were defending this part of England all came from the north but were not necessarily Northumbrian. Sir Edward Stanley had been frightened by the raid on the Ribble and had done his job well. The men of Yorkshire and Westmoreland were well prepared for war.

There would be no sumpter to carry my plate and poor Lion had to endure both me and armour as we headed north. Sir William knew horses and he husbanded them well. He insisted not only on grazing when we stopped but also ensured that the horses were given cereal. The farmers complained but Sir William had the authority of the Earl of Surrey and Lord Dacre. Lion fared better than he had on my journey north. I had bought him as a disguise but there was still life in the old horse and he responded well to the rigours of the road.

His archers were good scouts. They were not all his men, Lord Dacre had added some local men from the Wooler area and they acted as both scouts and purveyors of valuable intelligence. We traversed the land looking for danger and ready to respond to any news of men who were scouting. I spoke often with Sir William and we both expected, with a Scottish muster imminent, that the Scots would send men south to scout out the land. They were the men we sought. We would deny the enemy intelligence and keep them in the dark. We were north of Wooler, close to Lowick when we heard that Lord Home and the Scots had pre-empted the actual invasion and were raiding the plains around Wooler and Milfield. This was more than a scouting expedition. It was a full raid. We heard rumours of ten thousand men. That seemed like an exaggeration but even if it was less than that figure our six hundred men would be outnumbered,

Egbert and Alan were the two local men and Sir William consulted them immediately. He knew when to use local knowledge.

"You know the local Scottish lords, who is it that is likely to command this raid?"

Egbert rubbed his chin, "Lord Home. He is not afraid of Ford and Etal Castle for both have tiny garrisons. He can easily cross the Tweed and raid Wooler. It is a large plain, my lord, and there are many animals. We are often raided by small bands of men, clans like the Kerrs, Armstrongs and Pringles often take cattle, horses and sheep but this is a mighty raid."

"And where can we stop him?"

Alan jumped in immediately, "Milfield, my lord. The road north passes close to the Till and there is a thick wood just north of Milfield. The Scots have to pass by if they are to return to Scotland and as this raid is days old then they will be returning soon. It is their way." He paused, "It is my home, my lord, or was until my family were killed in a raid."

Egbert said, "It is just six miles southwest of here, my lord, we can be there in under two hours and catch them as they head north."

Alan nodded, "Aye, lord and they will be laden. You cannot drive sheep and cattle quickly."

A decisive man, Sir William summoned the local levy to join us, adding almost a hundred men to our ranks and sent a rider, one of his hobilars, back to Newcastle with the news. That done we then followed our two scouts. If we failed then at least Baron Dacre would know of the raid and its perpetrator.

It was clear when we neared Milfield that it had already been partly raided but they had not taken the animals. The villagers had taken the animals into the woods to hide them. The headman, Ethelbert, told us that they knew the Scots would return, "They took the plate and vestments from the church and the treasure from the homes as well as food but they did not encumber themselves with animals. They are as cunning as foxes and expect to take them on their return." He shook his head, "My lord, there are more than five thousand of them. They cut a huge swathe through the countryside."

Sir William nodded, "Then we all have the opportunity to make Scottish widows do we not?" Sir William was an old campaigner. He would not admit defeat until he was dead or taken prisoner.

The wood only lined the eastern side of the road, descending to the Till and the western side was made up of open fields. There was also a great deal of broom, the yellow-flowered shrub that grew so well in the north. It would help to disguise us. We dismounted and left the horses to be watched by the boys and younger men from the village along with their own animals. We lined the woods with archers and the hobilars interspersed themselves along the line. There were only two hundred archers and as the enemy numbers were between five and ten thousand then they would only be able to dent their numbers but they were our most potent weapon. It would be the archers' task to cull the Scots and the hobilars while the handful of Sir William's men at arms and I would protect them. I managed to acquire a billhook from Ethelbert. It had belonged to his brother who had been killed by the Scots when they had attacked Milfield on their way south. We would have less than a thousand men to take on the army which was anything from five thousand to ten thousand men in total.

As Ethelbert handed the billhook to me, he said, "Put it to good use, captain. My brother was a brave man, a little reckless but he did not deserve to be cut down by border bandits."

I did not say it but I knew that the raid had been prompted by the raid of the men of Ford on Jedburgh. It was tit for tat.

I found myself between Egbert and Alan, who chatted to me as we embedded some stakes before us. They would be disguised by the broom, "You are a long way from home, captain."

I nodded, "My men will already be heading for Newcastle and the muster." I replied enigmatically. I could not tell them that I was a spy and I think I left them with the opinion that I sought glory. I did not.

Thousands of men driving animals before them make a great noise. We knew they were coming long before we saw them. The animals complained and metal jangled. The men sang and bantered. As with all raiders one of the first things they had taken was ale and wine from the churches. They must have thought that with no sign of pursuit, they had got away with the raid, the animals and the treasure. Their celebrations would be premature. It was late in the afternoon and Sir William had impressed upon everyone, especially the men of Milfield, that the order to attack would be his and his alone. His horn would signal the shower of arrows that would fall upon the Scots.

There were Milfield men close to us and when the smell of burning from the houses they were destroying reached us and the pall of smoke drifted towards us, it took all their self-control not to pre-empt the attack. Edgar and Alan counselled them, "We can rebuild homes but let us wait until we have these barbarians where we want them. They will not escape our wrath. Sir William strikes me as a good leader. We might be outnumbered but we have surprise."

I nodded, "It is clear that they do not know we are here and as the sun is lowering in the sky and yon field has a fence around it, I believe that we may have the perfect place to stop them."

It proved even better than Sir William might have hoped for, obligingly, the Scots camped across the road from where we waited. They tethered their horses and the huge herd of captured horses, on the far side of the plain. The other animals were penned in by a wall of horses and a hedgerow. It was August and they would not need either tents or hovels but they lit fires and slaughtered two bulls. They did not belong to the men of Milfield whose own animals were within the woods but the act added fuel to the anger of the waiting warriors.

Sir William chose his moment perfectly. The last of the Scots had tramped into the camp and were about to tether their horses when the horn sounded. The nearest Scottish soldiers were just fifty yards from us but the broom on both sides of the road hid us from view. Our archers were good bowmen. They were descended from the archers of Agincourt and Crécy. Their forebears had destroyed the Scots at the battle of Falkirk Bridge and Neville's Cross.

They could loose ten arrows a minute and the Scots began to die.

It took five flights before the Scots even knew what had struck them but when they did it became clear where their enemy lay and they rushed through the broom to get at the archers. I stood braced knowing that I had two men to protect and that they would keep loosing as long as they could and would be oblivious to danger. The first Scot who parted the yellow shrub levelled his spear at Egbert. The billhook I used was not as good as mine but it mattered not for I knew how to use it. I flicked the spearhead to the side and then jabbed with the short point of the billhook. His momentum propelled him onto the tip and the corner of bill finished the job begun by the spike. The arrows of Sir William's archers were decimating the Scots but some men made it across the road to attack us. None had the pike and most used a spear, sword or axe. The billhook was the perfect weapon to use and I swept it before me. Often that stopped them and then one of the archers would simply lower his bow a little and drive an arrow through leather, flesh and bone. It was a mad few moments as Scottish soldiers, some half-drunk already, raced at us. It was the same all along our thin line of warriors. My billhook was a surprise and the two archers flanking me also added to the slaughter.

Two men were almost my undoing. A handful of men raced over in a group. They were obviously shield brothers. With swords and bucklers, they ran directly at the three of us. Clearly outnumbering us they would, unless we used skill, overwhelm us. Egbert and Alan slew two immediately. I swung the billhook at the arm of the first man and the edge bit into the flesh to break bone. His scream was feral. The second man who faced me saw his chance and he lunged at me. Had I been using my own billhook I would have rammed the point at the base of the billhook into him but the one I used had no such adornment. Instead, I swung the bottom of the bill to smash into his knee. He lost his footing and I struck as he hit the ground, I smacked the shaft into the back of his head. The wounded man swung his sword at me but the wound had weakened him and I parried the blow with my billhook. The man I had stunned began to rise. I jabbed the point of the billhook at the wounded man and he could not raise his buckler. The point drove into his chest and I quickly pulled it out and swung the billhook to take the head from the rising man. Alan and Egbert killed the last two. The rest of the archers continued to rain death on the Scots and no more crossed the road.

Sir William shouted, "Men at arms and hobilars, mount your horses."

I handed the billhook to Ethelbert. Alan said, "You use that billhook like a fencing master uses his sword. That was smart work, captain."

I nodded, "And it is good to know that the archers of the north are so skilful."

The boys holding the horses were ready and I mounted Lion. The rest had done him good but I would still have to husband him. I followed the other riders and we crossed a plain filled with Scottish bodies. By my estimate, more than five hundred had been slain and the wounded who survived would be prisoners. I doubted that there would be many for the men of Milfield were angry. Only the lords would be taken and that would be for ransom. Lord Home and many of his men had mounted their horses and fled towards Ford Castle and the border. While the castle was not a major obstacle it would determine the route the Scots would take. They would have to avoid the castle walls and my local knowledge came to the fore. I knew where they would ride and I took the line of least resistance and rode further to the south than the rest. We were not an organised column that followed Lord Home and his disintegrating warband. We were small groups of horsemen. I found myself riding alongside six hobilars and two mounted men at arms. I was the only one plated. The rest had mail and metal studded jakkes. They carried spears and two of the hobilars had latches. My plate made them think I might have been a knight and they grouped around me. Sir William and the majority of the riders were closer to Ford. They would cut off many of the Scots but I knew that Lord Home would be heading for the ford over the Tweed. I knew it well.

We crashed through some bushes and I saw them just forty paces from us. I might not have recognised the knight for I had only seen him once before but I knew his banner and battle standard carried by the knight. The hobilars whooped for joy and spurred their horses as they saw rich prey ahead. Orders from me would have been futile and so, along with the men at arms I rode at Lord Home. His capture would be a severe blow to king James and might make him reconsider his decision to invade. The men with him were his bodyguards but I guessed, as I saw one fall to the bolt from a hobilar's latch, that they were not as familiar with fighting mounted as the border horse. I rode at the man at arms with the mail jakke who tried to wheel his horse to take me on. He flailed with his sword and I struck at his left arm, the one holding the reins. He had mail covering his arms but even so, my sword hurt him and he dropped his reins. His horse reared and I rammed my sword under his chin. He tumbled to the ground. We were not having it our own way, however. Lord Home, his standard bearer and a third knight had disposed of three hobilars, even as another five border horsemen rode to our aid. The hobilars were good at fighting lightly armed men but the plated knights were too good for them. I rode directly at Lord Home but the standard bearer spurred his horse to place himself between me and his lord.

I wore no spurs and he did. To a knight, that means he is fighting a commoner and that he, the knight, should win. The smile on his face showed me that he was confident, over-confident. He flicked his sword at me, his hands as fast as I had ever seen. I had been trained well and I riposted and stabbed at the same time. My tip scratched across his tunic, tearing it and scraping along his breastplate. His eyes registered his shock. Holding the standard meant that he could not use the reins and he was skilfully guiding his horse with his knees. I had reins and I whipped Lion's head around and urged him towards the knight's back. There was a slight gap between his breastplate and faulds. I swung the edge of my sword towards the gap and sliced into flesh and his spine. It was a mortal blow and as he spread his arms in a crucifix he and the standard fell from the mighty warhorse. I dug my heels into Lion's flanks to get to Lord Home but one of the knights who had been unhorsed rammed his spear into the chest of my brave mount. It cost the knight his life as Lion's body crushed him but threw me from the saddle. By the time I had recovered my feet, the Scottish lord had fled with the last of his men. Just one man at arms and a hobilar, of those that had followed me, remained.

I had just picked up the standard when Sir William and the bulk of the men rode in, "A mighty prize, Captain James, and Lord Home?"

"Fled across the ford."

He shook his head, "We shall follow but our prey has escaped. I will see you back at Milfield. Well done."

I walked over to Lion and stroked his head. He had died quickly for he was an old horse but I would have wished for a better end. He should have come home to Ecclestone and enjoyed grazing on the green. The hobilar was picking over the dead knights and John, the man at arms, led over the standard bearer's mount, "I know it will not compensate for the loss of such a brave beast but it is something. You fight well, captain. When I followed the captain of billmen I wondered if I would have to guard you. That was mightily done."

"Aye, but the greatest prize evaded us." I waved an arm, "Profit from the dead for you deserve it."

We took the plate, mail, coins and weapons from the dead and put them on the backs of the horses of the Scottish warriors. Our own dead we placed on the mounts that had survived. They would be buried in the churchyard at Milfield. We walked back and reached the village well after dark. We unsaddled and tended to our horses. As I took off the saddle, I saw that the squire had burned the horse's name into the leather. The horse was called Duncan. As I led him to the water trough I said, "I will give you a good home, Duncan, but I wish that Lion had not given his life for me."

With the archers guarding the field full of captives we buried our dead. Sir William and his weary men rode in just as the women of Milfield fetched a horsemeat stew for us to eat. The Scottish horses killed in the skirmish had not been wasted.

"He escaped us but we have a mighty victory and the loss of the standard will hurt him." He dismounted, "Come, captain, I would eat with you for you served your king and country well today and I would learn more about you."

I enjoyed his company for he was a warrior who had served England and the north. He was not a young man and yet he had willingly ridden a weary horse into Scotland seeking his prey. I told him all that I could about my life but the secrets of Perkin Warbeck and the service to King Henry remained that way. "And what now, my lord?"

"The earl wanted us to stay in the field until the Scots came. Well, they have come. I have learned that they burned and raided seven villages. We need to return the animals that were taken. As for the treasure taken," he shrugged, "I am not sure that they will get that back. The bodies of the Scots have been looted already. They will have to address their claims to the court. When we defeat the Scots then it is they who will have to compensate the people of Wooler."

"You are that confident that we can win, my lord?" I was too but I wanted to know why the knight appeared so confident.

"Aye, for today we were outnumbered by almost eight to one and yet we slew hundreds and lost few. If we meet them in open battle then they will lose."

"And what if King James chooses his battlefield wisely?"

"You are right, captain, and we should not count on victory before they have drawn swords. So far as I know, this Scottish king has yet to lead men in war. Our own king is making his reputation in France. Perhaps King James will do the same." He smiled, "The Earl of Surrey and his sons are good men and I trust to the archers and billmen of England."

The next day the knights and those with property were separated from the rest of the captives. They would be sent to Newcastle and await their ransom. That still left us with almost a thousand men. Sir William had their weapons and mail taken from them and then their boots. I know that they expected to be hanged and even the humiliation of marching home barefoot seemed a small price to pay for their lives. They might fight us again but a man who marches many miles barefoot will take some time to recover. The men of Lord Home had suffered and if we saw them on the battlefield would not fear them. The Home standard I carried would be a severe blow to their confidence.

It took almost ten days to return the animals and to distribute some of the treasure we had taken from the dead. We were about to return north to Ford when the news came that the Scottish army was heading south, for Norham and Ford. Etal had been abandoned and Sir William wisely led us back to Newcastle. Word was sent to the Earl of Surrey who was still at Pontefract and as we headed south and east, we warned all that we passed of the plague that was about to descend. The preliminaries were over and the next time I drew my sword it would be in a battle for the north.

Chapter 11

Norham August 1513

By the time we reached Newcastle riders told us that both Norham and Ford were under siege. The Scots had brought bombards with them and Lord Dacre knew that it would only be a matter of time before they fell. Norman-built castles could not withstand bombards and gunpowder. The muster had begun and the town of Newcastle as well as the moor to the north of the town were filled with contingents of warriors. Sir Edward was there already and the men of Lancashire, all seven thousand of them, were on the place they called the Town Moor. Sir Edward was in the castle and before I could join my men and my son, I had to speak with the high and the mighty in the Great Hall of Newcastle Castle.

Lord Dacre was in a good mood when he heard of our victory. "It may make the Scottish king reconsider his decision."

Sir William counselled caution, "My lord, Norham and Ford will fall and Berwick will be besieged. Even if King James chooses not to attack, the Earl of Surrey, when he comes, will have to retake those castles if only to protect the border."

I felt that I had to support the Yorkshireman, "Sir William is right, my lord, for Lord Home brought seven thousand men south on a cattle raid. If they took just that number, with their bombards then all three castles would easily fall and then there is just Morpeth to bar his way here to Newcastle."

Lord Dacre shook his head, "You are wrong, Sir William. Norham and the other castles did not stop Lord Home's raid. The days of the border castles are over but what you say about King James fighting defensively is interesting. You seem, Captain James, to have a better grasp on the land than many men, where would you think that they would fight to hold us?"

I had an idea in my head but I did not wish to risk making a fool of myself. I said nothing.

Sir William said, softly, "Come, Captain James, I know that you have in that clever head of yours an idea. Tell us and let us be the judge of its merits."

I nodded, "As you know, Sir William, the Scots like the route to England across the Tweed and through Wooler. Thanks to your victory they know that the plain of Milfield does not suit them but, further north and west there are two ridges which run southwest to northeast. Flodden Edge and Branxton Ridge which would allow them to use their cannons to great effect and make a killing field over which our men would have to march."

Lord Dacre nodded, "Then I would have you show me these ridges. The Earl of Surrey will need our intelligence when he comes north. The day after tomorrow you should be prepared to ride. I will bring border horsemen with me."

Sir Edward said, "I have told Lord Dacre of your previous services to this country. Once more, James of Eccleston, you will serve your king."

Once more I would have to leave my men. When I finally detached myself from what was a council of war I rode to our camp. I saw Ralf almost immediately and rode my new horse to the horse lines. I was greeted by cheers and I felt humbled. James and John were both there as were the hobilars. I found myself surrounded by men eager to speak with me.

Ralf shouted, "Away with you and let the captain greet his son and foster son." There was no malice in his voice.

Ned said, "I will tend to your horse, captain."

"He is a warhorse, Ned, and his name is Duncan. Until last week he belonged to a Scottish knight."

Ralf grinned as John brought me a barrel on which to sit, "I can see that you have had an interesting time, captain."

James fetched me food and I gave them an account of my time. They deserved the truth and now that it was over there was nothing to be gained from keeping it hidden.

John nodded, "Then if the Scots have been beaten already, we shall have an easy time of it."

"Do not be fooled by our initial victory. We surprised them and we shall not do that easily again. We have time before the battle lines will be drawn. Ralf, I need you and our hobilars to ride forth the day after tomorrow. We are to act as scouts."

James was full of excitement and I knew why. When I had run away to war none of the problems of the march seemed important. It was the new experience and the companionship of other warriors that made it seem like an adventure. Until he had faced an enemy then he would not know what war was all about. All that he would do, hopefully, in this campaign would be to hold the horses. I put from my mind his fate if we should lose. He was not a child and the Scots would kill him. We had to win and that meant that I would ride north once more into danger with Lord Dacre for there was no alternative.

As I ate, I spoke with Ralf as captain to captain. I wanted to know the mood of the men. Ralf was pleased with how they had endured the march north. He would not be fighting with the billmen, it would be me who was leading them but he had walked rather than rode the long miles from Eccleston. "They are in good heart, captain, but I cannot say the same for some of the other levies. I heard grumblings that it was the Stanley men who would have to bear the brunt of the fighting again. They wondered about the men of Yorkshire and Westmoreland."

I tapped his new tunic. It was adorned with the Stanley eagle claw symbol. "I see Sir Edward has marked all our men."

He laughed, "Aye, and we have your tunic for you."

That was no bad thing for while it would mark me as a Stanley man the tabard-type tunic would hide my breast plate and back plate. When I fought, they would be the only armour I would wear. I turned to James, "And your boots, they did not chafe?"

"No, father, they are well made and mother gave me a salve to apply to my feet. Gammer Alice in the village made it. The smell is pungent but it has kept my feet free from blisters." He nodded to the wagon, "We have your billhook there and mother sent spare clothes in case you need them."

"This will be our camp until we return from the north and that will not be long. I cannot see the border castles holding for a sustained period and once the floodgates are opened then the Scots will fill the land with their men." I smiled at him, "So, how is your mother?"

"Well, but tired for she has grandfather and grandmother under her feet."

I laughed, "Do not worry. She will be happy that they are both safe and your mother enjoys caring for others. She is the kindest woman I know."

I was relieved that nothing untoward had occurred while I was away. A warrior with worries made mistakes.

I took advantage, the next day, of my position and I went to the castle and bathed. When I had been with Perkin Warbeck I had been treated well and accustomed to smelling less like a horse and more like a flower. I knew that it would only be temporary but taking my new clothes and bathing seemed to invigorate me. Whilst in the castle I saw some of the other gentlemen and captains of billmen I had previously met. They had been summoned to receive new orders. Lord Dacre and I might be riding forth but plans had to be in place for the order of march and supplies, especially of arrows, had to be organised. They all knew, thanks to my absence from the march, that I had been in the borderlands for some time and they were all anxious to know what we faced. I told them all that I knew and that was not much. Lord Home's attack had involved more men than I had expected and the fact that it had been sent a week before the army moved south told me and the other captains that we would be well outnumbered when we fought.

By the time I reached our camp, I had a better idea of the size of our army. The Earl of Surrey was at York where he was collecting not only levies but also the holy banners that had served the English so well at the Battle of the Standards and at Neville's Cross. He would then go to Durham to speak with the Bishop of Durham and bring the men of the Palatinate and St Cuthbert's banner. It would be that banner which would both attract Scottish attacks and inspire fear. I could not see the earl arriving before the week was out.

That evening as I sat with my men and ate, I discussed with Ralf our numbers, "We have less than eighteen thousand men here at the moment. I would hope that the earl might bring another couple of thousand or so but the Scots may have twice that number. He will also have cannons and," I spread my arm, "we do not have a great number of them as yet."

Ralf nodded, "Aye, you are right." He smiled, "Yet I have hopes that this battle may secure not only the northern border but bring peace. I know that when I followed you south, I wished to become a man at arms but Elizabeth is with child and even with just the income from you, Captain James, we can have a good life. I hope to fight bravely in this battle and to take Scottish lords for ransom. I would still be a warrior but I hope for some years before I need to use my skills again."

I nodded, "I understand your thoughts, Ralf. When Jane had James here then my life changed. My father fought in a civil war when men had to choose sides. We fight here to defend our land from an invader. King Henry can enjoy peace with this victory." It was a dream and although I spoke the words with sincerity in my heart, I knew that kings were never happy with what they had. They always wanted more.

I did not wear plate as I mounted Duncan. None of the men who rode with us burdened our animals. We did not seek battle but information and the one hundred men who rode north from Newcastle rode like Border Reivers. It would be a three-day ride and we headed for Rothbury where we would spend the night and gather more intelligence. I rode with Lord Dacre rather than Ralf and his lordship questioned me all the way north. I could not answer many of his questions for this was not my land but his questions promoted thoughts in my head that proved, in the end, useful.

Rothbury had no castle but there were bastle houses and we were accommodated by farmers, the tenants of Henry Percy, who were more than happy to feed and house us knowing that we were their salvation when the Scottish hordes descended.

I led him to the place where Ralf and I had stopped on the way back from burying Sir Edward of Hedingham and rode with his staff to the ridge that overlooked the tiny hamlet of Flodden. I pointed to Ford Castle in the distance. There were Scottish soldiers entrenched around it but the booming of bombards came from further north, at Norham. "See, my lord, how close is the border? This is England and a better place to defend I have yet to see."

He nodded, "Aye, I can hear their cannons. If they placed them on this ridge with their spears to defend them then we would have to bleed our way to the top and there be massacred."

One of his knights, Sir Walter said, "But what is to stop them, my lord, from heading further south?"

Lord Dacre shook his head, "As Sir William showed the Scots at Milfield, the open plains do not suit the schiltrons of Scotland. Our heavy horses combined with our archers would cut them to pieces. I hope that Norham will last as long as it can for we need the men that the Earl of Surrey will bring." He suddenly seemed to make the decision. He mounted his horse, "Come, we will risk riding close to Norham and see the threat we face at close hand. Captain James, you and your man know the castle better than most. Take us as close as you can and we will assess the danger. The earl will want facts and not conjecture when he arrives."

It was lucky that this was familiar territory for the Scots had built many camps around the castles. They were building trenches and emplacements for their guns but they also had light horsemen who were raiding the countryside for food to feed what was clearly a huge army. I counted on the fact that we might be taken for Scottish horsemen. Our cloaks hid our liveries. I took us, not down the roads, but across fields and through the copses and woods that filled the land between the villages. God smiled on us for we reached Norham from the northeast and were unseen. It meant that we approached Norham from the direction of the nearby Berwick Castle. Berwick had the advantage that it could be supplied by sea and there were ships anchored in the estuary to prevent the Scots from assaulting the northernmost English fortress.

With our men watching with loaded latches, I rode with Lord Dacre and Sir Walter through the woods that lay just four hundred paces from their trenches. We sheltered between two huge oaks whose branches and leaves hid us from view. It was like a huge anthill as men dug trenches, built earth ramparts and hauled on ropes to pull the guns into position. They seemed immune from the attentions of the defenders. That made sense to me for those within would not want to waste powder, bolts and arrows on men who would be hard to hit and were not the fighters who would attack the walls when they were sufficiently weakened. The attention of the Scottish engineers was on the castle. They had begun to bombard the walls for I could see the pockmarks where stones had struck the curtain wall. I was not an expert in cannons but Sir Walter was.

"These guns will break down the outer walls easily, Lord Dacre, and that will give them clear lines to attack the inner curtain wall and the keep. If it lasts five days I will be surprised. It matters not how many men lie within it is the age of the walls that will cause Norham to fall and that means Ford will soon follow."

Lord Dacre nodded, the disappointment clearly etched upon his face. He had obviously hoped for a longer period of grace. He shook his head, "And we are no wiser as to numbers."

I pointed to the men who we could see, "My lord these are not the knights but the labourers. From the number we can see here then I think there could be twenty thousand or more labourers. Add to that their warriors, the knights, gallowglasses and highlanders and it would be double. The bulk of their army will be across the Tweed or in Norham village."

"You are right, we have seen enough. Let us return to the men."

Our luck deserted us as we left the shelter of the woods. We suddenly found ourselves face to face with forty horsemen who had been raiding the land towards Bamburgh which lay due east of Norham. It was lucky that it was my twenty hobilars who led us for they had loaded latches and they raised and loosed them before the Scots could even register that they had found English horsemen outside the castle. Men were unhorsed and others wheeled away, leaving a gap that could be exploited.

I drew my sword and shouted, "Charge!" as my men reloaded and loosed their latches for a second time. More riders were unhorsed and as they tried to draw weapons we galloped through their centre. I slashed at a horseman who was trying to draw his sword. I did not have the luxury of time to aim but I knocked him from his mount which, freed from a rider, fled through the other Scotsmen, disordering them.

Lord Dacre was a good warrior and he and Sir Walter, both plated, drove a wedge through the horsemen who disappeared before us. We had to get away as quickly as we could and I knew that they would soon recover and summon heavier horsemen from the other side of the castle and the village. I did not wait for an order but rode at the head of my men, towards the road that led north to Berwick. I knew that it crossed the main road that led south and we could make quicker time that way. Duncan was a good horse and easily outstripped the lighter horses of my other men. I reached the crossroads and saw the banners of Berwick in the distance to the north. The road was empty and I wheeled Duncan south. Lord Dacre joined me as we rode down the ancient Roman highway built from cobbles and kept repaired by the Bishop of Durham's men in Norham.

"A strange route, captain."

"It will take time to follow us and I hope to be out of sight and well on the road south before they reach here. I am gambling that they will seek us north towards Berwick. That would make more sense than a long fifty-mile ride south. We ride hard for Morpeth, my lord."

"Not back to Rothbury? It is a longer ride to Morpeth."

"But on a better road and there they have a castle." I shrugged, "I am sorry, my lord, I had little time to conjure a better plan and I cast the bones. The alternative was to head south directly and then we would have had a running fight."

In the end, I was vindicated for we were not pursued. The ancient Roman Road was long and straight. The Romans liked to see enemies coming and when we stopped to rest at the top of a long rise, we were able to see two miles behind us and there was no one following. We were hungry and our horses were exhausted but we reached the sanctuary that was Morpeth and rested there for the rest of the night.

Chapter 12

The Borders August 1513

We reached Newcastle on the same day that the Earl of Surrey reached York. He was still many days away from us and while we had more than half of the army, Lord Dacre did not feel confident in leading such a large body of men. The Earl of Surrey had fought at Bosworth and was a wily old general. My men and I were glad of the opportunity to rest. As soon as the earl arrived then we knew we would be marching once more.

We had done more than our fair share of work thus far and we were able just to practise and rest. It was harvest time and there was plenty of food. When the Earl of Surrey's son, Sir Thomas, arrived with the fleet then our numbers were bolstered by more than a thousand marines. They were good men who could not only use cannons and bombards but were able to fight with a billhook or boarding pike. It took time for them to land as they had to bring guns ashore but, for me, it was gratifying to see that we now had some artillery as well. The Town Moor was filled with tents and men from all over the north. It had grown because now the foot soldiers had arrived from the rest of England and we had a sea of men.

When the earl did arrive, with the last of the army, it was to a depressed camp for we had heard, from riders, that Norham had finally fallen. This came a day after the news that Ford was taken. King James occupied Norham but slighted Etal and Ford.

James was with us and frowned when he heard the word, "Slighted, father? King James insulted them?"

Ralf smiled and ruffled James' hair. The two had become close on the march north. I think impending fatherhood had changed Ralf more than a little, "It means, young warrior, that the Scots have made Ford and Etal indefensible. They can still be used as homes but cannot defend themselves against an enemy. The two lords will have to rebuild."

It had been the Bastard Heron who had brought the news. You had to admire the man who seemed to have more lives than a cat. He and his renowned border horsemen had escaped by a whisker and ridden through the Scots who had finally taken the three jewels of the north. The reason for the delay in the arrival of the earl became obvious when we saw the horses and draught animals drawing the sakers and serpentines. I was not summoned to the council of war but I did not mind. I recognised that the men who were there, Sir William Bulmer, Lord Dacre, Sir Marmaduke Constable, Sir Thomas Howard and Sir William Percy, all knew their business. The Town Moor was overflowing and men had come from all over Lancashire, Cheshire and Yorkshire. None had travelled as far as we had but as the tenants of Whitby Abbey had sent their billmen and archers then it was clear that the north had rallied to thwart the intentions of the Scottish king.

Ralf enjoyed numbers and he estimated that we had more than twenty-five thousand men. That seemed a huge army but from what I had seen the Scottish horde was greater. The problem as I saw it was that the earl's position in Newcastle kept him too far from the enemy. The last we had heard was that King James and his enormous army were at Norham and slighting castles took time but we would have to move soon. The earl proved his worth and ordered the army to march north to Bolton, just west of Alnwick castle where we would be in a position to counter whatever plans the Scots had. He had not enjoyed more than a night in Newcastle before he marched once more.

It was merely thirty miles but we were a long metal snake and the last elements did not reach Bolton until the fourth of September. The earl and the majority of his council did not reach it until the fifth. Thomas Howard, the Lord Admiral, commanded the vanguard and Lord Dacre had recommended that my men, along with Sir William Bulmer, should be part of it. The result was that as soon as we arrived at Bolton and while a defensive camp was made, Sir William and I led our hobilars to scout out the Scots. Ralf and I donned our breastplates and helmets. Our hobilars made sure that they had their latches and bolts in their sheaves.

As soon as we reached Wooler, thirteen miles from our camp, we had news of the Scots. They were close. We could have returned immediately to the earl with that information but the two of us were experienced enough as warriors to know that this needed a military eye and not that of a shepherd who had seen the saltire. Sir William did, however, send a rider back to Bolton suggesting that the earl might shift the army to Wooler.

It was just seven miles from Wooler to Flodden and we spied the Scots forming up on the ridge above the village. As we reined in and watched them from afar, I realised that Lord Dacre and I had underestimated their numbers. From what I saw and the banners we counted, there had to be more than forty thousand men. The position, now that I saw the men milling along its edge, was even more formidable. The land on one side was too high and steep for men to ascend whilst, on the other, it was a bog. An attacking army would need to advance up a slope that would sap energy from men's legs and was without cover of any kind. Even worse was that their position, on the ridge, meant that if we attacked our men would be slaughtered long before they could reach the top. It was a perfect place to have bombards and cannons.

Sir William looked at me and nodded, "Lord Dacre said that you had identified this as the perfect place for the Scots to halt us and you are right." He pointed, "There is nowhere for us to place our cannons. Counter battery fire is the only answer to the Scottish batteries."

One of his knights, Sir Ralph Prestbury said, "My lord, they have seen us, we should leave." I saw agitation on the ridge. The men there were foot soldiers but they had to have horsemen close by and they would soon chase us away.

"Aye, we should but as our animals have just ridden twenty miles we should rest them, at least for a while, besides, we need to know if there is another way we could stop them."

Another of his knights, Sir Geoffrey Barwick, said, "The earl needs to do nothing, my lord. Let the Scots have this English ridge. If they squat on the ridge then they cannot ravage the countryside."

Sir William laughed, "These are the borderlands. While their army occupies the ridge then our route north is barred and they could raid as far east as the coast. The land to the west could be threatened too. No, Sir Geoffrey, the Scottish king has chosen well and we will have to shift him. Unless there is another route then it will need the blood of Englishmen to wash the Scots from our land."

It was then that the Scots reacted to what they saw as an insult. We were spying on them and they did not like it. More than a hundred horsemen detached themselves and hurtled down the slope towards us. I saw, as we wheeled and fled back to Wooler, that they gained speed quickly and that told me the slope was steeper than it looked from afar and that it was firm. Balls would bounce along it and take out files of advancing men. Our horses were tired and the Scots gradually reined us in. Wooler was just two miles away when we could hear not only their hooves but the shouts and insults from riders who clearly thought that they had us.

I pointed ahead, just beyond the farm of Humbleton, "My lord, the road there dips at the ford over the stream and there is a wood. Our horses are wearying and if we were hurt this close to Wooler then it would dishearten all. Let us turn and bloody their noses."

"You are right." He shouted above the sound of our hooves, "At the ford, halt, spread out and we will give these Scots a smack on the nose to show them what they face."

I knew that my men had loaded latches already and while the Scots outnumbered us, we would outnumber those who rode at the fore.

Sir William and I reached the ford first and, after crossing it, for the stream was narrow, turned our horses, drew our swords and waited. Our men joined us and spread out. I saw the first riders and they were eager young Scotsmen. They were the ones who were plated and rode war horses. I took them to be knights. Behind them rode their border horsemen and I saw that they were armed not with latches but with spears. We had just thirty-three latches but the men using them understood their weapons well and as the knights and the first warriors splashed into the stream, they did not waste their bolts. Sir William was flanked by his knights and I had Ralf to my left. The five of us were protected by metal and the Scottish knights had to draw their weapons. They rode up to us and I found myself facing a knight whose sword was longer than mine but, as our blades crashed together, I realised that it was an ancient and clumsy weapon. The cracks of latches and the whizzing of bolts told me that our hobilars now had targets, the men without plate. There were cries as men and horses were hit and then the splash of riders falling into the stream. As my sword flicked away the heavier Scottish one, I saw my chance and lunged with the tip. The Scottish knight, like me, was wearing a breastplate but his arms, like mine, were unprotected. My sword drew blood and the sword fell from his hand. I raised my sword to end his life but he wheeled his mount around and picked his way across the stream that was now littered with bodies. Sir William had killed his opponent and the latches were now hitting men as they reached the stream. Ralf and my hobilars also had sword skills and with better swords than the Scots the duels were unequal. Like the man I had wounded when the Scottish horseman was cut, they fled. More men were wounded that day than died.

The Scottish voice that shouted, "Back!" marked the end of the skirmish. Whoever led them now knew that we had seen their lines and that they could do little about it. Whatever honour they might have regained now floated down the stream and lay littered in the ford.

We waited until we were certain that they had endured enough and then our hobilars retrieved the eight horses that wandered in the stream and the weapons and treasure from the twelve bodies that lay in the water. I saw that Sir Geoffrey had been wounded by a spear but other than that we were whole.

We headed back to Wooler and when I saw the Tudor dragon banner flying above the rapidly growing camp then I knew that the Earl of Surrey had arrived. Duncan had performed well and John and James had found some wizened old apples as a reward for him. I would look after my new horse.

The council of war was held the next day and I was asked to attend. I realised later that both Sir Edward Stanley and Sir William Bulmer, not to mention Lord Dacre, all held me in high esteem but when I entered the commandeered barn, I felt like a very small fish indeed.

There was a pursuivant present, Thomas Hawley, Rouge Croix. The Rouge Croix was a relatively minor pursuivant and I guessed that the more important ones were with the king in France. His Scottish equivalent, the Islay Herald, would be the senior Scottish herald.

Sir William reported to the earl who, as my part in the reconnaissance was mentioned, studied me closely. He nodded when the knight had finished, "And, Captain James, what is your view of the Scottish position?" He saw frowns appear on the faces of some of those present, not least his son the Lord Admiral. "Despite your somewhat lowly status, I have heard good reports of you and I would value your opinion."

"If we attack up the slope we will be slaughtered. If we do nothing or skulk away then the Scottish king has won."

The old earl smiled, "Succinctly put. I have heard from Lord Heron of Ford that there may be an alternative route. What say you two, our most recent scouts?"

Sir William shook his head, "I know not."

I nodded, "There is another ridge to the northwest of Flodden close to the village of Branxton and it is protected by a small burn. It would afford our guns the opportunity to fire at the Scots and the ground below is boggy. That, my lord, would disrupt their pikes." I could not say so but I had witnessed the effect of uneven ground at Galashiels when I had trained the levy. On solid ground, they could move quickly and smoothly but the boggy ground would suck at their feet and I guessed descending slopes would also have an effect.

The earl smiled, "That concurs precisely with the words of Lord Heron."

The Lord Admiral said, "But how would we get around the enemy? What is to stop them from attacking us in line of march?"

Sir William smiled, "The same reason as their choice of position. They have a strong defence and cannot quit their ridge. They cannot easily attack except down the slope. King James has fixed himself to the ridge. It is, from what Lord Dacre has told me, a formidable position but it cannot easily be shifted." He stroked his beard, "Besides if he does attack us in line of march then we are making him do that which he does not want to do."

Lord Dacre had a map which he studied, "And what of the two slighted castles, Etal and Ford? We have to pass them."

I was on more familiar ground now. "When I was here some years ago in the service of the old king, I had cause to serve close to Twesilhaugh. That castle was destroyed but not the bridge over the Till. The guns and wagons could use that and the foot and horse cross the Heaton Ford which is close by." I remembered the area well. We had chased Perkin Warbeck when his attempt to claim the crown had failed.

The Lord Admiral looked at the map, "Could we do the march in one day?"

I knew that a small group of men could but not an army the size of ours and therein lay another problem. It would take the whole army a long time to be in position on the ridge, "No, my lord. We would need to camp north of here."

Lord Dacre jabbed his finger at the map, "Here, close to Barnmoor we could camp and if we put men on the top of this moor, what is it called?" He peered at the map, "Watch Law, then we would be forewarned of an attack."

The earl peered around the others, "Has anyone a better plan?" His words were greeted by silence. He turned to Thomas Hawley, "Then, pursuivant, it is you who will deliver the message to this Scottish king that he either quits the field or gives battle." The old earl had put his ultimatum to parchment already and he handed it to Sir Thomas. "If you would, pursuivant, read my words so that all may hear."

The brightly dressed courtier took the parchment and read, "King James, contrary to your oath and league, and unnaturally against all reason and conscience, you are guilty of burning, spoiling and destroying and cruelly murdering the King of England's subjects. I demand that you quit this land and make reparations to those you have harmed."

Men nodded for it was the right tone and the Rouge Croix left us to head to the ridge at Flodden. We immediately broke camp. As I passed him Sir Marmaduke Constable took me by the arm. Like the earl, the Sheriff of Yorkshire was also seventy years old but still rode to war plated and ready for battle, "Young man I admire your fortitude in voicing an opinion in such august company. Your rank and age bespeak someone who is callow and inexperienced but your words were those of a veteran. England is lucky to have young men such as you to fight for her."

"Thank you, my lord, and I am happy that we are led by such men as you."

As I headed back to my men I reflected on the fact that the Earl of Surrey and Marmaduke Constable as well as Baron Dacre, had fought against King Henry and were now fighting for his son. It was England that was important and not the man who ruled it.

We rode with the Lord Admiral and his vanguard. The hobilars formed a curtain to the west of us for almost as soon as we had left Wooler to head towards Barnmoor we were seen as we crossed the Milfield Plain. The blackened and burnt-out villages were a testament to the fate of the borders. It was a blur in the distance but we heard the horns on Flodden Edge and saw activity.

Sir Thomas turned to me, "Captain James come with me and bring your hobilars. I would ascend Watch Law and view the enemy."

"Yes, my lord, Ralf bring the men."

John and James were becoming used to being abandoned. The family that was my company would watch them as though they were their own.

The knight had ten knight companions with him and I think he wanted the hobilars in case he had to flee. We could and would be sacrificed if he had to escape. There were tracks up the slope to the top of one of the only places that overlooked Flodden. The path hid us from Flodden Edge and we saw nothing as we ascended. As we neared the top, I saw the artillery pieces turn to face us. The admiral was no doubt used to being fired upon by cannons. He and his brother, Edmund, had been the ones who had brought the Scottish privateer, Andrew Barton, to battle and captured his three ships, *Unicorn*, *Lion* and *Jenny Pirwyn*. The Scottish knight had been beheaded after death and the action still rankled with the Scots who felt he had been murdered. Perhaps they recognised his livery for as we stopped, we saw the puffs of smoke and the belch of flame from some of the guns and then heard the rumble a moment later as they opened fire. Some of the horses became skittish but the admiral merely smiled, "If this is an example of their skills then my gunners will show them real gunnery." He turned to me, "Well, captain of billmen, you, it seems, do have skills." He turned to one of his companions, "See, William, we can see the two castles from here and, if I am not mistaken, the bridge, ford, and the castle that was destroyed."

"Aye my lord, it is not far at all."

Sir Thomas said, "Where is this other ridge of which you speak?"

"If you look beyond the smoke from the guns, you can see it. There are no trees but it lies about one and a half miles from Flodden Edge."

He laughed, "Better and better. We can place our guns there and then the boot is on the other foot. The Scots will have to shift us from the ridge for we bar their way home. It is they who will have to endure shot and shell and then face our billmen. I have seen enough. Let us ride to Barnmoor before one of those gunners gets lucky."

I had seen guns on the battlefield and the worst place for them to fire was at a slope leading to a crest. On the flat, the balls would bounce as boys did skimming stones. I had heard they did the same at sea. The balls the Scots had fired had merely either ploughed into the earth many hundreds of paces below us or flown harmlessly above our heads.

By the time we reached the camp, fires were lit and food was cooking.

We were on short rations for the men who lived north of Newcastle had raided and looted the supply wagons bringing us food. The lack of food meant that we needed to bring the Scots to battle within a day or two. If not, then the army would begin to starve and a starving, outnumbered army was more prone to flight.

Flodden

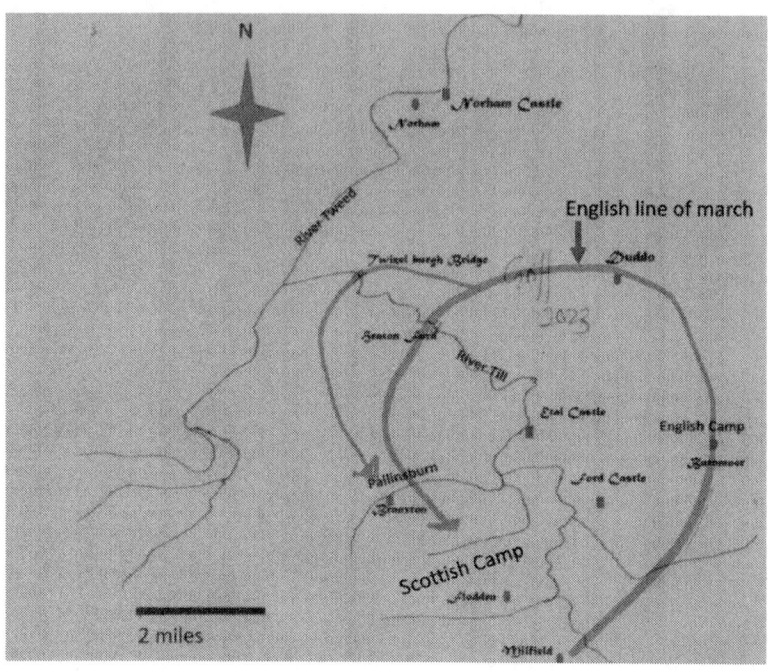

Chapter 13

Branxton Edge September 1513

My fear had been that the Scots might send horsemen to the ford and the bridge. We would not discover if they had an idea of our intentions until we rode there the next day. I had learned not to worry about what might happen. We had made our plans and I thought that they were good ones. If they were at the ford and the bridge then we would have a fight on our hands. I was confident now that we had the beating of the Scottish borderers. As we sat around a fire eating a watery stew, we spoke of what the Scots might do and what our response might be. Thanks to my time with the Pringle family I had a better insight into the Scottish mind. They were more confident that their king would lead them to victory. David Pringle had boasted, when he had returned from Edinburgh, of the huge numbers of men that they had. He spoke of French officers training the pikemen in the Swiss techniques. They had proved very successful in the Empire and France, I wondered if they would work as well in the rough, upland country of the borders.

John and James had not been with us when we had scouted and they pestered us with questions. I had told Ralf of the council of war but my son and foster son were in the dark. My hobilars apart, my men were in the same position and I knew that they would be talking of the prospective battle around their fires. I endured the questions.

"So, father, if the Scots know of this bridge and this ford, will they not contest our crossing of it?"

Ralf laughed and smiled at my son, "You have a clever one here, captain, he has worked out that the Scots must have crossed the ford and the bridge in order to get to Flodden." His face became serious, "And he makes a good point. What if they do contest it?"

"Then we have a skirmish battle and at the crossings they cannot use their cannons, nor will their pikes be of any use. We have better horsemen than they do and our archers are the finest in the world. If they fight then it will be like

Milfield but multiplied. There we had a mere two hundred longbowmen. Here we have more than two thousand."

I dipped some stale bread into the thin stew until it softened.

John said, "Then what will they do?"

I pointed the stale bread north, "The Scots may think that, as they outnumber us, our movement north means we intend to flee to Berwick and await reinforcements. If we did that then the Scots would have free rein to loot and ravage Northumberland, the Tyne Valley and England. They would, in effect, have what they wanted, Northumberland. They would fortify the castles and then it would be we who would have to assault. I think that they will let us move north and it will only be when they see us at Branxton Edge that they will react."

John said, brightly, "Then we will have won."

Ralf laughed, "We will have to endure an attack by wild men first, John. The Scots may not be the best led nor do they have the best of weapons but their soldiers are fearless and tenacious. All that we can do is hold them and hope that they bleed themselves into defeat. The best soldiers that King Henry has, the thousands of bowmen and serried ranks of men at arms and knights, are in France and Flanders challenging the French to enable the king to win land. Here we fight to keep land."

James nodded and took it all in. Ralf was right. My son had a clever mind.

The next morning, well before dawn, we broke camp and headed north. I led the vanguard towards the Heaton Ford and we reached it in an hour. To my relief, we did not have to fight to cross it. Memories kept flooding back. The fight to capture Perkin Warbeck and the death of Sir Edward Hedingham were but two. I wondered about the fate of Gerald of Etal. Had he escaped or had he died defending his castle? Once across and while Sir Thomas oversaw the passage of the vanguard I rode to the bridge. It was still intact and my men and I guarded it until the first of the wagons and the animals pulling the artillery pieces arrived. Lord Dacre's border marchers joined the hobilars of the vanguard to keep a thin screen of horsemen to protect us. The earl was marching in line of battle. Sir Edmund Howard would command the right wing and next to his men would be his brother and his father. The last to reach the battle would be Sir Edward Stanley with the Lancashire men and the Yorkshire men led by Sir Marmaduke Constable. Lord Dacre would lead the horsemen and they would be placed on the right of the line, supporting the right wing. The guns had to be across almost first as they had to be hauled across Pallinsburn and that would take time.

Once on the other side of the Till, the men were marshalled into their battles. Sir Edmund had the command of the vanguard. The Earl of Surrey arrived before the main body. For a seventy-year-old, he was as active as any. He shouted as men crossed the Till, "I doubt not that you will serve the King and me truly this day!" It was typical of the man that he used such simple words to inspire his men.

The men were then formed into a line of march so that they could take their positions up on the edge. The admiral's young brother commanded what would be our right flank. He commanded three thousand men and they were made of the men of Cheshire, as well as men from the Abbey of the Royal Vale and some marines. I knew that I would be fighting with Sir Edward on the left wing but I waved to men I had known, the men of the Stanley lands in Cheshire. They wore the same livery as I did. I saw Sir Edmund frown when he heard some of the comments. They were clearly unhappy at being commanded by one who was not a Stanley.

"Captain James, why do we not fight with you and the other Stanley men?"

"Let Sir Edward lead us and we alone will defeat these jackanapes."

I waved at them, feeling somewhat embarrassed for Sir Edmund, "Fear not for we are well led."

The largest of our battles was the centre one and there were nine thousand men marching behind the Earl of Surrey. They were the best of our men. There were a thousand of the marines brought by the admiral as well as two thousand men from the Palatinate. They were eager for vengeance. The

Queen of the Borders, Norham, was a Durham castle. They had Sir William Bulmer with the standard of St Cuthbert. Then there were the Northumbrian knights. Sir Edward led the men of Lancashire and Craven too.

The Pallinsburn took time to cross and then we had to ascend the steep slope of Branxton Edge. Until we reached the top then the Scots would have no idea where we were and so we ascended the slope in the same battles that we would fight. Already almost two-thirds of the army had begun to ascend the ridge but Sir Edward and the billmen of Lancashire were tardy and had not yet crossed Heaton ford. Sir Thomas waved impatiently to me, "Captain James, if you please." He wished me to accompany him.

"Yes, my lord," I turned my horse to join my billmen. "Take care, Ralf. You have had one wound. Do not suffer another."

"I will, Captain James." He would be with Lord Dacre who led our mounted knights and our hobilars. They would be our only reserve. The Lord of the Western Marches had more than three thousand men and Lord Heron of Ford would fight with them along with eighteen hundred men on foot led by Bishop Stanley. Wherever you looked you could see the eagle claw livery. The last to cross, before the rearguard of Sir Marmaduke and Sir Edward, were the five thousand men of Yorkshire, led by the Earl of Surrey.

Sir Marmaduke had ridden ahead to view where he would be fighting and to encourage his men to ascend the slope. He waved as I left. He would command the left wing where his two thousand men included the Percy men and a thousand men of Lancashire. I was proud that Lancashire would feature so prominently in this battle. James and John had used two of the captured horses and were not with the rest of the billmen and Ecclestone men. They were with me. I gestured for them to follow me. Their task, hopefully, would be as observers and horse holders. They would not be happy to be relegated to such a role but I would and I knew that Jane would thank me for it, if I survived.

We had four miles to march and Sir Edmund, as the marshal, did his job and harried the five-mile column of men. If the Scots had known of our position, they could have fallen upon us but they seemed blind to our line of march.

I spurred Duncan to catch up with the vanguard and reached the crest of Branxton Edge. As I reached the centre I saw the men of the vanguard, including the Cheshire grumblers, forming up on the far right of our line. Of the Scots, I could see nothing. John said, "Do you wish to dismount yet, captain?"

I shook my head and pointed to the dead ground behind the edge, "You two go and find somewhere with grazing. I will join you with Duncan when I can." The two headed off. Being amongst the first meant that they had the best chance to find a good, safe spot.

I turned my attention back to the battlefield. There was a muddy morass that ran from my left to just right of where our centre would be. Neither side would wish to advance over that ground. On our right, it was slightly higher and drier. Sir Edmund Thomas would have his work cut out there. Already the sakers and serpentines were being placed to face the Scottish attack although, as I looked, I saw nothing of the Scots. Then I spied smoke spiralling from where I had taken the Scots to be camped and I then witnessed the arrival of a magnificently armoured King James. The banners rose over the ridge and the mounted Scottish knights appeared. It had been some years since I had seen him but I recognised him. I also recognised Lord Home. The other Scottish nobles also appeared to be familiar but I could not identify them except for Sir John Maxwell. I recognised his livery. I saw them spying on us and arms were gesticulated. It was then that they fetched out their great bombards. Huge lines of men hauled them to the top of the ridge. They would have dwarfed our sakers and serpentines had they been placed next to each other and it appeared that they had more ordnance than we did. Our men would be in for a battering.

Sir Edmund rode over to me, "Captain James, be so good as to tell my father and brother that they need to hurry, look."

As I followed his pointing finger, I saw the first of the pikemen as they appeared over the ridge. It was like a rolling wall as pike after pike, held perfectly vertically, rose over the ridge. "Yes, my lord." I knew the size of the problem. Our men had endured a long march and were spread out on the road. All that the Scots had needed to do, once they knew where we were, was to turn around and begin to fire their ordinance. If they attacked now, while we were forming up, then all the effort of our outflanking manoeuvre would have been in vain.

I saw the main battle, they were crossing the Pallinsburn. Whilst not an obstacle it was slowing the progress of the men as they crossed and the slope of Branxton Edge hid the danger from them. The earl had moved from the Till and was now exhorting the men he would lead.

"My lord, the enemy warriors are marshalling into position and your son urges speed."

He nodded, "Find the admiral and tell him."

I smiled, the earl was not in the least flustered. "Yes, my lord."

When I reached the admiral, he was helping men to haul guns across the muddy burn. I told him and he shook his head, "This land is not cooperating, Captain James." He shielded his eyes, "Sir Edward and the doughty men of Lancashire appear to be missing. Be so good as to find your lord and urge him to join us with all speed." Sir Edward commanded seven thousand men and they were, in my somewhat prejudiced view, the best in the army.

"Yes, Sir Thomas."

I wondered what had delayed them. I found them a short time later. They had lost sight of Sir Marmaduke's men ahead of them and were heading not south and west but south. Had I not reached them then they would have wandered around lost and we would lose the battle. If they continued on this path then they would find themselves between the two armies and that would be a disaster for Sir Edward was vital to the earl's plans. They would be the rock that would protect the left wing and stop the Scots from getting back over the Till.

I stood in my stirrups and shouted, "Sir Edward! Sir Edward! This way."

He turned and ordered his men to follow him. When he reached me, he said, "I know not this land it all looks the same to me."

I pointed to the hill behind me, "We have no time to lose, my lord. The Scots are forming their lines and their guns are about ready to open fire."

He turned in his saddle, "Stanley men, we must run to the battle. Are you with me?"

There was a huge cheer and Sir Edward and I led his mounted men to get to the battle as quickly as possible. The jingle of metal and the pounding feet behind us was a comfort but I wondered if we would be in time. Already the pall of smoke from behind the Scottish lines was drifting and I saw its fog above the ridge. Even Duncan struggled up the slope and as we crested the top the smoke from the Scottish fires partly obscured the ground but through it, I could see the pikes. In the short time I had been absent the ridge before us, just six hundred paces away, was filled with rank upon rank of pikes. There were also ranks of Highlanders armed with deadly-looking axes and long swords and, facing the earl and his son, Sir Edmund, were the Scottish artillery pieces. It was clear where they would attack. The Scottish left and the centre were the strongest elements in their army. As the smoke drifted and the men of Lancashire began to climb the ridge and were marched into position, I counted the guns. There were at least five bombards which threw a shot weighing sixty pounds, as well as two huge eighteen-pound culverins, four smaller culverins and half a dozen of the culverins moyenne which sent a larger shot than our serpentines. The Scottish army had the weight of shot on their side. They had more guns and heavier guns than we did. We had twenty-two smaller cannons to face this barrage. The only advantages we held were that our gunners could fire faster and as they were manned by marines, had better gunners.

Sir Edward shouted, "Captain James, I need you to earn your pay and command the billmen of Lancashire."

"I am coming, my lord."

I spurred Duncan and rode along the reverse slope of Branxton Ridge. The ground had been empty just an hour before but now there were barrels of powder, the tethered horses that had pulled the guns and the healers who were waiting for their first patients. I saw that they had taken over Branxton Church. It was as good a place as any for men either to be healed or to die. I saw John and James. They had unsaddled their horses and the two animals were happily grazing. I rode over and dismounted.

"Has the battle begun, father?"

I smiled, "You will hear and smell the start."

"Smell?"

"The cannons stink when they fire and the air will be filled with a pestilential smell that comes from Hades. You watch Duncan. John, fetch my billhook."

John had brought my billhook in a hessian sack and, after taking it out he handed it to me. He said, "The healers have asked for us to help them. We are to carry the wounded from the field." It was almost a request.

My heart sank but I knew that there could be no idle bystanders in this battle. I nodded my agreement, "Take care then and keep your heads down. Do not go near any wounded Scotsman. They will see your eagle's claw and wounded or not they will try to slay you." I hugged James and clasped John's arm. "May God watch over you."

One of the healers, a priest, made the sign of the cross and said, "Amen."

I hurried to the top of the ridge and saw that Sir Edward had managed to get our men in line. The sakers and serpentines were in position and even as I looked, I saw the enemy guns belch smoke and flame. The battle of Flodden Field had begun.

A Lord Bothwell and the reserve
B Earl of Argyll and the Highlanders
C King James and the Earl of Montrose
D Scottish Artillery
E Lords Home and Huntley

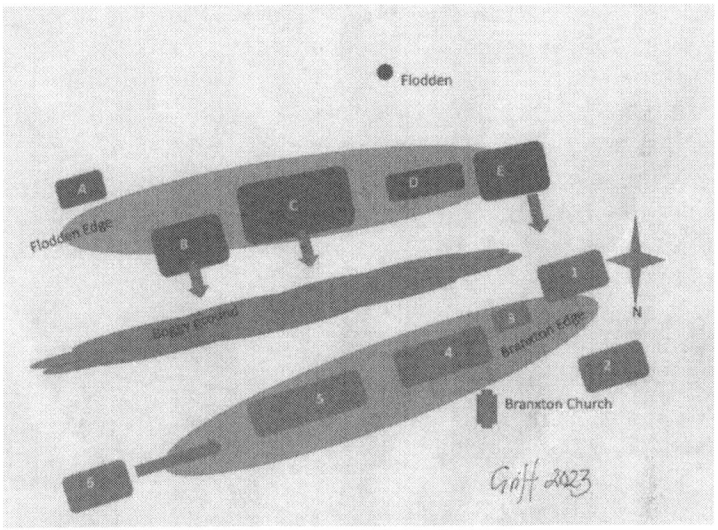

The Battle of Flodden

1 Sir Edmund Howard
2 Lord Dacre
3 English artillery
4 Lord Admiral Howard
5 The Earl of Surrey
6 Sir Edward Stanley

Chapter 14

The Battle of Flodden September 9th, 1513

The tardy arrival of our men, the billmen and archers of Ecclestone meant that even as the artillery pieces blasted away, sending smoke to fill the dell, Sir Edward was still marshalling the men into position. It looked like less than a third of our men were ready to face the attack which would clearly begin as soon as the bombards had done their work. The remainder of the men were still trudging across the burn. I ran to help him and my familiar voice soon brought order to what had looked, as I raced to join them, like chaos. He had echeloned them back and that helped but I shifted two of the companies around so that the stronger one, mine, was closer to the Earl of Surrey's men. The guns banged away and we could see little because of the smoke.

"Come, men of Ecclestone. We shall fight close to the earl!"

Sir Edward pointed back towards the burn, "More than half of our men are still to arrive. I will go and hurry them. Take command, Captain James. The battle has yet to start."

I sought out Richard who often deputised for me as we crested the rise and saw the enormous wall of pikes across the shallow valley, "Well, lieutenant, you have marched with our men, are they in good heart?"

He looked up at the enemy who opposed us. I saw that the banners of the King of Scotland were amongst the battle that we would face. "They outnumber us and those pikes look fearfully long, Captain James."

I nodded, "But it takes skill to march slowly and keep together. When I viewed the ground from the ridge, I saw that the bottom was boggy. It is hard to see them keeping that formation."

Just then a messenger, one of the earl's knights, rode to us, "Where is Lord Stanley, Captain James?"

I gestured towards the burn, "He has gone to fetch the rest of our men."

"The earl asks you to bring your billmen closer to his battle and protect his left flank. Have your archers stand behind."

"Yes, my lord." He wheeled his horse to ride back to the earl. I cupped my hands, "Close up and move to your right. Archers form up behind the billmen. On my command, march." I paused, "March!" We had practised this many times and the men moved, crablike but in perfect time. We were lucky that the ground was relatively flat and dry. The movement also afforded us a better view of the fire of the cannons. I realised that the lighter serpentines and sakers were sending four balls for every one of the heavier Scottish ones. The English gunners, marines and sailors, were also aiming their balls at the enemy guns. The Scottish were aiming at the billmen. When a ball struck, it did terrible damage but more balls ploughed into the ground before them than struck flesh. The soggy, boggy ground did not help them. Our right flank, however, was suffering for Lord Home had begun his march first and was now closing with Sir Edmund and his men. There the drier ground allowed the balls to bounce. I saw a file of men all fall to one lucky bouncing ball. The Scottish pikes were still advancing and the two Scottish lords, Home and Huntly were marching slowly to ensure that they all arrived together and to allow the guns to kill as many of the men as they could. I spied Sir Edmund as he waved his sword. Like his father, he knew the value of encouraging men with words. I could not hear them but I knew what he was doing. Would the men of Cheshire stand?

The explosion amongst the Scottish guns evoked a cheer from our line as a ball struck first a bombard and then the powder next to it. A column of fire leapt into the air and the bombard was destroyed. Burning wood and powder hit other barrels of powder and there were more small explosions amongst the Scottish guns. Even though it was a thousand paces from us I saw some of the gunners flee. That was the turning point in the battle of the cannons. As the Scottish fire lessened, for some other gunners had also fled, so the English guns were able to strike the remaining gunners.

When the bombards and culverins ceased their fire there was
a cheer and then our sakers and serpentines began to fire into
the ranks of pikemen. The pikemen in the main battle had
not been able to advance for fear of being struck by their
own guns. Lord Home had no such constriction. Again there
were cheers but I knew what would happen and it did. The
Scottish horns and drums signalled the charge.

Their cannons gone, King James was ordering a general
advance. The Scots had begun to marshal their men into
huge columns. When marching with a long pike, the column
was an easier formation and meant faster progress. When
they struck even if the men at the front were slain the
pressure from behind would drive over their enemy. The
problem the Scottish would face was that we were on a slope
and I knew that was the only thing that could save us.

I heard the Earl of Surrey shout, "We have the banner of
St Cuthbert with us! Trust in God and fight for England and
King Henry."

It would be some time before we engaged but idle men
had time to think and to fear what was coming. I shouted, in
the absence of Sir Edward, the orders, "Bills forward.
Archers nock!"

All along our line captains gave their commands. We
presented our bills and behind us, the archers, commanded
by their own captains, would select arrows and wait for the
command to draw. An archer could not hold the full draw for
more than a heartbeat. They would draw back and release in
one motion but with the Sottish columns still more than six
hundred paces from us there was no opportunity to release.
Arrows and the strength of the archers would not be wasted.
I was aware of movement to our left and behind us and knew
that it was the bulk of our men struggling up the slope to join
us.

From my position, I was able to see across to Sir Edmund
and our right flank. They were the weakest of our battles and
also the ones who had endured the most savage of the
artillery barrage. They also had one thousand disenchanted
Cheshire men who would rather be fighting with us under
the Stanley banner but their biggest problem was that the

Scots who advanced towards them, the men under Lord
Home and Lord Huntly, had the flattest and driest ground.
There was little to stop their pikes. It also meant that they
would reach Lord Edmund before the two bigger Scottish
battles, the enormous one facing us led by King James and
the marginally smaller one led by the Earl of Montrose,
engaged with the earl and the Lord Admiral. Our sakers and
serpentines were carving lines through the battle led by the
Scottish king but cannons need to be cleaned and the rate of
fire was not enough to deter the Scots who were led by their
king. It would take them some time to cross the flooded
ground, drainage ditch and the bog and reach us.

Before that happened I heard the clash as Lord Home led
his men to smash into Sir Edmund and our right flank. The
cannonade and the lack of heart must have contributed to
what happened next for the billmen there were struck so hard
and so many fell that they broke and fled back over the ridge
towards Branxton Church. Even as they broke, I heard
voices from the Lord Admiral's battle to echelon and face
the new threat. Our right flank was in tatters and there was
nothing now to prevent Lord Home from attacking the flank
of the Lord Admiral's men. The Scottish cheers from the
battle commanded by King James echoed across the field.
With our left flank not yet secure as Sir Edward and the
remainder of the men were still in line of march and our right
wing in tatters then we would be surrounded and
slaughtered. My son and foster son were close to the right
wing and I could do nothing. I prayed that they would take
my horse and join the flight of the men of Cheshire but even
as the thought flitted into my head, I knew that it was a false
hope. They would stay and they would die. I resolved to take
as many Scotsmen with me as I could.

I heard the horns from my right and saw Lord Dacre
leading his horsemen to rescue what they could of the
beleaguered Sir Edmund, he and his knights had not fled and
I could see his banner surrounded by a sea of Scottish pikes
and swords. Lord Dacre, along with Ralf and my hobilars as
well as the redoubtable Sir William, were the only hope for
Sir Edmund but even if he was rescued the horsemen could

do little against pikes. It would be a stay of execution and
when Lord Home reformed his men they would fall upon the
flank of the men led by the Lord Admiral. I looked up at the
sky. It was late afternoon and darkness would soon envelop
us. Perhaps, I thought, that might be our salvation. We might
be able to slip away under cover of darkness and with our
tails between our legs, scuttle back to the Tyne Valley.

The battle between the horsemen and the Scottish raged
on and it was hard to see what was happening. I could
imagine. Sir Edmund and any men who had not run would
be trying to reach the safety of the Lord Admiral and his
men. The border horse, knights and men at arms would be
doing their best to hurt the pikes as much as they could.
There was no way I could identify Ralf and my hobilars for
they wore, like many others, the Stanley livery. I could only
pray that their lives were not being thrown away.

The Scottish pikes were using the Swiss formation. Four
hundred and fifty men in each block of twenty files of
pikemen. Having seen the success on their left the two huge
battles in their centre advanced and by advance, I mean ran.
Even as they descended to the boggy ground, I saw that they
were not as tight as they ought to have been and when I
heard the horns to our right, both Scottish and English,
sound the recall I knew that Lord Dacre and his English
horsemen had held Lord Home. The Scottish battle had
halted at the top of the high ground. Miraculously he did not
reform his men and march down to attack the Lord Admiral.
The lack of Scottish horses now came to hurt them. Perhaps
when we had bloodied them at Norham and at the ford we
had hurt them more than we knew. There was light at the end
of the tunnel for it meant the Lord Admiral would not now
be outflanked. The sun beginning to dip behind a wall of
clouds also brought more of our men led by Sir Edward. His
knights formed up next to the Earl of Surrey.

I watched as a rider with a blood-soaked tabard galloped
and shouted to the Earl of Surrey, "The right wing broke, my
lord, but Lord Dacre has held firm. The Lord Admiral
advises you that now we will have to endure the attack by
the king's battle."

He said nothing but studied the enemy warriors who were now almost within the range of arrows.

Richard shouted and pointed, "Captain James, they have discarded their boots!"

The ground had been so wet that many men had taken off their boots to have a better purchase on the slick turf.

Sir Edward shouted, "Archers prepare!"

My captains of archers knew best but even I could see that there was little point in sending arrows at the front ranks. There King James had packed it with his knights and men at arms. They were plated men against whom arrows would be ineffective. They had good helmets, many of them with visors and even bodkins would not penetrate. I heard the archer centenars giving their orders to send their arrow against the rear ranks, the ones who wore no armour. It would be our front ranks who would have to fight the pikes of the Scots and I looked at them as they ascended the slope towards us. It was a solid wall of pikes no longer. The slope and the slippery turf had spread them out and there were spaces between some files where there should not have been. I saw the king's banner and realised it was heading for the Earl of Surrey fighting beneath the Tudor Standard. The Scottish king was gambling now that his enormous battle of fifteen thousand men would destroy the nine thousand men of the Earl of Surrey.

As I looked at the front ranks approaching us, I saw the livery of the Pringles. Fate had thrown me into a battle to face the men I had helped to train. I realised that the Pringle men were closer together. I had trained them too well and when they struck, we would suffer more than most. It was Davy Pringle who recognised me and his reckless anger could not be contained.

"Treacherous bastard!" He screamed the words at me and men turned to look at me.

Even as his father shouted, "Davy, keep with us." His son ignored him and raced at me with his pike.

Pikes are most effective when used en masse. Twenty odd pikes stabbing at a rank of men would cause damage. A single man had no such opportunity. Davy's pike waved before him for there was too much whip in the shaft. It moved up and down as well as left to right. The pike head looked as though it would hit me and then miss me. It was a wild erratic motion and I remained calm. Timing my blow well, I swung my billhook at the wood and hacked through it. The pike head fell leaving him with a long piece of kindling. His speed had brought him closer to me and, lowering my billhook, I lunged with my spike. He wore a gorget and had a breastplate but his sallet was an open one. My tip slid over his gorget and drove up under his chin and into his skull. It was a quick death and he fell at my feet.

His father screamed, "No!" and disobeyed his own orders. He, his son, James, along with his best men, as well as Caleb ran at us. They were all trying to get at me and I knew why. I had betrayed them. I was just pleased that the two younger sons were not in the front rank.

The men alongside whom I fought were my best billmen and none of us was nonplussed at the wild attack. Had the Pringle clan continued their steady march they might have enjoyed more success but our sharp billhooks smashed through the pikes and as Sir David, Caleb and the others in the front rank hurled their now useless weapons at us we swung our billhooks. This time I was not as lucky as when I had fought Davy. My billhook smashed against the side of Sir David's helmet. I stunned him and I used the hook to pull the disorientated knight towards me. I used the shaft to smash into his face. His nose erupted and I knew that he would be temporarily blinded. I raised my billhook as the Scottish knight drew his sword from over his back. I rammed the bottom spike into his sabaton. His metal shoe slowed down the iron point but did not stop it and I hit flesh. As he screamed in pain, I slashed my billhook across his face. Reeling he fell back and I smashed my billhook into his shoulder. There was a gap between his gorget and shoulder piece. Mail was there to protect it but my billhook cut through it as though it was parchment. Even as he fell back, I knew he was dead or soon would be.

I had no time for self-congratulation for the rest of the pikes reached us and a pike, aimed at my face, struck the side of my helmet and then slid over my shoulder. Edwin, behind me, hacked off the end and then rammed his spike at the middle of the unarmoured man.

A voice from behind shouted, "Captain James!"

I felt, rather than saw the claidheamh-mòr wielded by Caleb come down towards me. Here I did not have the ground to dance and dodge as I had at Smailholm. The strike from the pike had disorientated me slightly and I would have been a dead man if I had not such natural instincts. My hands worked as though another was making them do so. The billhook came up and managed, I know not how, to make the huge weapon miss me. Sparks flew as the metal blades connected and clashed. The ringing of the weapons showed how true both were.

Caleb spat his words at me, "I knew you were no Flemish warrior. Had I known you were an English spy I would have gutted you."

Caleb was a skilled fighter but his anger had blinded him. He was wasting words while staring into my eyes and not watching my hands. The tip of his claidheamh-mòr was embedded in the ground and I was able to use the blade of my billhook to slice across his arm. Like most of the Scots who were not knights his arms were bare and the billhook sliced through to the bone. He roared in anger and raised his claidheamh-mòr. The roar made those around him shy away for the mighty blade could easily have caught them on the backswing. It allowed me a swing to his side. He wore a breastplate but, like me, no backplate. The billhook hacked into his side but he was a tough man and he brought the sword down. He was wounded and I was not. I stepped away from the downward swing and brought my billhook around to hack into his unprotected neck.

"Go to God for you were a brave man, Caleb." The head flew from his body.

Even as I said the words James Pringle ran at me with his long sword held in two hands. The arrow that slammed into his face was a well-aimed one and went into his mouth and knocked him from his feet.

The deaths of the knight and his best warrior enraged the Pringle warriors and they forgot all that I had drilled into them. Along with the two younger sons, William and Malcolm, they raced at us over slippery ground that was now slick with blood. We were no longer a continuous line for men had died. My lieutenant, Richard, lay dead at my side but the men who ran were without plate or mail and the archers behind us sent their arrows on a flat trajectory to kill them before they could close with us. Sir David's sons died within a few feet of their father. They had gone to war but their pikes, lying in their hands, were without blood. Their deaths had been pointless. The wild attack had ended the charge of their column but I saw another forming up. I recognised the standard and the livery. It was Sir John Maxwell. There was no way that he could know that I was the man who had rescued the hostages but I suppose he knew that men from Lancashire had been responsible and Sir Edward's standard told him that he was facing the men of Lancashire. He led them himself.

"Take the wounded to the rear. Reform!" Where were Sir Edward and the rest of the men? I felt vulnerable.

This time there would be no wild rush and Sir John Maxwell was bringing his two hundred men forward in a steady march. He was to the right of King James whose own battle had yet to engage. Perhaps he sought to impress his king and be given an even bigger manor in England when they won. He was exhorting his men on. With a visored helmet and plate covering his entire body, he was an opponent to be feared. I braced myself. A few more strikes would blunt my billhook and I would have to smash rather than cut. However, as Sir John was encased in plate, I would have to do that in any case. They were still forty paces from us and I took the opportunity to slip one of the daggers from my boot into my left hand. Although the Maxwell men were not racing towards us, they still had problems. The ground was already damp and the blood from the Pringle dead had made it slick and slippery. Even though the commoners had taken off their boots they were finding it hard to get a grip on the ground. Sir John and the knights had a bigger problem.

Flodden

Their metal sabatons were not meant for marching on blood-soaked ground. The result was that, as they began to avoid slick puddles of water and blood so gaps appeared. That was all a good billman needed, a gap and as Sir John and his men tried to run the last few feet towards us, we simply stepped inside the wavering pikes. Arrows slammed into the knights and men at arms and the men in our second rank chopped pikes in two. I brought my billhook down hard on Sir John's right-hand side. The plate was dented and from behind the visored mask, I heard a shout of pain. I moved the curved head sideways to hit him in the side of the helmet. This time I did not even make a dent but I knew that such a blow would disorientate a man. The knight dropped his now useless pike and his hands went behind him to pull his sword. I used the dagger in my left hand to drive into his eyehole. It was a bodkin dagger with a long point. I struck first his eye and his scream of pain ended when the point entered the brain. Sir John Maxwell died at my feet and the dead of Clifton were avenged.

The noise from the battle now sounded like a weaponsmith's workshop as billhooks battered against plate armour making it ring like a bell. I was able to raise my billhook and bring it down on the next man to approach me for his pike's head had missed my shoulder and the shaft rested on my plate. He wore a good helmet and my billhook was no longer sharp but, even so, I still dented it so much that I must have also cracked his skull. He fell. We had killed the plated men and now were faced with men without helmets and no armour. The archers behind us, whilst tired, were still able to send arrow after arrow to slam into unprotected bodies and heads. We hit heads that had no helmet to slow the blow and a billhook, even a blunted one, can still split a head or cut into a neck. They were brave men and fought on beyond reason but eventually, they broke and tried to flee. It was wasted effort for our billhooks and our archers' arrows killed when they struck unprotected backs.

The main battles on both sides were now completely disordered and the columns of pikes were no longer a real threat. Many men had discarded the now useless weapons and drawn swords. The only Scottish warriors who had any protection were the five thousand Highlanders under the command of the Earl of Argyll. They had bucklers as well as their swords. The rest all used swords, war hammers or axes. It was a bloody battle with no quarter given. I saw a plated knight fighting one of Sir Edward's household warriors. The Scot had a fine helmet but the Englishman drove his rondel dagger through the eye hole and the Scottish knight expired.

The deaths of the Maxwell warriors gave us breathing space and I shouted, "Ecclestone, reform."

Sir Edward had finally brought the rest of our men with sharp billhooks into position and hearing my command added, "Stanley warriors, we will go to the aid of the earl."

I could see King James' banner and the earl's. They were less than a hundred paces apart. The earl was seventy years old and, great warrior though he was, I doubted that he would be able to defeat the younger King James especially as he would be surrounded by his best knights. It was clear that King James and his household knights were trying to end the battle by taking the earl's standard and killing the veteran warrior. Our line turned so that we were at an oblique angle. It was a risk for Sir Edward to do so as it invited an attack by the highlanders but as they had been the reserve, they were still hurrying up the slope to get at us. Without plate or mail, they relied on their swords and ferocious attacks to win. Sir Edward was hoping that we might win before they arrived.

We turned and I gave the command to march. We would not be marching in column formation but we would have the slope to aid us. This time we would have the impetus and we would be attacking the flank of King James' battle.

Sir Edward shouted, "Archers, unleash an arrow storm." He was asking much from archers who had been sending arrows, intermittently, for more than an hour.

As we were only three ranks deep, we had the advantage that our archers could be close behind us. All the men that I led came from Ecclestone, Parr, Windle and Sutton. I could ride to any of their homes in an hour and we all knew each other well. They knew my voice and they knew my

168

commands. There was rivalry on the practice ground but not beyond it and we marched in perfect unison. The other Stanley billmen and the rows of knights and men at arms were to our left and the men of the king's battle were in for a shock. It was the arrows that warned them of our imminent arrival and they turned to face the new threat from their right. They saw a wall of menacingly sharp billhooks and then the arrows descended on men who were without armour, many who had no helmets and none had a shield. They began to fall as we neared them and were helpless to defend themselves against our billhooks. After the first ten blows, I had finally blunted my billhook. By that time we were spread out for men had to be finished off. You did not leave a wounded Scotsman who might hamstring a passing billman. We killed them all before we moved on. I was lucky and my kills were all quick ones. The skills I had inherited from my father and had been honed in the last twenty years served me well and I wasted neither effort nor breath as I slew quickly.

I spied the king. I recognised not only the livery but the face. He had household knights wearing the same livery but I knew King James. He was older and not as lean as he had been. His helmet had gone and he wore just his coif. He had discarded his pike and was wielding a sword and using a dagger to fend off the weapons that tried to end his life. His household knights had taken an oath and they were dying as they fulfilled that oath.

This was now a battle not of lines but of individuals and groups of men. I ran, with some of the knights who had followed Sir Edward Stanley. One was too eager and was hacked in the leg by a Scottish knight wielding a great sword and then in the neck, by the king. A battlefield is no place for honour and you had to assume that more than one man might try to kill you. The other Stanley knights, seeing the fate of their comrade slowed and approached the band of royal knights warily. Around us, the battle raged. It ebbed and flowed as men died and fresh ones came to take their place but Sir Edward's clever move had trapped one side of the Scottish army and hemmed it in. I did not know it as I swung my billhook at the leg of a Scottish knight, but Lord Dacre and the Bastard Heron had helped to rally Sir Edmund's men and they were pressing on the other flank. The tables had been turned and it was the Scottish army, huge though it was, that was in danger of being outflanked and surrounded. My billhook was no longer sharp but the now ragged head still tore into a knight's leg and the force of my blow broke his thighbone. As he tumbled, I rammed my spike through his eyehole and he perished.

More of Sir Edward's knights had fallen, as had the king's men, and the Scottish king was more exposed. As he slew Sir Richard Ferris of Hornby, I brought my billhook down at the king's left arm and smashed into it. Not only was the bone broken but the flesh was hacked through and the hand could no longer grip. Sir Walter of Prestbury and Sir Roger of Meols did not give the wounded king a chance and both struck at the same time, allowing him no opportunity to defend himself. One sword came through his body while a second rammed into his side and an arrow came from, seemingly nowhere, and hit him in the jaw. The last strike slashed his throat as he fell to the ground on Flodden field.

As he slid to the ground the last of his knights hurled themselves at the warriors who had killed their king and a bloody battle ensued. I had to defend myself from a wild knight who wielded a claidheamh-mòr. Luckily for me, he was wearier than I was and as he struggled to lift the weapon again, I swung my billhook in a mighty arc and smashed the blunted blade into the side of his helmet. He had already been struck many times and the speed of my billhook allied to its inherent strength smashed through the weakened metal and into his skull. As he tumbled to the ground, I saw Sir Roger slain by the last of King James' knights. He saw me and came towards me. I was now wearying. Holding my billhook in two hands I rammed it at his head as he came towards me. The slippery, blood-soaked ground came to my aid and he stumbled. It allowed me to adjust my strike and drive the spike into his helmet, through the eyepiece and into his head. The strike jammed my billhook in the visor and as he fell so the billhook was torn from my hands. I drew my sword and rondel dagger. I looked down at the Scottish king's body. I had saved his life once and now I had been partly responsible for his death. He lay unnoticed for the battle still raged on. I realised that I had become isolated and I looked for the eagle's claw banner and the Tudor one. The Earl of Surrey's banner was just fifty feet from me and that meant my men, the men of Ecclestone lay to the south of me.

Darkness was falling and some, those who could, were fleeing north. I do not think that they knew their king was dead. I was the only one who remained from those who had witnessed the death of King James of Scotland.

A battlefield is a treacherous place and in the half darkness of dusk, a hand came to trip me as I hurried for the safety of my billmen. I rolled as I fell and that saved my life for as the highlander rose to split my skull with his long sword, I was able to whip the edge of my razor-sharp and as yet unused sword across his bare leg. It grated along the bone and as it severed tendons, the leg gave way and I rolled again to escape his fall. Rising I hacked through the back of his neck. I rejoined my men. My heart sank when I saw that at least ten had died.

Dick shook his head, "Captain, you have lost your billhook."

"My sword shall serve me now."

The training we had shared meant that my company was the only one still in any kind of formation and the highlanders spied us. They were brave men and must have decided that they could still win the battle by defeating us. There had been thousands of them and now there were hundreds. The Stanley banner still fluttered above our heads for Sir Edward's standard bearer had planted it in the ground before we had advanced. They would get to the Earl of Surrey through us.

"Brace for these are wild men with swords and bucklers."

I knew that I would have my work cut out. I had been fighting all afternoon and the weight of plate hung heavily on me. It was fortunate that the wild men of Argyll came at us like wild beasts intent on wiping us from the face of the earth for it meant that they did not strike us together but piecemeal and two billhooks were able to take one highlander. While a highlander's buckler could block one billhook the second could take a limb or a life before he was in range. The first eight men died quickly and then the body of men struck our line.

I still had my rondel and I fended off, not without some difficulty, the sword that came at me. Highlanders were barelegged and I slashed with my sword at his thigh. I then inclined my head and butted him in the face. His conical helmet with the nasal offered him some protection but blood spurted and he reeled. Before he could raise his sword again, although he tried, I rammed my rondel under his armpit and into his body. Allied to the wound in his leg as well as the broken nose, it was too much for his body and the sword slipped from his hand and he fell at my feet. Mindful of the trip I sank my sword into his throat to ensure he did not rise like Lazarus to hurt another of my men.

The highlanders were brave men and fought to the last. Our archers closed with them and used their knives and short swords to do what their spent arrows could not. By the time the last of them had been sent to God the battle was virtually over. Men were still dying in the darkness but the Scots had fled the field of Flodden. Even in the half-dark, I saw the banner of St Cuthbert and the Tudor banner still held aloft. No more men came at us and we were too weary to seek more enemies While the battle was over the dying would continue.

A weary Sir Edward, bareheaded, came over to me, "It is over Captain James and you and your men deserve great praise for their efforts."

I sheathed my weapons and after taking it off hung my helmet from my sword's hilt, "King James lies dead, yonder my lord and he is surrounded by many of your men. The Stanley crest was well served this day."

"The king is dead?" I nodded, "Then let us take this news to the earl and you can find your son."

My son, John and Ralf had been in my mind from the moment that I had slain the last highlander. We headed across a battlefield filled with human carrion stripping and robbing the dead. Wounded Scotsmen would soon have their throats slit. The only wounded who would be tended would be the English and already the healers were helping them.

The earl was whole and was with the Lord Admiral when we made our way through the press of men. He looked at Sir Edward as we approached. Sir Edward bowed his head, "The king is dead my lord."

"You have seen his body?"

Sir Edward shook his head, "No, but Captain James has. Speak."

I turned and pointed behind me, "He lies in the darkness my lord not fifty feet from your banner. He was trying to get to you when he was struck down by two of Sir Edward's knights and a Stanley arrow." I did not know for certain if it was a Stanley arrow but the fletch looked like one my archers used. I did not mention my own part. I wanted to get home.

The earl smiled, "You have done well, Captain James of Ecclestone and you shall be rewarded."

"May I be permitted to find my son and foster son, my lord?"

"Of course."

I headed up the slope for the fighting had moved from Branxton Edge and then down the other side to the church. I saw the cloak-covered bodies outside and the candles from within gave the place an eerie look. Even as I descended, I saw John and James bringing a body from inside. The healers had not been able to save the man. James' face broke into a grin, "You are alive!" They laid the body neatly next to the others and then James ran to me to hug me. "Each time a man with the eagle claw was brought in I feared it would be you."

"No, I am whole but we have lost brothers in arms."

The healer came out, "You two, let us go to the field. I am sure there will be others who need my ministrations." He recognised me, "Captain James, these two youths have contributed as much to this victory as any but I need them for a little while longer."

I nodded and left them. They were safe and as any Scot who might wish them harm was now dead, I could eat and drink with my men. By the time I reached the ridge where my men had lit a fire, some had been across to the deserted Scottish encampment and brought food and ale. It might well have been taken from English farms but it was food. As I walked into the firelight I was greeted by cheers. They moved apart so that I could sit on one of the logs they had dragged there. As I ate, I heard of the ends that had befallen those who had died. None had run and all had died well. That would afford their families little comfort but we decided, as we ate, to pool the money we had taken and divide it so that the families of the dead men would have coins to buy food. As they were also men who had leased land from me, I would ensure that their families did not suffer. The only youths who had come to war were James and John. It meant that the elder son would now shoulder the family responsibilities. That was our way.

Although I was tired, I set sentries and stood the first watch until Lauds. I had barely been asleep an hour when I was shaken awake by Will, "Sorry to wake you, Captain James, but the hobilars have just walked their weary mounts in. I thought you might wish to speak to them."

"You did right, Will."

Ralf was alive as were all but one of my hobilars. Saul had died. I clasped Ralf's arm, "John and James live too."

He beamed, "That had been my worry." He supped some of the ale and pointed north-west, "Lord Dacre led us to harry them back to the Tweed. We waited there and fought those who were tardy leaving the field. They have abandoned Etal and Ford but still cling to Norham. Lord Dacre thinks that it will fall before too long." He held up a purse. "We did well from the Scots."

I nodded and told him that we planned to compensate the families and he agreed.

It was as we were speaking that a weary pair joined us. John and James had not fought with weapons but they had served their king and country. Without their help, many men would have died and I know that the experience changed them. As we all rolled into our blankets, we knew that from this day forth we would be the men who had fought at Flodden. My father's generation had used the accolade, 'I fought at Bosworth' we would do the same for Flodden.

Chapter 15

Newcastle September 1513

We did not have a long period of rest. The army was sent back to Newcastle with the captured guns while the earl and his sons, along with Lord Dacre, went to demand the surrender of Norham. The Scottish garrison soon agreed and Lord Dacre caught up with us as we approached Morpeth. I learned, from Sir William, who had accompanied the earl that Gerald of Etal had survived and had been one of the prisoners released from Norham. I was relieved. I rode with Sir Edward and learned that he was now Lord Monteagle. He had been rewarded with the title for his services and the Stanley contribution to the victory.

It was as we left Morpeth that the Lord Admiral nudged his horse next to mine, "Captain James, you were promised the manor of Ecclestone but my father feels, as I do, that your efforts deserve more. When we reach Newcastle, you shall be dubbed a knight and given your spurs. You shouldered the responsibility of leading the Stanley men and that deserves a reward."

"Thank you, my lord."

"It was well earned. The army shall soon be paid off and dismissed but there is a price to your spurs. Someone must take the news of our victory to the king. I shall provide the ship but one who witnessed the death of the Scottish king should be the one to deliver it, that shall be you."

It was disappointing. I knew that the sea voyage not to mention the task of finding the king could take two months. I would not be home to see my child and I would be lucky if I was able to see my home by Christmas. I nodded, "Yes, my lord." I hesitated, "I think the men might have preferred to be paid until they reach their home. My men will take ten days to reach home."

He shook his head, "The French war costs us money and my father thinks to save the king money. Besides, I know that your men took enough plunder to make them rich men."

Whilst that was true, I knew my men would not see it that way. They had been promised pay to fight for the king and they had fought hard for their plunder. This was not the way to win the loyalty of an army. The next time they were asked they might baulk.

The dubbing ceremony in the castle was not the special one I might have hoped for. There were many men so knighted for I was not the only one who had attracted the eye of a Howard but when I emerged, I was greeted by a huge cheer from the men I had led. It was enough. The spurs I had been given were not new ones. I suspected that they were part of the booty taken from the dead Scottish knights, there had been many of them. It was a plain, homely pair and would need work from a weaponsmith to fit properly. I was not precious about such things but I would wear them as it would tell others that I was a knight and who knew when that might prove useful. Perhaps I would have my blacksmith make me a good pair for special occasions. Jane would like that.

I was not given the opportunity to enjoy the celebrations on the Town Moor for I was summoned to the side of the earl who gave me a letter to the king with a full account of the battle and his actions. The knighthoods and titles would not be legal until sanctioned by the king. Lord Dacre, Sir William and Sir Marmaduke were fulsome in their praise and I enjoyed a goblet of wine with them before I was escorted to the quay along with Ralf, John and James. There was a sally port and stone steps led from the castle to the river. Waiting at the ship, the six hundred ton *'Regent'*, were the Lord Admiral and Lord Monteagle. Knowing that they wished to speak to me I turned to Ralf. I gave him the hasty letter I had managed to pen once I knew I would not be going home, "Give this to Jane and tell her that the three of us will be home as soon as we can. I know that the men will be in good hands with you to lead them, Captain Ralf."

He nodded, "And I will ensure that all is well at your home." He clasped James' arm in a warrior handshake, "And you, young James, will soon be home when you can decide if you wish to follow in the footsteps of your father or ride to war. You and John are now warriors. Many men owe their lives to you. I was told that you never shirked once and took men who were close to the front line to be healed. That was bravely done."

He nodded, "I learned much in the church. When men are close to death, they use anyone nearby as a confessional. It was a chastening experience, Captain Ralf."

"Farewell, Sir James, and God Speed."

We had not brought either my plate or my weapons. Ralf would see that they were taken back to my hall. We each had a bag we carried over our shoulders and we headed up the gangplank. The two lords were speaking with the captain.

"Sir James, this is Captain Jem Oldcastle and he will take you to Calais and return thence to Southampton."

I smiled for this was the first time my title had been used by another noble. I saw the grins on the faces of John and James and realised that it had taken them by surprise too.

The captain beamed. "An honour, Sir James. I will show these young sea dogs to your cabin."

Lord Monteagle handed me a document with a seal upon it. "Here is the letter you must deliver, intact, to the king. I know not where in Flanders he is to be found but I trust in your skills. Do not let others know of the victory. The king must be the first to hear the news."

"Yes, my lord."

He gave me a second document, "As was promised when we met at Lancaster, this is your reward, the manor of Ecclestone. With the rights come responsibilities. When time allows, I beg you to visit Lathom where you will be informed what they are. I will leave you now with Sir Thomas."

Before he headed down the gangplank, Sir Thomas took out a purse and handed it to me, "These are for expenses on the road but I also have this for you," he handed me a royal warrant. "This can be used in the king's name to be given horses and shelter for the night. You will need the purse for, at the moment, England only owns Calais. That may change. Upon your return, you may use it to provide yourself with comfort on the journey back to Ecclestone." He leaned in,

"You were too modest, James, you were the one who almost severed King James' hand. Why did you not speak of it to my father?"

"I was brought up not to boast of such things but how did you know? The other knights and warriors all died."

"The Stanley archer who sent the arrow into King James' jaw saw you and he reported it to Sir Edward. Had my father known he would have included that detail in the letter. I believe that the king will be happy that he has men such as you who serve him."

The captain came back with John and James, "Admiral, the tide…"

He nodded, "I know better than any, Captain Jem. Fare ye well."

He strode off down the gangplank and as soon as he reached the quay the gangplank was hauled aboard and the ship was readied to leave. The first mate ordered men up the ratlines and they stood ready to loose the sails. I took the boys to the side where we could watch without being in the way. It appeared complicated and the commands could have been in Chinese for all that we understood but within a few moments the sails were half-lowered and the ropes untied. The Tyne took us towards the sea and the captain steered a careful course between the colliers and other ships that were busily plying their trade. We looked back at the castle where, even now, men were being paid off and headed towards the remains of the old Roman Bridge that had stood for centuries. Once past the stone pillars the river widened and I saw the old Roman fort on the south bank and the abbey and the castle on the north side. Newcastle was now vital to King Henry and would be well-defended against any Scottish incursion. We turned south when we were well clear of South Shields.

"It was strange to hear you called Sir James, Father."

"It was to me too but I daresay I will get used to it in time. What I know is that it will not change me."

John shook his head, "You cannot know that, sir. A title would change the life of any man."

I smiled for there was one thing I did know, a title and the
lifestyle that came with it could prove fatal as Perkin
Warbeck had discovered. I said, gently, "Trust me, John, the
title is just that and the man within this frame is the same one
who ran away to war all those years ago. I am more pleased
for James' mother for she will be Lady Jane and she
deserves that title." I also knew that Mary de Clifton would
be beside herself with joy when she discovered that I had
been knighted. I doubted that she would ever wish to leave
my hall. "Come, let us get settled in our cabin while there is
still light. This is your first voyage and it will take some
getting used to."

We had a cabin beneath the steps leading to the forward
fighting platform. It was normally used, the first mate told
us, to store spare weapons but they had been moved below
decks. We were given three canvas bags that we hung from
hooks and placed our bags on the floor. There was no
aperture through which light could come and the slats on the
door would only allow a little light to shine. I gave them
each a lesson in how to climb into the bags while there was
still light. They seemed confident that they would be able to
do so in the dark but I knew it would be harder. That would
be a better lesson for them than my words.

The crew were pleasant fellows and made the trip easier
than it might have been. They were honoured to be escorting
a hero of Flodden and, as we went on deck to watch the coast
of Durham slip by, answered all the questions posed by my
son and foster son. We dined each night with the captain and
he told us of battles he had fought under the former Lord
Admiral, Sir Thomas' brother, Edward. He had died in battle
and the Howard family was held in high regard by the whole
crew.

"I know that the admiral said we would be there to take
you back to Southampton, my lord, but that is dependent
upon the men we have been asked to ferry back to England.
There was a battle and some men were hurt. They will be
sent to Calais so that we can take them home. This warship
will become a ferry for a while. When I have taken them to

Southampton I will return to Calais and await you there. I hope you understand."

"If you have to leave while we are still with the king, Captain Jem, do not worry. I have a warrant and I am sure that there are many ships that ply the seas between Calais and England."

The captain looked relieved and our open discussion enabled the rest of the trip to pass pleasantly. As we neared the busy port of Calais, Captain Jem took me to one side. "Sir James, a word of warning. I was asked, nay, commanded, by the Lord Admiral to give no details of the battle until you have delivered the message to the king."

I nodded. Sir Thomas Howard wanted his family to be accorded the honours of the victory and for the king to know of their part rather than hearing of the victory first. "Thank you for the warning, captain. I will heed it."

He smiled and looked relieved, "The king keeps a stable at the port. I have often brought messengers. If you present your warrant you can leave within an hour of our docking on good horses. That might be wisest."

I had planned on visiting Jean le Casserole, the old friend who had helped me before but that would have to wait until our return. The captain was right, speed was everything. King Henry would regard any delay as an insult. I returned to the cabin we had been given and saw that John and James had packed our bags. "Not a word about Flodden until we reach the king."

They nodded seriously. Although, as they could speak neither French nor Flemish I doubted that the matter would arise. As we bade farewell and stepped down the gangplank, I realised that I was visiting Calais and did not need to be in disguise. I could be me and this would be the first time it had been so in this land. I also knew that I could use my new title. A mere James of Ecclestone could be ignored by King Henry's horse master but Sir James of Ecclestone, bearing important documents could not. As we tacked our way into the anchorage, I heard the bells of a distant house of God tolling sext. It took a good hour for us to finally tie up at a recently vacated berth. What I did not have time for was a visit to my old friend Jean le Casserole. That was a pleasure for another time.

A sobering sight was the wagons with the wounded waiting to be loaded aboard the ship. These were not the lords or gentlemen but the ordinary yeomen of England. I suppose they were luckier than in times past for at least there was a ship to take them back to England. For many, the life to which they would return would be different. Those who were crippled by war would need to rely on the goodwill of family or friends. For some, it would mean life as a beggar. I saw the two boys looking at the men. The healers had bandaged them but, even so, they were a reminder of death. The boys had cared for such men at Branxton Church. Now they saw the next stage in the lives of the wounded warriors of England.

After even a few days at sea, our legs were wobbly and the walk across the cobbles was uncomfortable. In the event the horse master was ready for us, "We heard from a Newcastle ship that there had been a battle against the Scots and I was waiting for a messenger. You are lucky, Sir James. I have three good rouncys for you."

He waved over two ostlers and they began to saddle the animals.

"Do you know where the king and his army are to be found?"

He pointed east, "He has just won a victory at Tournai. It is eighty miles or so east of here." He paused, "These are good animals, my lord but they will not do the journey in a day." He looked at the sky. "I would suggest two. Do you know the roads?"

I nodded, "I have served here before."

"Then you know that this is not England." He nodded to the warrant, "And that means nothing here. The innkeepers will rook you and it is good that you are armed for there are brigands and bandits aplenty. Do not ride in the dark and be mindful of travelling with companions you do not know, no matter how plausible is their story."

It was sage advice and I slipped him a coin I had taken from a dead Scotsman. "Thank you, my friend."

As I fastened the bag on the back of the saddle, I realised that I should not have brought the boys. I was used to being on my own and living off my wits. They were unprepared for this. I had forgotten that Flanders could be a dangerous place. When the two had done as I had done, I waved them over. "This may be a dangerous journey. Do not think of it as a ride back home in England but as a hazard-filled ride behind enemy lines. Keep your wits about you and do not be afraid to draw your swords. They are sharp?"

They both nodded and John said, "When we headed north to the muster Captain Ralf made us present our blades each day to ensure that they were sharp."

"And your rondels?"

"Yes, Sir James."

"Good, then let us ride. When we reach the open road then ride next to me but while we are in this busy town, we must ride single file." We mounted. The three horses were English and responded to our commands well. They were used to having a variety of different riders.

"Good luck, Sir James." The horse master waved us off and there was a cheer from '*Regent*' as the sailors there waved too. I waved back and smiled to myself. My last forays had seen me sneak in and out of Calais. I was no longer King Henry's spy and I could ride openly.

It was as we left the port and entered the town proper that I released we should have changed our tabards. We still wore the Stanley livery and the Englishmen we met as we wound our way through the port recognised it. We were accosted by a couple of archers, "My lord, you have come from England?"

"I have."

"We hear that the Scots were given a bloody nose." I said nothing and he continued, "Lord Home and his horsemen were sent packing back across the border, we were told. Is that true?"

I breathed a sigh of relief. The victory was not Flodden but the encounter at Milfield. I could speak of that."

"Aye, he brought seven thousand men to attack Wooler but Sir William of Brancepath and Wilton with two hundred mounted longbowmen and a few hundred hobilars sent him on his way."

The centenar turned to his companion, "See, I told you we should have stayed in England. You said the French were richer than the Scots. Well, our purses have few French coins." He looked up at me, "Were you there, my lord?"

"I was."

"God bless you then, my lord." He smiled at the boys, "And you squires, were you there?"

They both looked at me and I shook my head, "Their time will come and now I have many miles to ride."

We left the town and headed along the quieter road, for it was the afternoon, east.

"Are we squires, Father?"

"Would you wish to be? There is much more work involved than you do at present."

John shrugged, "We have served at table and I did not mind that for we were fed well."

"You need to be able to read and write, play the rote and compose poetry."

James grinned, "I can read and write already."

"I cannot."

"Well, John, I shall teach you."

I shook my head, "I am more than happy for you to be my squires but you do not make such a hasty decision while we ride through Flanders. When we are in Ecclestone you can make your mind up. You should know, after Flodden, the dangers of making hasty decisions. King James might be alive today had he not been hasty."

James had a curious mind, "What do you mean?"

"The Scots had the best of the first encounter but the boggy ground did not suit the Scottish pikes which fought in the Swiss manner. The king should have pulled back his men from the centre and sent his reserves around to his left where he had already won."

"And we would have lost?"

"No John, but the Scots would not have lost. All that they had to do was to hold the field. The earl's strategy was a bold one but a risky one. We either won or we would have been trapped by a superior army with no way back to England. Now, let us make haste for I would be in an inn before darkness falls."

I knew that there were inns along the road. I knew the area better than most Englishmen but I remembered that there were none that we could make before darkness. Then I remembered the Abbey at Watten. Watten was a small village close to a ford and the Abbey was the only place that might accommodate us. We managed to reach it before dark. I think that if I had been James of Ecclestone, the billman, then we might have been refused but my spurs and the royal warrant meant that the prior did not wish to upset the English king who had just defeated the French. We were grudgingly given a cell to share and a bowl of potage and yeoman's bread. We were, of course, charged, but the coins came from the purse I had been given. We retired early. The boys and I were woken three times by matins, lauds and prime as the monks went to their prayers. The breakfast of porridge was without either salt or honey but it would keep us going.

I knew we would not make Tournai before dark and as we rode and the boys chattered like magpies, I wracked my memory for a mental map of Flanders. Lille seemed the most likely place to find a bed but it was close to French-held territory and there would be risks. Life was full of risks and I hoped that there might be an English presence there. We had seen no other English travellers along the road. My French and Flemish ensured that we were greeted politely when we did stop. It also let the land know that there were three Englishmen wearing the Stanley livery travelling in Flanders. I cursed my lack of foresight. We had other clothes that were anonymous but they were heading back to Ecclestone with Ralf.

As we neared the citadel in Lille, in the late afternoon, I reined in, "Whilst we might enjoy better accommodation and food than we did last night this is a place of danger. Try not to speak for this is a land riven by war and King Henry is seen as an invader by many. Lille has been Flemish, Burgundian and French. It was also, hundreds of years ago,

English. Better that we keep silent than risk drawing attention to ourselves."

The inn I chose was in the better part of the city and therefore more expensive but I did not wish to risk staying in the less salubrious quarter. It was not my money that I was spending. We shared a room. That was inevitable. Without our cloaks about our shoulders, the Stanley livery was even more obvious and I saw that we were the centre of some men's attention. Even without opening our mouths, we had told Lille and any enemies that we were English. When we had stabled the horses the ostler had welcomed the three horses like old friends. He rubbed their manes and when he saw my questioning look said, "This is the fifth time I have looked after these horses in the last four months. They must know this road well. I will say this, you English choose good horses."

I had my precious parchments in a satchel I carried across my body. Even when I ate it was with me although I placed it under the table while I used my knife to cut the food. The satchel was a burden. I had never delivered a more valuable item. As we ate the more than passable stew, I felt miserable. Had I been alone, the Tudor spy, then I would not have worried, but I had two young men in my charge and I could not do as I had when last I had been here and felt in danger. We retired as soon as we had finished the meal.

I tried to pay for the rooms and stabling to enable a quick start but the innkeeper would have none of it. "You will need breakfast, my lord. Do not worry, I rise early and no matter what time you wish to leave there will be food and I can present you with an accurate bill."

I knew he meant well but it did not suit me. I liked the freedom of choosing the time when I moved.

That night I sharpened all my weapons. I not only had my sword and rondel but two daggers in the tops of my boots. The various wars and battles in which I had fought had furnished me well.

I was awake an hour before dawn. I wanted to get my message delivered as quickly as I could and then get back to England. By now my men would be within touching distance of Ecclestone. I was also anxious to get on the road as soon as I could.

True to his word the innkeeper was ready with food and he chatted amiably to us as he totted up the charges. He cheerily presented me with my account and I counted out the coins while John and James filled up on the bread, ham and cheese.

"They have good appetites."

"Didn't we all at that age?"

"True my lord. It is a shame you are not staying longer."

"And why is that?"

"Your presence makes money for me. You were the subject of much chatter last night after you had retired to bed and men drank and spoke of you long after the times they usually left. They all spent more than they normally do."

I laughed uneasily, "I am an uninteresting fellow."

"No, you are not. You speak Flemish like a local and yet you are a knight wearing the livery of a noble English family. One of the men drinking spied that while you are English your spurs are of a Scottish design. Men enjoy speaking of such puzzles."

His words made me glad that I was leaving. When we reached the stable, I slipped the ostler a coin and he beamed, "You and your horses have made me more coins in one day than I usually get in a week."

"How is that? I just paid what I normally pay an ostler."

"And a generous payment it is but no, it was others who paid me coppers just to come and look at your horses. They are good horses but did not seem to me worth the three sous that they gave me. Perhaps they wished to buy them," he shrugged, "I know not but the coins will be put to good use."

I was now worried. The only reason for men to identify our horses would be if they wished to recognise them from a distance and that meant an ambush. Perhaps they had been intrigued by the satchel that never left my sight or the curious case of the spurs had intrigued them. I worried that there might be an ambush.

As we left the city I said, "We ride hard and will be even more vigilant than we were yesterday."

"You fear trouble, Sir James?"

"Let us say, John, I do not like the scrutiny to which we were subjected. Watch me and follow whatever I do."

My fears were confirmed just five miles from the city. We had left most of the farms and dwellings far behind us. Ahead I saw a crossroads and a gallows. The crossroads were just a couple of feet higher than the land around and in this part of the world that was almost high ground. We were twenty paces from it when the five men rose from where they had lain concealed. I immediately slowed from the trot and my hand went to my sword, masked by my cloak. The two boys were slightly behind me and I took in the five assailants, for I knew that was what they were, in an instant. There was one behind the crossroads sign and as he had a good sword then I took him to be the leader. To his right was a man with a club and to his right the most dangerous of the five, a man with a crossbow. It had a windlass to wind it and it was an incredibly accurate weapon. At the same time, it was heavy. On the other side of the crossroad sign was a man, small of stature with a short sword and the last man, the youngest and scrawniest of them held a spear with a fire-hardened tip.

I kept walking my horse but slowly. My suspicions that they meant us harm were confirmed when the man behind the sign spoke. He knew we were English for he spoke to us, not in Flemish but in heavily accented English. These had been the men in the inn with the questions and the desire to see our horses. He was French and as he spoke, I recognised the livery of a French soldier. He had deserted, at some point, from the French army. "Milord, you are clearly a rich man and we are poor old soldiers. Give us your horses, your purses and that clearly important satchel and you may have your lives."

If the documents I had been carrying had not been so important I might have possibly agreed to their demands but I knew that as soon as we handed over our purses, they would kill us and take our horses. I prayed that I knew my son and foster son well for I drew my sword, hoping that they would emulate me and I spurred my horse towards the crossbowman. More to distract them as much as anything I shouted, as I dug my heels in the horse's sides, "An Englishman does not make deals with snakes. Boys, ride!"

As I headed for the crossbowman I counted on a couple of things. One was that they might have expected me to take the direct road. Secondly, the crossbowman had to lift and loose the bolt. Raising and aiming the end of the cumbersome weapon was not easy and the end wobbled. However, at a range of ten paces, he could not miss. I gambled he would aim for the biggest target, my body and I leant down and prepared to sweep the sword across him. I heard the crack of the crossbow and felt its wind as it sailed over my head. He did not want to risk killing the horse. He had no time to reload before my sword hacked across his body, striking both his chest and the crossbow. Blood spurted and the ruined weapon fell to the ground. I rode at the club man who was between me and their leader. A club is a nasty weapon but was not as long as my sword and I fooled him by swinging my horse to my right as I leaned over the left of my horse. He had begun his swing and struck air. My horse's shoulder knocked him to the ground and the leader whirled to face me. John and James had passed the crossroads sign and were heading down the Tournai Road. Whatever happened, they had survived.

Cursing at me the leader drew his dagger, "Cunning Englishman! I shall have your satchel and your…"

I did not discover what else he would have for I was close enough to stand in my stirrups and bring my sword down. He made a cross with his sword and dagger but the force of my swing was too powerful and I struck his skull. I did not think it was a mortal blow but it incapacitated him. As I wheeled my horse to my left, I saw that the other two, the one with the short sword and the one with the improvised spear were nursing injuries. My son and foster son had acquitted themselves well.

They were waiting for me two hundred paces down the road and I slowed. The ambushers had neither horse nor crossbow and so long as we kept heading for Tournai then we were safe. "Are you hurt?"

There was elation on both their faces and each held their swords for me to see. There was blood on them. "No, father. They were too concerned with you and we barrelled past them. I slashed wildly but I think I must have hit him."

"You did, as did you, John. I am proud of you both. Now let us put distance between us."

They wiped and sheathed their swords as did I. "Sir James, how did they know what we carried? I did not see them in the inn last night."

"Then be more vigilant. The leader was there but not the others. It would have been simple for them to discover where we were headed and a five-mile stroll to the crossroads ensured a good place to rob us."

James looked over his shoulder, "What would they have done if they had taken us?"

This was no time for the white lies of childhood, "They would have slit our throats, taken our clothes and left our bodies for the vermin to eat." As lessons go it was the most valuable one I had taught so far.

Chapter 16

Tournai 1513

King Henry was not at his camp but in the newly captured city of Tournai. The siege had been successful and the king was now enjoying, along with the spoils of war, a roof over his head. It was the middle of the afternoon when we reached the tented camp for the journey had taken longer than I had thought. I left the two boys in the camp. I was recognised by some of the Essex billmen alongside whom I had fought. My friend Stephen was a Captain of Billmen and was somewhere close by. Wilfred, the billman I recognised, promised to watch the boys until I returned. I knew then that they would be as safe as if they were guarded in the Tower of London. I headed into the city which still showed signs of conflict. There were holes in the walls and burnt parts of the city. Some rooves had been damaged and would need repair before the winter rains came. There was also a contrast in the people I saw. The English soldiers strode almost arrogantly through the streets while the Flemish folk had hangdog expressions and a slumped demeanour. The market stalls I saw were bare. Tournai was paying the price for defying an invader.

I saw the royal standard which was atop the Hotel de Ville and I reined in. There were yeomen of the guard with halberds at the door and an equerry in royal regalia. I fastened my horse to a post and headed up the steps. The two yeomen crossed their halberds and looked straight ahead.

The equerry spoke and I recognised in him a pompous little man who liked to make people look and feel small. He was of limited stature and almost rotund. There might be little food in Tournai but this equerry would ensure he had his share of it. I had met many of his type at the royal court when I had accompanied Perkin Warbeck to Mechelen. He was unimportant and had been relegated to speaking to those who came to the door. He would make the most of his position. "Yes?" There was a sneering tone in his voice and he pointedly looked down at me.

I kept calm. "I am Sir James of Ecclestone and the Lord Admiral has sent me with despatches for the king."

My name aroused interest in one of the yeomen for he turned his head to study me. The equerry held out an imperious hand, "I will take it and then you can be gone."

My eyes narrowed, "My title is Sir James if you please, and I was commanded by the Lord Admiral, Sir Thomas Howard, to deliver this into the king's hands and not some grubby little man in a brightly coloured tabard."

He coloured, "I have never heard of a Sir James of Ecclestone."

"And that is understandable for I was only given my spurs after... recently."

"I cannot allow you to pass." He looked up in the air as though he had spied something of interest there.

I smiled and turned, "Then pray to tell the king that I came to deliver my message but was refused entry. I shall return to the army camp where I will await his pleasure. Perhaps the king will enjoy a stroll to meet me."

I began to descend the steps. The equerry said, "The king will be angry," I did not turn and he added, "Sir James."

I stopped and turned, "Aye, but with you and not me for what I deliver is news that the king waits to hear. It is not nice, it is important."

One of the yeomen said, "Sir James, are you the James of Ecclestone who was a captain of billmen?"

I turned and ascended to speak to the yeomen who had both pointedly lowered their halberds, "I still am."

The yeoman turned to the equerry, "This knight is a warrior of note and I believe that the king knows him. Certainly, his father did." He smiled at me, "I served old King Henry too and remember one of your visits to the castle."

That decided the equerry, "Very well, follow me...Sir James."

I waited and said to the yeoman, "Thank you, friend. I may have my spurs but within my chest beats the heart of a billman."

"Aye, and from what I have heard a mighty one."

192

"Ahem!" With his hands on his hips, the equerry looked like a petulant child.

I shook my head and smiled at the yeoman, "I do not think I will ever get used to pompous little men." I waved my hand, "Lead on!"

The court was in what must have been a sort of great hall. The walls were made of carved wood and looked to depict an ancient battle of some type. Candles burned in sconces and there was a buzz for it was filled with soldiers and courtiers, not all were English and I recognised a few faces from my time at the Burgundian Court at Mechelen. I had changed too much for them to recognise me and I saw only interest rather than remembrance, The Holy Roman Emperor was now an ally of King Henry and all were friends, for the moment. I doubted that any of those who had been at the court of the Duchess of Burgundy would recognise me for then I had been a fresh-faced youth with barely a whisker on his face. I followed and then the equerry stopped, twenty paces from the king and held up a hand while he approached his superior, a herald. I stopped and was well aware of being the centre of attention. Men whispered behind gloved hands. The equerry approached the herald who listened and then looked at me. He went to the king who was seated at a table. Two clerks hovered behind him with more parchments. Their ink-stained fingers marked their profession. The king was dealing with affairs of state and the courtiers and nobles who waited and buzzed in the hall would have to wait until there was an opportunity to speak to him. It explained the sudden interest in me. The herald waved me over and I approached. There was wine before the king and his hands clutched the stem of the goblet but he was studying maps and parchments and he did not look up.

The herald said, quietly, "Sir James of Ecclestone?" I gave the slightest of bows. He nodded at my livery, "You serve the Stanley family."

"I do." Unsure of his rank I added, "Sir."

"And you have messages from the Lord Admiral?"

I nodded, "I do." I hesitated, "There has been a battle."

"Just so. Wait here, Sir James, and I will inform the king." He added, almost apologetically, "He is very busy for this night there is a feast to celebrate our victory here and he wishes all to be in order before then." The contrast in the herald and equerry was a marked one. The equerry would rise no further. He would never become a pursuivant and the elevated office of herald was so far beyond him that he could live to be a hundred and never attain it.

He approached the king and whispered in his ear. The king looked up and frowned. He waved me forward and I dropped to my knee a few paces from him. I knew, from his father, that kings liked distance between themselves and any visitor.

I took the parchment from my satchel and held it before me. I did not speak loudly but loud enough for the king, the herald and the yeomen to hear my words, "My liege, I have come from Newcastle upon the orders of the Lord Admiral, his father, the Earl of Surrey, along with the men of Northumberland, Lancashire and Cheshire, who have won a great victory for Your Majesty and your realm. The Scots have been defeated and their king lies dead."

His eyes narrowed but he took the parchment and examined the seal. He was a careful man. Until he saw the signatures of the Earl of Surrey then this could all be some trick to make a fool of the young King of England. He took a knife and slit it open. He began to read and I was aware that the whole hall was silent and seemed to be holding its breath.

He read it and then looked at me. He seemed to study my face and then read again. This time, after he had re-read it, he stood and held it aloft, "By the grace of God and thanks to the Earl of Surrey and the men of the North of England, our country has been saved from the savage deprivations of the Scots! The invaders have been killed in great numbers and their king lies dead."

Cheers rang out for all knew what it meant. Queen Ann of France had been the instigator of the invasion. She had written to King James and begged him to attack England. It was an attempt to save her husband's kingdom. Our victory meant that King Henry now had the ascendancy in France.

His victory at Tournai was now of even more importance. England would not need to send soldiers home to defend the borders. The hastily cobbled force of farmers and yeomen had done all that had been necessary.

He seemed suddenly aware that I was still kneeling, "Rise." He bellowed at a servant, "Bring this knight a drink for he deserves one and we have finished with the business of the day. Leave us alone." His words were for the assembled knights who, disappointed, began to slowly head for the door.

The yeomen must have done this on numerous occasions for they deftly directed the nobles, soldiers and courtiers to the doors. The equerry stood looking a little lost until the herald, like a man shooing away an annoying pet, waved him towards the door. I saw, as the room was emptied, tables against the walls and I guessed that as soon as the king had finished his business then the tables would be moved and then laid for what would now be a victory speech. Silence descended and I was brought some wine. The footsteps of the servant now echoed on the stone floor of the ancient hall. The wine was of the best quality and I sipped it. The king studied me and then patted the parchment.

"You are James of Ecclestone, one-time captain of billmen and now a knight of the realm?" I nodded. "Were you one of those that killed King James?" I realised that the letter must have said that the men of Stanley were the ones who had slain the king.

I shook my head, "I can put a hand on heart and say that although I wounded him it was others who killed him and the ones who slew him now lie on the field of Flodden."

He seemed relieved. "Good, for it is a bad habit to get into, killing kings," he sipped his own wine. "It is clear that you were at the battle and I believe you are an honest fellow. I have read Howard's account. Now I would hear your version of the battle."

Even when I had been at Mechelen I had not had to endure such an interrogation. Even as I began the account, I decided to tell the truth. As my mother would have said, '*tell the truth and shame the devil*'. It took some time. I did not hide the near disaster of the collapse of the right nor the tardy arrival of the Stanley men. When the king returned to England there would be others who would tell the tale and I wanted the king to know that I spoke the truth.

"The Lord Admiral says thirty thousand Scotsmen perished."

"I could not say, King Henry, for I did not count them. What I do know is that we slew five Scotsmen for every one of ours that was slain and that the killing went on well after dark."

His eyes narrowed, "I know you, do I not?"

"I had the honour to serve your father and latterly did some service for you and Cardinal Wolsey."

He beamed and banged the table as it all came back to him, "The spy! By God but you are a useful fellow." He waved an arm and said, "Turn around." I did as he asked but knew not why. "This will not do. Whence did you get those spurs?"

"I was given them in Newcastle Castle by the earl when I was dubbed. I believe, my lord, they were from the spoils of Flodden and taken from some dead Scottish knight."

"And they are poor ones at that." He turned to the herald, "Cecil, send for my second-best spurs." As the herald hurried off, he added, "You deserve something for your efforts."

"There is no need, King Henry."

Once more, his eyes narrowed and his mouth pursed, "I am King of England and I decide if there is a need and there is. Men who serve me and serve me well must be rewarded and a new set of spurs is the least that I can do."

"Sorry, King Henry."

The scowl changed to a smile, "And your modesty is understandable. You were brought up a commoner and have been elevated. You have a manor?"

"I do, King Henry, Ecclestone."

"Of course, you serve the Stanley family. You should have more for your service and I would have you serve me again." A servant brought the spurs and they were magnificent. He handed them to Cecil, the herald who gave them to the king. "Kneel." I knelt. "I cannot dub you a second time even though you deserve to be knighted by a king but I give these to you, Sir James of Ecclestone, for service to the one true king of England." I took them and rose. As I did our eyes met and his face erupted as he remembered something else, "You were the fellow who brought Warbeck to book! My father was too kind and Warbeck should have been hung drawn and quartered before he could ever do mischief again. You shall dine with us this night."

"King Henry, I have only these clothes with me and they have not been washed since Flodden." In truth, I did not want to dine in the Great Hall. Others might enjoy the honour but not me.

"Better and better. They are the clothes of a warrior and I would be surrounded by such men." He stood and headed towards the door that led to the bed chambers.

The herald took my arm to guide me out of the main doors. Once the doors closed behind us, I said, "Have I got time to ride to the camp and see my people?"

"Of course, and it does you great credit that you think of such matters but do not be tardy. The king does not like latecomers."

The equerry was still waiting without. Cecil said to him, "Sir James is to be admitted at any time and brought to either me or the king, do you understand?"

Although he had been talking to the equerry the two yeomen took great delight in snapping to attention and banging their halberds on the steps. "Yes, my lord!"

The equerry almost jumped from his skin and added his own weaker, "Yes, my lord."

When I reached the camp, I saw John and James surrounded by billmen, amongst them Stephen, my brother in arms and they were in animated conversation. I knew they were talking about Flodden. The story they told would change over the years but this would be the truest version, the first one that they recounted. As I approached, they all burst into applause and cheers. I shook my head as I was led to an upturned barrel by Stephen. I wagged a finger at James, "I thought I said no mention of the battle."

He adopted an innocent look, "But the king knows now, does he not?"

I shook my head and turned to Stephen, I clasped his arm, "Good to see you, old friend." Nodding at the two youths I said, "Children, eh?"

"James does you great credit. I look forward to the meal this night so that I can hear all from your lips, old friend."

I shook my head, "This night I dine with the king." I handed the spurs to James, "Hold these for me, will you? They are a gift from the king."

Stephen laughed, "And I knew you when you were just a billman, now you rub shoulders with the great and the good."

I said, quietly, "The great? Aye. The good?" I waggled my hand and he laughed.

Between us, we managed to clean the tabard as much as we could and Stephen loaned me a pair of breeks that did not stink of horse sweat. We polished my boots and as James fitted my spurs I combed my hair. I did not look as wild as I had when I had presented myself to the equerry. After I had finished and mounted my horse, I realised why the royal servant had been so reluctant to allow such a wild-looking man into the king's presence. Perhaps his disdain was a little justified.

I arrived in plenty of time but most of the seats at the lower tables had been taken. The herald called Cecil must have been looking for me. I was greeted as soon as I entered the hall, now lit by even more candles, and with tables already laden with food and jugs of wine.

He nodded to a servant who was clearly expecting me, "This way, Sir James." I knew from his accent that he was Flemish.

As I followed the servant, I saw that this was an all-male gathering. We were at war and King Henry had no time for gowns and women, at least not here. I knew the rumours and that the court in England was filled with potential bedmates for the king but here he was all business. He was a young

king trying to impress the Holy Roman Emperor and show
the King of France that the King of England was a foe to be
respected. I knew that if there was a young woman then she
would be in his bedchamber and awaiting patiently his
return. Mechelen had taught me such things. I was taken to
the head table and I saw that I was in a place of honour close
to the king. I knew then that I would not enjoy the food or
the drink. I would be too busy choosing my words and
worrying about offending someone. The etiquette was not a
problem. I had dined with the Duchess of Burgundy at
Mechelen many times. As Jane had pointed out to me, my
manners were impeccable.

I was almost alone at the table for the ones who would be
seated with me were the most important men in this part of
Flanders. I felt exposed as though every eye was upon me. It
was like Mechelen all over again except that now I was not
in disguise, I was not hiding. I was aware that their eyes
were assessing me. My tabard identified me as a Stanley
man and some would have seen my arrival. There would be
speculation and I knew that there might be some who sought
me out. If I was seated at the high table then I was a conduit
to the king. There would be nobles who would try to use me
for their own ends. When the servant came to pour my wine,
I was grateful for it afforded me the chance to hide, albeit
briefly, from their gaze. I did not meet their eyes. That was
the old James, the spy. As I put the wine down, I saw that I
was no longer the focus of the eyes in the room. They would
await the next stranger but they would still speak of the
travelled stranger who had been accorded a place at the high
table.

I looked along the three tables and searched for faces I
knew. In the past, I would have worried that there was
someone who might recognise me and expose my identity. I
was no long King Henry's spy, I was King Henry's knight.
My name would be known. I saw knights I had known when
I had served Sir Edward at Hedingham. One of them, Sir
Giles, must have recognised me for he raised his goblet in a
toast and I returned it. There were other familiar faces but, as
my eyes neared the last table, the one furthest from the king

and therefore the men of least importance, I felt a cold shudder. I recognised another face from the past but this one was not a friendly one. Without staring but flicking my gaze to others I searched my memory for the man's identity. I knew him but he had aged and changed. He had fine clothes and a trimmed beard. He had also put on weight but it suddenly came to me. He was the Growler.

The Growler had been with those who had served the White Rose in Paris and Mechelen and the aborted attempt to put Perkin Warbeck on the English throne. Most had been killed after the failed landing at Deal. I had thought the Growler had suffered the same fate but he was there. I had never known his name, or if I had it was forgotten but he was the most dangerous of the men I had met and when he spoke, he growled his words threateningly. The name had stuck. It was as I studied him that I remembered the suspicion from those that I had met after I had visited the inn in Paris. The ones who had taken me to the Pont Neuf had kept their identities hidden from me. The only one whose name had been given to me was Sir John Bardolph. He had died but I was always grateful to him for, along with the mercenaries they had hired, he had made me into a man who could use a sword and pretend to be a gentleman. The Growler was always suspicious of me. What was Growler doing here? It could not be part of a Yorkist threat. That was long gone, Sir Thomas Howard and Sir Marmaduke Constable had been Yorkists and now served the king. If it was not a Yorkist plot then why else was he here? The thought briefly crossed my mind that he could have become a loyal Englishman but I dismissed it as soon as it came to me. The Growler was not like that. He was one of the most unpleasant men I had ever met and that list was a long one.

My thoughts were disrupted when a bejewelled hand was placed on my shoulder. There was a strong smell of perfume and I looked up and saw Sir Thomas Wolsey. He was the master politician and ran a network of spies. I began to rise but his hand on my shoulder restrained me.

"Keep your seat, Sir James. You have earned the right to sit at the high table." He sat on one side of me and four men sat to my left. I guessed that the king would be seated to the right of Cardinal Wolsey. "You have done great things for one so lowly born and, while we eat, I would hear from your lips the story of Flodden Field."

I guessed then that the king must have spoken to his closest adviser. "Thank you, Cardinal. I did not know you were in Flanders."

He spread his hands as a servant poured wine, "And where else should I be, Sir James, other than at the side of the king? I am not a warrior, I am a man of peace but a practical one. I have read the despatch from the Lord Admiral and pored over the names of the dead. Tell me of Lord Home."

"Lord Home?"

"It is clear from both the admiral's missive and your oral account that Lord Home broke Sir Edmund Thomas and then did nothing after. He could have saved his king but did not. Why I wonder?"

I sipped my wine, "I did not mention it and as I did not read the letter, I know not what was told but did it mention Milfield?"

He frowned, "Milfield?" He had clearly not heard of the Ill Raid.

"In August Lord Home led seven thousand men to raid Wooler. Sir William of Brancepath and Wilton led a few hundred of us to ambush them on their way home. We slew a thousand and captured Lord Home's banner. All that I can think was he regarded his initial victory at Flodden as enough and did not wish to risk another defeat."

"Seven thousand defeated by less than a thousand? I am no soldier but I find it hard to believe that such a paltry number could defeat so many."

"Two hundred longbowmen, backed by five hundred billmen, added to surprise, can do much."

He nodded and smiled, "Better and better. The king shall know of this." The cardinal was astute. By informing the king he would be associated with the victory and rise even higher in the king's standing. "It is always good to know the politics of an enemy, Queen Margaret is the king's sister and her son is an infant. It is not they who will rule Scotland but the lords who survived Flodden. Lord Home and Lord Huntly may have aspirations. The information you have given me is most useful and I shall use it judiciously. I am pleased that you are seated close to me. I shall pick your mind in the same manner as we pick over the bones of the fine fowl that shall be served to us."

I knew then that he was far more than a man of God.

He leaned closer to me and said, "You are not the only man I have sent to serve the king and discover information. I have learned that there is no such thing as useless information. There is just information that you have yet to find a use for." He nodded behind him and I saw four men. I had taken them to be servants but his next words made me realise they were not. "John and the others are here to protect the king and me. They may look like servants but they were men like you and now elevated to serve me." He smiled, "They are not knights and will look at your spurs enviously but they are men like you, Sir James." I saw that they were, indeed, all warriors. They each had a muscled build and one or two still bore scars on their faces and hands. The cardinal was not just a churchman and a politician, and his words confirmed what I already knew, he was also a spymaster.

Our conversation was ended by a fanfare and we all rose as King Henry and his chief guests entered; they were the most senior of his allies. He sat and, a heartbeat later, we did too. He nodded to the cardinal who said Grace and without further ado the array of food was fetched in. Had I not been at Mechelen then I might have been more impressed. As it was, I had tasted such delicacies before and the Growler was still on my mind. The king and the cardinal talked over me and I kept glancing not only at Growler but also those seated with him. They were his confederates and I would memorise their features.

The cardinal took great delight in recounting the Milfield ambush as though he had taken part. Those seated close to the king listened eagerly too. The cardinal made it sound glorious, a handful of Englishmen thwarting a Scottish noble who was intent on ravaging farmers and their families. I saw the wry smile on the king's face and he nodded at me, "Your knighthood was well deserved. Tell me, Sir James, how was it that mere billmen could defeat knights and pikemen?"

"A bill is a handy weapon, King Henry. There is a blade as there is on a poleaxe and a spike but there is also a hook. A horseman might be plated but a hook can pull a knight from his mount and a felled knight is like an upturned crab. Billmen know the weak spots in plate armour."

"Perhaps I should retain you here for I have need of experienced warriors."

My heart sank and I returned a weak smile. Fortunately one of the foreign lords to his right attracted his attention to ask a question, presumably about my explanation, and I was left alone for the cardinal spoke with one of his people. I had never really enjoyed such feasts at Mechelen and the thought that I might be kept from my family for longer made my spirits sink to my boots. I kept looking over to Growler and tried to piece together his story. I did not recognise any of the lords with him but there was no reason why I should have. I began to think that it was an innocent happenstance and that Growler could have reformed or fallen on his feet through some good luck. I was an example of such events. When I had run away to join Lord Clifford, I could never have imagined how my life would have turned out. I was clutching at straws I knew but the spy side of my head told me that this was a sinister encounter.

When Cardinal Wolsey next spoke, I almost jumped out of my skin. "Your Grace?"

"I said, Sir James, you seem preoccupied and you keep glancing at those men at the lower end of yonder table." He lowered his voice even more and almost whispered in my ear, "What is amiss?" I hesitated. I had sworn an oath to keep secret all that had happened in my time as King Henry's spy. The cardinal was a very clever man, "I know you are a man with secrets, Sir James. I have spoken with the men who sent you to do the king's bidding. I may not know all the details of what you did but I am aware that you served your country, perhaps, in a way which is best kept secret.

Tell me what disturbs you, and regard this as a rather noisy confessional."

I sighed and spoke in the whispered way I had in the church at Ecclestone, "When I was trying to get to Perkin Warbeck, that man there with the green tunic and waxed beard, worked for the Yorkists. I had not seen him since the invasion at Deal. Perhaps this is all innocent and he is reformed I know but it nags at me. I know that the Yorkists have given up but…"

He smiled, "And how do you know that?" I turned and looked at him, "We still find cells of men who wish for a different dynasty but most of them are in England. I cannot see what they would have to gain from this." He waved heavily ringed fingers and the largest of the men who had stood behind us came forward to bend closer to him. I think he was the man the cardinal had called John for I heard the name spoken. The cardinal spoke and after nodding the man disappeared. "You can always come to me if you have suspicions about the safety of the realm or the king. Part of my job is to ensure that he remains safe. I thank you for your honesty. This may be nothing but John has a good eye and ear. He will help us uncover the truth." He smiled as the puddings came. Cardinal Wolsey liked his food.

I watched the man called John while I ate the posset. He deftly took a platter from one of the servants and headed down to the Growler and his confederates. When he reached them, he smiled and said something. I heard laughter from two of the men. One said something to him and he put the platter down and left. He returned a short while later with another plate of delicacies. He spoke with the men for a short time. He returned not long before the king rose to signal the end of the feast. The cardinal's man spoke to the cardinal for some time. The king rose as did we all. The cardinal said a prayer and the king left, attended by his yeomen of the guard. I knew that Queen Katherine was not with the king and I guessed that there would be some bedmate waiting for the king in his chamber. He smiled and nodded as he passed me.

Flodden

I was going to leave too but the cardinal gestured to my seat, "Sit, my friend, the night is young and we have a fine dessert wine from Spain. The king's marriage might not have resulted in strong male heirs but we do have the best of wines as a result of the Spanish." I sat and, reluctantly, took the proffered goblet. He leaned closer to me, "You have a good memory and good instincts, Sir James, and your knighthood is well merited. The men at the lower end of the table purport to be Flemish warriors. There are four of them and they performed good service in the siege of this city. I am suspicious for no one saw them during the actual assault and as the other Flemish soldiers who took part in the attack died then there is none to verify their story. Had you not mentioned this, Growler, I might have overlooked them. You are sure he was English?"

"When I met him, cardinal, I was not fluent in Flemish and his English was without an accent. He is English and I would guess from the north."

"And you would know." He put his hands together as though in prayer and closed his eyes. He was not praying, however, he was thinking. Cardinal Wolsey was a very clever man. Some said too clever for his own good. He opened them and smiled. "Tomorrow, come back to this hall at sext."

"I was hoping that, my mission completed, I could return home to Ecclestone."

"Your ship will be waiting for you. The wounded men from the siege will already be travelling back on the *'Regent'*. Those who have been released from service will leave at the end of the week. You can stay until then for your king needs you still." He nodded to my tabard. "Change that and do not wear your spurs when you next come. You have a cloak with a cowl and hood?" I nodded, "Then wear that. I would have your face hidden. My man here will greet you at the gate."

I left half of the dessert wine for, delicious though it was, it had begun to taste of vinegar. I was becoming embroiled in yet another plot and such matters rarely ended well. My past continued to shape my future.

Stephen, John and James were seated around the fire when I returned. "So, James, sorry, I should address you as Sir James, now, when do you return to England?"

I shook my head and smiled at Stephen, "I will always be James to a brother in arms and I know not the answer to your question. I was told at the end of the week but who knows for Cardinal Wolsey still has need of me. We are to return to England with the men released from service."

Stephen beamed, "Better and better for my company is soon to be released and I shall be travelling home." I raised my eyebrows and he shrugged, "We were of some service at the Battle of the Spurs but we were of little use in the siege. The campaigning season is over and releasing the billmen saves the king his gold. This war has been expensive and, as yet, has yielded the king little save the approbation of the emperor. The new pope, it seems, is not as belligerent as the old one. I think that this war is over. Still, my men and I have made a profit and I would rather spend the winter in our warm hall than in these tents in a pestilential Flanders."

"Then I pray that I will only have to endure a week of this and then come home with you. It will be good to see Sam again and let him meet James."

I felt better after his words. I might be forced to stay in Flanders and delay my journey home but at least we would be travelling in company. We would not have to risk brigands, bandits and deserters. James and John had become seasoned campaigners. Their march to Flodden and our time in the north had given them skills that would last a lifetime. They had made me a cosy and relatively comfortable bed in the tent provided by Stephen. The wine and the food I enjoyed ensured that I slept well.

Chapter 17

Tournai 1513

When I rose the sun was up and that was a rarity for me as I was normally awake before dawn. We had some time before I needed to meet with the cardinal and so after we had breakfasted, we headed into Tournai. Stephen had not yet availed himself of the opportunity to buy things for his wife and as this would be his best opportunity, we accompanied him. Mindful of the cardinal's words I had the boys discard their Stanley tabards and we wore simple attire. I had an almost full purse. I did not think it would need to be returned and I, too, sought gifts for those at home in Ecclestone.

Captain Stephen's standing amongst the warriors was clear not only in the camp but also when we were in Tournai. Whenever we met other billmen and archers he was warmly greeted. He, for his part, was generous enough to introduce me. The result was that I recounted the battle of Flodden six times before we reached the market of Tournai. We pottered around paying less for items that we would be taking back with us. The traders were forced to lower their prices for the siege meant that their normal clientele was absent and soldiers never pay too much. An hour before sext we had bought enough and retired to an inn for some beer. They made good beer in Flanders and it met with our approval. The boys would make a last few purchases for the family and then return to the camp. They were enjoying being with Stephen and their experiences at Flodden meant that there was always a ready audience to hear of the defeat of our old enemy. I reluctantly left them and headed for the meeting with the cardinal's man.

He was waiting for me at the bottom of the steps. I was punctual. Even as he greeted me the first peel of sext rang out. "Come with me, Sir James." I never discovered his name but, in the daylight and as I followed him not into the hall but towards the citadel, I was able to assess him better. He was a soldier. His face showed that he had endured fists and there was a scar which ran down the side of his head.

The hair did not grow properly there. He was not simply a servant, he served the cardinal in other ways. I worked out that he was another of the cardinal's men. John and the others had been just a part of the secret army of Cardinal Wolsey. As we neared the citadel he said, "Your hood, Sir James." I pulled the hood up. It completely hid my face. "If you would be so good as to keep it up until the cardinal asks you to reveal yourself and say nothing until you are asked."

"Of course."

He smiled, "All will become clear, Sir James. Everything that the cardinal does is for a purpose."

There were no questions at the gate and we entered the citadel which showed clear evidence of the bombardment. Once inside we headed for the keep where, once again, we were not hindered and we descended, lit by burning brands, to the lower portion of the keep. I knew where we were going. These were the dungeons where prisoners were kept. The walls ran with damp. Anyone who spent more than a month or two in the dungeons would be doomed to death. The deeper we went then the ranker became the smell. It was a mixture of sweat, blood, urine, and human faeces. It made my hogbog at home smell like a pleasant nosegay. The guard on the door of the room was another of what I now thought of as the cardinal's guards and he silently opened the door to a surprisingly large though low-ceilinged chamber. The cardinal was seated at a table and picking at some chicken. There were four guards within and I saw the Growler and the others who had been with him. One of the guards was the one who had gleaned the information the previous night, John. He nodded acknowledgement at me. The four men had clearly been tortured. Bare-chested, they bore the signs of burning brands. One had a mangled right hand and one of them had lost the fingernails on his left hand.

The cardinal looked up and smiled. "Ah, you have come. This should not take long."

The four men looked up at me. They could not see my face but I knew they were studying both my build and clothes to identify me.

The cardinal turned his attention to the four bound men, "You still maintain that you are Flemish soldiers serving with the imperial troops?"

The one with the mangled hand spoke and I saw that he had lost teeth.

"We are, why do you not believe us?"

"Because your accent does not seem local." He waved a hand at me, "I have brought with me one who can detect such things." He nodded to the man who had brought me and he went to lift up Growler's face. I could see that he had also been beaten but lost fewer teeth. His left hand looked like it had broken fingers too. "You, the silent one. Thus far you have not spoken. Speak some Flemish for my friend here."

Growler looked up at me. He could still not see my face. He spoke but his words were distorted because he had lost teeth. However, even distorted it was clear he had learned a few phrases, "I am Philippe of Lille and a hired sword."

The cardinal laughed, "Even without my friend here I know that you are not Flemish and you have lied despite the torture. I am King Henry's protector. I suspect you all of treachery. I can and will put you on the rack if my questions are not truthfully answered. Your end can be both painful and without any relief or absolution. I need to know who you really are and what is your purpose."

They remained stubbornly silent and the cardinal wiped his mouth on his napkin, drank some wine and dabbed his mouth, "You, the one who claims to be Philippe of Lille, you were part of the plot to put the usurper, Perkin Warbeck on the English throne. As such you are guilty of treason and can be hanged drawn and quartered. If you speak then I might commute that sentence."

This time he spat out his words, and blood, in English, "That is a lie!"

He turned to me, "Would you care to reveal your identity?"

I carefully took the hood and, whilst keeping my face down pulled it back. When I lifted my face Growler stared at me and after a moment tried to rise, "You, the traitor! I thought you dead else I would have sought you out! Many men died because of you. I will rip your heart out."

He could not rise because he was restrained and his outburst seemed to amuse the cardinal, "A better admission of guilt I have yet to hear. Give me your real name for the time for deception is over,"

Realising he could not move he slumped in the seat, "Guy of Guisborough and that is all that I will say. You can torture me all you like but I will not betray my friends." He spat a bloody gob of phlegm at me. It missed and landed on the floor. For his pains, he was struck in the side of the head.

"Then you shall die as will these other three. If, however, one of you is willing to speak then only the other three will die and the one who speaks will be freed."

They all looked at each other. The man who was clearly the leader of the cardinal's men said, "Cardinal, if I might suggest?" The cardinal waved an imperious arm. "Let us put each one in a cell and that way we can question them a little easier."

The cardinal's reply told me that this was pre-planned, "An excellent suggestion, John, make it so." He looked at me, "And we have done with you..." he paused, "friend."

He was not taking any chances revealing my true identity.

The door was opened and I made my way from the stinking foetid torture chamber. When I reached the bailey, I breathed deeply. Even the smell of the hay and horses from the stable seemed somehow cleaner than the stink of the dungeon and imminent death. I also felt dirty even though I had touched nothing. I went to the horse trough and washed both my face and hands. I dried them on my cloak. I left the citadel and headed for the camp feeling lighter of step. I had exorcised the ghost of the past and now I could go home with Stephen and his billmen. My service to the cardinal was at an end.

After the horror of the dungeon the camp seemed, in contrast, a lively and happy place. I enjoyed the company of billmen. I might now be a knight but I was determined that it would not change me and being with Stephen and the other billmen confirmed my decision. Stephen and I spoke of Sam and his family. Stephen also had a child and we shared stories. For James and John, this was their idea of heaven. They had no duties and they, too, were asked to recount their adventures in the short war. As I told them, two days before we were due to leave for Calais, that would be their future. Having fought in such an important battle men would speak of it for the rest of their lives.

It was that night, as we were preparing our meal that a messenger came from the cardinal, summoning me. Stephen frowned, "Will this delay your departure?"

I shrugged, "I know not but I can see no reason why it should." I paused, "But on the morrow, if I have not returned then take John and James with you. I will follow if I am delayed and meet you in Hedingham."

Even as I said it, I knew that men like Cardinal Wolsey would not worry about inconveniencing me. I was a tool to be used. This time I was taken not to the keep and the dungeon but to a small chamber in the hall in which we had dined my first night in Tournai. King Henry was also there. Some of his yeomen were also present but no one else. It was a secret meeting. The king sat and the cardinal hovered close to his shoulder. I bowed as the king spoke, "Once again you have served England." He glowered at the cardinal. "And no blame can be attached to you. Thanks to your words we discovered a plot to assassinate me, now at my moment of glory and before I have an heir to safeguard England and its future. France might have failed to defeat me here or to use an ally to cause mischief but the King of France and that bitch of a wife are treacherous snakes." His face reddened and he waved an arm, "This rage will bring on the ill humours." I think he was trying to shift the bad mood which had somehow descended. I wondered what had happened since the feast to bring on such a change. "Carry on, Wolsey, you can tell him of your failure. Try not to disappoint me again or it will be you who enjoys the dungeons." He tossed a small purse to me, "Thank you Ecclestone, you will serve me again."

He left with his four yeomen and the cardinal and I were left alone. The cardinal sat. He looked shrunken, "The king is right and I have failed him." I had no idea what was going on but I knew that this was not the time for questions. He would tell me what I needed to know in his own good time. "The king is right, I discovered the plot and pride conspired with hubris to bring about disaster. All four of the prisoners informed on the others in a bid to save their skins. Three were Frenchmen and Guy of Guisborough was the token Englishmen yet he was crucial to the plot. It would be his use of English that would allow him to get close to the king."

I could not contain my curiosity, "But how?"

"The king is due to hunt next week and Guy of Guisborough would be part of the hunt. The king needs beaters. He was to use a latch and secrete himself in the woods."

"But any could have done that."

He smiled, "The other three knew what Guy of Guisborough did not, that they expected the Englishman to be caught and that we would believe it was an English plot. His Yorkist sympathies would be unearthed and civil strife would ensue when the king culled all those with Yorkist links. A clever plan."

I was still in the dark, "But why is the king angry? We know the plot and we have the plotters."

He shook his head, "We have two, or their bodies at least but Guy of Guisborough and a Frenchman, Guillaume d'Abbeville, if that was his real name, escaped. They managed to overcome and kill John, my most trusted of guards and escaped last night. I have men hunting for them but another matter was uncovered during the interrogation, there is a web of French spies here and in England. Once out of the citadel, they had safehouses to which they could flee. Men are searching now but they will be long gone. This is not England and here I do not have the men to hunt as I would in England."

My heart sank for I knew what was coming. I asked, "And why do you tell me?"

He looked sad, and for the first time since I had met him, he looked like a priest and sympathy was in his eyes, "For we believe that Guy of Guisborough will hunt you down.

Indeed the French plotters themselves may wish to wreak revenge on you." His smile was not a happy one but one of resignation, "I too may well be a target for them but, thankfully, I am a harder target. You, in contrast, are an easy one."

"But he knows not my name."

"He does for you were identified at the feast. John, when he discovered their identity also discovered that many men at that table asked about the unknown knight so favoured by the king. The honour that was done to you may prove to be a fatal one. Take care, James." The use of my Christian name rather than my title seemed to underscore his words. I was being abandoned but short of men standing guard on me and my family it was hard to see what else he could do. "You will be safe until you reach England. What was not planned may prove to be your temporary salvation. Marching to Calais with billmen now seems the perfect protection. The '*Regent*' will also be a sanctuary for you but the road twixt Southampton and Ecclestone is a long one. There are still enemies of both the king and the house of Tudor in England and Guy of Guisborough, not to mention the French, have allies there." He smiled, "You still have your warrant and if you survive this journey home then the king will heap more honours upon you."

"I care not for honours. I would have my life back." I could not and did not hide the bitterness in my voice. I agreed with the king that the cardinal and his men had failed.

"A man can never go back. When you first agreed to spy on Perkin Warbeck then your life was changed." He made the sign of the cross and then handed me a crucifix. "This was given to me by Pope Leo. I pray that it will help you."

I placed it about my neck but knew that my sword and rondel would be of more use. Not only was I in danger but my family and friends too. As I walked back to the camp, in the darkening dusk, I found myself looking over my shoulder. It was as I did so that I saw the two yeomen who had been on duty when I had arrived in Tournai. They were following me and showed that the cardinal was watching over me, albeit for a short time. I had not been completely abandoned. As I entered the camp I turned and waved. They saluted me with their halberds. Perhaps the best thing would be for me to simply disappear and make my own way home. I dismissed the idea before I reached the campfire. All that would do would be to ensure I was a dead man and leave my family in the dark about my fate.

Stephen knew something was amiss before I even opened my mouth. I saw it on his face as he had seen it in my eyes. I gave a wan smile, "When we have eaten then we must talk but I need to eat and to think."

John and James were alerted by my tone but Stephen said, "Do not question your father. He will tell us when he is ready." He turned to his lieutenant, Edward, "When we have eaten, Edward, we would have some privacy."

"And that you shall have, captain."

I could see that John and James were desperate to know what had disturbed me so much but I had to think. Growler would want revenge and, I suspected, so would the French. While we were in France then we were in danger. The cardinal was right, the company of billmen, especially once they knew of the danger to me, would be good protection but would it be enough? It also meant that instead of heading directly for Ecclestone we would need to travel at least part of the way in England with the billmen. Once, however, we were alone then the three of us would be in danger. Speed would be the only answer and yet marching with billmen would slow us down.

Once we had eaten, I was no further forward in my thinking. The three of them looked expectantly at me. I sighed and told them what had happened. I omitted the part about the torture but all else was revealed.

James was bemused, "They are escaped prisoners and there are but two of them. What can they do?" He had come to know the billmen quite well and he waved a hand at their fires. "With eighty brave men, what have we to fear from two men."

I shook my head, "They are part of a hidden warband, James. The Frenchmen who sent them have many others at their beck and call. They might not be as concerned about vengeance as the two prisoners but you can be sure that they would wish to send a message to Cardinal Wolsey and the king that the men are still alive and there is still the threat of assassination. It is bad enough that I am left to look over my shoulder but quite another to have the king under the same threat."

Stephen had listened to all and he said, "Until we reach England, we are in danger." I was about to speak when he held up his hand, "Sorry, until we are north of London we are in danger. There may be agents in London and the southeast but the further north you go the safer you will be. My men and I will be with you until we reach Cambridge and by then you should be safe. You can buy good horses in Cambridge, I know a seller of horses who lives close by and then you can outrun them."

I said nothing for a moment and the three of them smiled as though Stephen had come up with a solution. "And so I draw my enemies to Ecclestone? Our three lives would be saved to put many more at risk." I shook my head, "However, I can think of no other solution. Perhaps the best thing would be if we were to invite an attack while we are protected by billmen."

"Perhaps," Stephen's eyes flicked to John and James, "And yet that would put others in danger too." He was right and I dismissed that idea straight away.

The next day was our last day and Stephen told his leaders of the possible attacks. They were angry. He did not mention the assassination attempt for the king and the cardinal insisted that none spoke of it. Instead, he spoke of vengeance against my person. What I did do was to seek three mail vests that we could wear beneath our tunics and our cloaks. They were easy enough to acquire as many such items had been taken when the siege had ended. Mail vests were seen as old-fashioned but I knew that they could turn a blade and we were more at risk from a knife in the back than a frontal attack. We also furnished the two youths with two extra blades to hide in their boots. When we left Tournai, I wished I had never come. No one from the king or the cardinal came to see us off. It was as though they had washed their hands of us. Perhaps they had. The generous side of me thought that they were making us safer.

We did not ride the horses but walked them. There was a good reason for that. Riding the horses made us stand out. Walking them gave us more anonymity and besides, we were moving at the pace of marching billmen. It took a few days to cross Flanders to Calais but it seemed to take much longer. The whole company was nervous. Each time I saw someone with a disfigured face my hand went to my sword. They were all false alarms and that was no good. It was more tiring than walking.

When we reached Calais and saw the masts of our ship I almost wept with relief. Stephen had been right. We were in more danger when in Flanders or France than in England but until we knew for certain that our two hunters were dead then we could not rest easy. As I boarded the ship, I looked towards Calais town. I had planned on introducing my son to Jean le Casserole. That could not now happen, not least because I did not want to draw any hunters to him.

Chapter 18

England 1513

This time the ship was rammed for we were not the only
company sailing back. There were other companies of
billmen. There were even some men at arms although their
horses were placed aboard a more suitable ship than a
warship. The '*Maryanne*' had no cabins but was able to
accommodate the ten horses that needed to be taken back to
England. I did not envy the squires who would accompany
them for the black skies out to the west did not bode well. I
was lucky for we boarded before the men at arms and, being
a knight, Captain Jem gave the three of us the tiny cabin in
the bow castle that we had shared on our way south. Stephen
joined us although we would only have one night to share
the constricting cabin. We stayed on deck while the ship was
loaded, despite the chilling wind. It was to look for pursuit.
Growler and any who wished to do us harm might well have
followed us or even have been waiting for our arrival.
Although only I would recognise either man, the others
would be able to look for suspicious behaviour or any men
showing unusual interest in us. We were chilled to the bone
by the time the warship was loaded and we were cast off to
head into the stormy waters of the English Channel. We had
seen no one but that gave me no comfort. They could have
been ahead of us and waiting in Southampton. It was only
when the ship turned into the choppy seas that we left our
viewpoint. We stayed on deck as long as we could but it was
clear that we were heading into a storm. Neither the captain
nor the sailors seemed put out by the prospect of a storm but
we were shepherded below decks. In our case, we would
enjoy a little light through the slats on the door but the bulk
of the men, billmen and men at arms included, would be
below decks where with the gun ports closed it would be a
Stygian darkness. Once we began to roll it would become a
foetid hole filled with the sounds and smells of retching.

While there was still a little light and with the door open,
we slung our hammocks and climbed in. I had done this

more frequently than the others and I closed the door and then hopped into the canvas. Our hammocks all touched and as we began to roll so we all swung and like babies in a cradle, we were rocked to sleep. Surprisingly, the sounds of the storm did not keep us awake. I had thought they would. In my case, I slept quickly and well because the first part of our journey had been successful and there had been no sign of pursuit. Once in England then we would have a better chance of spotting Growler and the Frenchman.

I woke in the early hours while it was still dark. I needed to rise to make water and I slipped out of the hammock. The deck was still tossing and I knew that was because of the bow and stern castle which accentuated the motion. The *'Maryanne'* had no fighting platforms and would be an easier ride. Barefooted I opened the door. It was black night but seemed lighter outside than within. The ship was tossing alarmingly. I went to the lee side and hung on to a sheet while I made water over the side. I had to use both hands to cling on when a rogue wave spilt over me and we rolled more alarmingly, I became soaked. As I turned to make my way back, I met a grinning sailor who smiled, "With a storm like this, my lord, you are as well peeing just outside the cabin and not risking being swept overboard. Below decks will stink of vomit and puke for days after this little lot."

I nodded for he was right. The sea was washing the decks clear. "Is the storm worsening?"

He shook his head. He had to shout because of the sounds of the storm, the waves and the cracking canvas, "No, but the captain has been forced to sail south so that we use the wind to have a safer journey to Southampton. It will add half a day to the voyage but it will be both safer and more comfortable when we turn."

I entered the cabin and stripped naked for I did not wish to lie in my hammock in clothes that were soaking wet. I found myself shivering and when I climbed back into the hammock, I wrapped my blanket tightly about me. I was soon asleep.

When the first rays of daylight flickered through the slats in the door, the motion was marginally easier and was less of a side-to-side movement. We must have turned, as the sailor had said, and we were heading north. I looked over and saw that the others were awake. I jumped from the hammock and James laughed, "Where are your clothes, father?"

"When you have seen forty summers then your bladder will necessitate a night visit. A wave decided to douse me."

I found dry clothes in my bag and donned them. I took the wet ones and went outside. The rain had ceased but the wind still blew strongly. I tied my wet clothes to a rope that held the bowsprit in place. The wind would dry them. As I turned, I saw billmen and men at arms lining the sides of the ship. The motion was easier and the fresh air would have been better than the hell below. I was ready for food. We had bought some in Calais and we sat on the steps that led up to the fighting platform of the bow castle to eat it. With the wind from the south, we had a little protection afforded by the sterncastle and the mast but we still enjoyed a fresh breeze in our faces. The spray acted like a damp face cloth. The bread we ate was damp but still relatively fresh and the ham and the cheese made up for it. We had bought a skin of wine and another of ale. The ale refreshed but the wine seemed to warm us. We enjoyed both.

The repast over, Stephen said, "I will go and see how my men fared." He headed to the ladder which led to the hold.

"Is that it, Sir James, are we safe?"

I shook my head, "Until the men who seek us are slain, no, John."

"But we have left France, father, and no one followed. How will they know where we are going?"

"The feast. I was the centre of interest and men wondered who was seated so close to the king. They will know that it was Sir James of Ecclestone. True, our home is many miles to the north but I am identified." My son's face fell. "I did not wish to bring this upon us but we are just pieces on a board that great men move around. I can think of many turns that might have been taken that would have resulted in a peaceful journey home but my past has caught up with me and for that, James and John I am sorry."

John smiled, "Sir James, it is who you are. I would not be here had you not given me hope and a new life after my father was slain. Had you not been at the battle of Flodden then who knows what the outcome might have been. You cannot change who you are or what you did and you are right, your life is not your own. Others, men like the cardinal, determine its direction. A man just has to live his life as best he can and trust to God. You are a good man, Sir James, and I cannot see you being abandoned by God."

"You are wise for one so young, John." His words gave me some comfort but, by all accounts, his father had been a good man and yet had suffered an inglorious death at the hands of robbers. God did not always save those that deserved to be saved.

When Stephen came back, he looked a little green about the gills, "I am glad that I know a knight and was accorded a cabin for below decks makes a man's stomach turn. My men will risk the sea and the storm rather than return below. It will not be a glorious march home for none of my men will be able to enjoy clean breeks and tabards. Our company shall stink our way north."

It was night by the time we docked in Southampton and clearly too late for men who were weary from vomiting and had not eaten, to march north. Before we left the ship the four of us scanned the people at the quay but none seemed to pose a threat and I saw neither the Growler nor the Frenchman. It was a reprieve and no more than that. I suppose I could have used the royal warrant to find horses for us but I wanted the company of the billmen for as long as I could. The constable accommodated us in the inner bailey of the castle. We were fed and men made shelters from cloaks. After being below decks the fresh air was seen as preferable. I was invited to dine with the constable for he wished to hear my account of Flodden but I declined. In my heart, I was still a billman and I wanted the anonymity of the company of billmen. Growler would recognise me but any of his supporters would only know who I was if someone used my name. I intended to hide with the billmen. My spurs were in my bag and I wore my plain cloak.

It would take two days for our band of warriors to get
north of the Thames and I believed that would be the most
dangerous time. Unlike the others, I feared that the fugitives
would have fled to England and arrived long before we did.
Dunkerque was close to Tournai and there would be
sympathisers there. A small ship could have landed them
along the Thames almost a week earlier and they could be
ahead of us. The southeast of England was a hotbed of
discontent and if there was a network of spies intent on
making mischief for King Henry then that is where they
would be found in greater numbers than anywhere else. The
inns of Southwick teemed with men who harboured
murderous intent and assassins could be hired for a couple of
crowns. We marched north warily. I think Stephen and his
company would have crossed the Thames at London Bridge
had we not been with them. As it was they showed loyalty to
me by heading for a crossing to the west of London, at
Brentford. It would be once we had crossed the river that our
paths would split.

It was one of Stephen's men who suggested that we use
the better road north to St Albans and part there. While it
added length to their journey it would be as quick and we
could all have one last night together in St Albans before we
headed northwest and they went to the northeast. I was
grateful for the billmen were good company and their eyes
watched where we three might not. Before we sought
accommodation, we bought three horses. Stephen did not
know the horse trader but he seemed to me an honest fellow
and with winter approaching he would be saved the price of
winter fodder. When we had left Southampton Stephen and I
had bought six sumpters to carry our war gear. Stephen took
five and we now had the sixth. I used some of the money
given to me at Newcastle to pay for food and shelter for the
billmen. It was the least I could do and the purse from King
Henry was still, as yet, untouched. I now realised that money
in itself was of no importance, it was how you used it that
mattered and I enjoyed spending it on billmen.

While the billmen enjoyed the ale and the food, the four
of us were involved in a more serious discussion. The further

from London we travelled, the safer we were for there were many routes which we could take.

"The shortest one is the one through Northampton and thence towards Cheshire."

I shook my head, "And that, Stephen, is the route a pursuer would expect us to take. Eventually, we will have to head through Cheshire for the closer we are to home the fewer alternatives are available. If we head north through Leicester and Derby we can then head northwest. Eventually, we will join up with the road that leads to Warrington and the crossing of the Mersey but by then I hope to have muddied our trail."

The others beamed at my plan which only added twenty miles or so to our journey and having marched from Southampton the prospect of riding was appealing. I was the spy, however, and there was a nagging doubt in my mind. I remembered that when Growler and the others had taken me, in Paris, I had not been expecting it. It had taken both me and Jean le Casserole by surprise. What had I not seen this time? I knew that there was something I was missing but I knew not what. There was little point in mentioning my fears to the other three for they had no experience of being threatened in this manner, I did.

"Tell Sam that I hoped to visit with him, but I will not be a harbinger of death and bring danger to Hedingham."

"He will understand, Sir James, but my wife as well as Sam will be sad to have missed the opportunity to speak with you."

"There will come a time when the land is at peace and I can visit."

The next morning it was a moving parting. Stephen had come to know John and James well. His own son was but a toddler and I think he saw his future. I could take little credit for John and James had largely been brought up by Jane but I was proud of my son. He had reacted well to every adversity and dealt with it in good humour. The billmen too had grown fond of the two youths who had kept their spirits up on the road. As for Stephen and me, we did not know when or if we would ever see each other again. I would have liked to have seen both Sam's and Stephen's families. I had lived in Hedingham and had friends there. As it was, I did not wish to put their lives in jeopardy.

We bade farewell and John led the sumpter. We waved until our friends disappeared from sight. It was as though a door to a sanctuary had slammed shut and I viewed the road ahead with trepidation and fear. The three of us were now alone. The horses I had bought were good hackneys. Although they were nowhere near as expensive as warhorses, they were not cheap but I viewed them as an investment. James was growing and now that I was a knight there would be times he would need to ride and a good horse was essential. My father-in-law could also use one. My life had changed once the Earl of Surrey touched my shoulders with his sword. Lord Monteagle, Sir Edward Stanley, was quite right, with the privileges came the responsibility.

The two boys were quieter than they had been before and I took that as a good sign that they were being vigilant. Every clip-clop behind us had our hands on our swords and until we saw the faces of those heading towards us, we feared an attack. We reached Leicester and I chose an inn close to the castle. We dined in a small dining room and I gave my name as Stephen of Hedingham in case we were noticed. My spurs were in my bags and John had learned not to call me my lord. No one took any interest in us and that pleased me.

We made Derby in one day and my decision to buy good horses was vindicated. The sumpter was suffering but not the hackneys. I asked the ostler to give all four animals extra feed. It was worth the handful of coins he was paid. As we ate, in another small dining room, we discussed our route. I needed the two of them to know my thinking. "We will head to Macclesfield tomorrow. It is only twenty-four miles from the river crossing at Warrington. If there was any other way across the Mersey, I would take it but Warrington is not far from our home. I am unfamiliar with the road from Macclesfield but then again our pursuers will be even less comfortable so far from home."

"Surely, father, they will have given up by now."

I shrugged, "I do not know. I would have given up in Tournai but then I am unlike the Growler and the others. They live in a world of intrigue. The opportunities to make a fortune are great but the dangers are equally high. They live for themselves and not for family. I do not understand them. Family has always been important to me. Even when I fell out with my father, I still valued my family. So, James, to answer your question I have to say I do not know but we must believe that they are out there somewhere and we must muddy our trail as much as we can."

Silence descended until John said, ominously, "Of course, my lord, they could guarantee to find us."

James said, "How?

"If they have identified your father then they know where our home is. They could be ahead of us already and waiting close to Ecclestone."

James looked shocked but I nodded my agreement, "John is quite right, my son. Snakes like these men can always find a rock to hide beneath. We will need to be vigilant even when we reach our home."

The road from Macclesfield was the worst of our journey. By that I mean that the surface of the road on which we travelled was rough stone covered with clay and gravel but worse than that, it was filled with places where we could be ambushed. Perhaps I was becoming overly nervous for I stopped at every place where we could be ambushed: blind rises, small woods, large buildings that looked to be unoccupied and sharp turns. It all added to the time it took. There was another thing, I was convinced that we were being followed. I saw nothing when I turned but my time as a spy had given me a sixth sense. I knew, even though my eyes told me differently, that we were being followed. As we were going so slowly the sense was even more acute for if it was innocent then whoever was following would catch us up. When we stopped to water our horses at Great Budworth I studied the road carefully, but the only travellers behind us were a couple of local merchants who had been to Macclesfield and were returning to their homes. It told me that we had taken far longer for the short journey. We could have been over the river by now had I not been so cautious.

It was getting on for dark when we descended from Walton Heath and I decided we could go faster for the river was not far ahead. We dug our heels in to make our horses go faster. Darkness was falling as the days were getting much shorter. In the distance, I could spy the smoke spiralling in the western sky. The river and Warrington were palpably close. The road made a slight turn around an overhanging beech tree and I was slightly unsighted for a moment. As I looked ahead, I saw six men in the centre of the road. They were an immovable obstacle. I recognised the two in the centre. It was the Growler and the Frenchman. Although their faces had healed and gloves covered their damaged hands I could still detect bruising on their faces. The other four, however, were unharmed and they, like the two escaped prisoners, held swords. We were doomed but it was not in my nature to simply surrender without a fight and I was working out a plan even as Growler spoke.

"You thought you had escaped justice, you treacherous spy. You have not. My friend and I knew where you would go and we have waited close by for a week. This is your only way home. Now you shall die and do so painfully. Sir Richard de la Pole, Sir John Bardolph and the others who died because of your betrayal and treachery shall be avenged."

My hand was on my sword. I hoped that James and John would remember the bandits who had attacked us close to Calais. This would be harder for these were not brigands, these were killers. "Let the boys go. You have me." I was ready for action and I was looking for an opportunity to strike.

Growler laughed, "Let them go? They shall be the first to die and they will do so painfully with you watching." I glanced over my shoulder and he laughed, "Do not think to flee. Ned!" Two men appeared on horses behind us. They must have been the men who had been following and suddenly everything became clear. When we had stopped so had they. When the merchants had come up the road they had hidden. I even knew where they had begun to follow us, Macclesfield. They were not trying to catch us but were there to stop us from escaping.

I decided to lull him by speaking, "I will not die easily you know, I…" I dug my heels in and my horse leapt forward. I was counting on the fact that he would wait to hear my words and in those moments of hesitation I had drawn my sword and reached him. His damaged hand tried to wheel his horse out of the way but it was plainly still hurting and he failed. I whipped my sword across the side of his head, knocking him into the Frenchman. "Ride! Ride!" My animal was not a warhorse but I was a warrior and I drew my dagger and rode at the man to my left. The falling Growler had made a gap and I prayed that James and John would use the gap. One of the horses clipped Growler's head and he lay still. The Frenchman with the damaged hand would also have the same difficulties as Growler. The man to my left brought down his sword but as I blocked it with my rondel dagger, I lunged at his middle. His sword almost beat down my left hand but he did not see my sword coming in the half-light and the blade slid in. I was aware of John and James spurring their horses and slashing wildly at the Frenchman. They had a chance. I had none for I heard the hooves of the two men coming from behind and I would not be able to take the last man on my left so easily. He turned his horse to block my escape and then drew, not a rondel dagger but a longer blade. He had two swords to my one. He grinned at me.

"We have been paid already, spy and we will do that for which we were paid. You are King Henry's man and we shall send your head to him so that he knows the price you have paid." He dug his heels in and stabbed at me. My rondel dagger could not stop it but it slowed it enough so that when it struck me the mail vest I wore stopped it from penetrating. It was then, as he thought he had me, that John and James appeared behind him. He looked around in shock as James slashed at his arm with his sword while John lunged with his. It was brave but foolish. We had slain two and wounded a third but there were still four others and John and James could not use surprise a second time.

"Ride, you fools, or my sacrifice will be in vain!"

I whirled my horse to face the other four men. If I was to die then I would take as many of them as I could. Just then I heard, from the Macclesfield Road, the sound of thundering hooves. Even as I fended off one sword and blocked a second with my dagger, I saw eight riders appear. They wore no livery and that meant they were probably enemies. Even if John and James fled, they would be caught. All three of us would die before we could reach the bridge to safety. When our attackers turned to look at the new threat I wondered at this strange turn of events. The eight riders surrounded the men and had swords at their throats before they even knew what was happening. The dead men, their horses and we three blocked their escape to the river and the eight men their route back to Macclesfield.

The leader looked vaguely familiar but as he had a helmet and cloak I could not be sure. "Thank you, Sir James. The cardinal hoped that this would be the outcome although you led us on a merry chase through England." Darkness had almost fallen and in the darkening gloom I could barely make out the man's features but I recognised his voice.

"Do I know you, sir?"

He nodded, "I stood behind you at the king's feast. I am Geoffrey Nym and I was one of John Webster's men. We all served the captain. These bastards slew him. Now we will take them and this time their interrogation will be even more painful. John was a good man and a great captain. Now we have some traitors to question about those others who skulk in England and the bodies of two that can be identified. We will interrogate them and seek their confederates. Thanks to you we will have rid England of those enemies who hide and we will have vengeance for John Webster."

He nodded and one of each pair of men dismounted and disarmed the four men. Their weapons were taken and their purses too. Their hands were bound behind their backs. They then lofted the wounded and unconscious Growler and bound him on his horse. With those four secured the four men went to the bodies. They took the purses from the dead men and tossed them to me. "Do you want their weapons, my lord?"

I shook my head. They slung the bodies over the backs of their horses and tied the reins to three of the other horses. Geoffrey Nym pointed to the north, "The bridge lies yonder. We will take shelter at Grappenhall. It is a mile or two away."

"You knew that they would come this way?"

He nodded, "Cardinal Wolsey told us that you were clever and resourceful however the enemy knew your name and where you lived. This is the shortest way home and all that they needed to do was to wait for you. Once we reached Macclesfield I knew where you would be crossing and I sent two men to guard the bridge and take any watchers. When we spied those two who followed you from Macclesfield we pressed closer than we had before. My two men wait at the bridge and another is at Grappenhall. It belongs to one of the cardinal's kin. When you see our two men tell them it is over. They will know where to find us."

With that, they led the men away. The Frenchman was glaring at me but I had no sympathy for him. Had I failed when I had been a spy then my end would be much the same as his. They would use torture to extract all the information he and Growler had and then execute them both. Their bodies and those of their confederates would never be found and the first that his associates would know of their end would be when the cardinal's men came for them. We had been used as bait. Although I did not like it, I knew that the lives of a poor knight and two boys were as nothing to a cardinal and a king who wished to hang on to power. I knew that we had been disposable. The coins that jingled in the purses I had in my saddlebags were well-earned.

We sheathed our swords and I said, "That was bravely done, boys, but unnecessary. I wanted you free and not lying dead on the road. Had the cardinal's men not found us then that would have been your fate.

"Sir James, how could we ride away and let you die?"

"Because I commanded it. When I command you obey." I knew, from their faces, that I had not convinced them.

As we neared the bridge two figures ghosted from the side. They were mounted and while they had no swords in their hands, I saw that their cloaks were pulled back to facilitate their drawing.

"I am Sir James of Ecclestone and Geoffrey Nym has the men you seek in his custody."

They grinned, "Thank you, my lord. This night we sleep in a bed and eat hot food. We are grateful to you." They dug in their heels and galloped off.

We clattered over the bridge, the lights from the houses on the northern bank a welcoming sight. I turned to the two boys and said, "We will not stay here this night. It is but ten miles from our home and our family. I would rather sleep in my own bed this night and for this part of our journey we know the way."

"Aye, father. That sounds like a good idea to me for I have much to tell Walter. He will be green with envy."

John nodded, "And Ralf will be pleased that we were able to put the skills he taught us to good use."

The last ten miles were in darkness but were lit by our laughter and the relief of having lives intact that had so nearly ended.

Epilogue

The gates were barred when we reached my hall and I smiled. Ralf was watching over my family. He could not have known about Growler but he had taken his responsibilities seriously and maintained a good watch. We dismounted and I banged on the door. I saw a light behind the door and one of my men grumbled, "Who, in the name of Beelzebub comes a-nocking at this ungodly hour? All decent folks are abed."

I laughed for I recognised the voice of old Joe, Joseph, who had been one of my father's friends. Fallen on hard times I had given him the job of gateman, "It is Captain James, Joe, and like you, we wish to be abed too."

"Sorry, sir!" I heard the bar being lifted and Joe bowed and scraped, "Sorry, sir. I did not know it was you."

I patted him on the back, "Fear not, Joe, I am not angry. We are just pleased to be back home. All is well?"

He nodded, "All is well. Captain Ralf did as he has done each night since he returned from Scotland. He waited until the watch was set before he left and we barred the gate."

"Good, then come with us while we stable these horses and you can return to your cell."

With four of us working it did not take long to tend to the horses. The stable was filled with the extra horses and I knew that I would need to build an even bigger one. We hoisted our bags and then headed for the hall. Joe had a key and he unlocked the door. There would be another hung inside to lock it behind us. Security was important to us and the last part of our journey had shown me that we could never relax that vigilance. The house was silent and I whispered, "Go to your chambers. We will not disturb the house. We are home and I am happy."

James nodded and, in the darkness, looked much older than he had when we had left. "And we will thank you now, father. You offered to give your life for us twice and we shall never forget that."

I nodded and headed up the stairs, hoping that they would not creak. I saw a light from our bedroom and wondered if I had disturbed Jane. I eased the door open and saw that there was a lit candle but my wife was not alone in our bed. There, lying asleep across her breast was a baby. Jane was also asleep. All of our adventures had driven it from my mind. Jane had told me that she was with child last Christmas and it was now the middle of October. The year had flown by.

I laid down my bag and undressed as quietly as I could. I knew that I stank of horse and of sweat but washing would disturb them and I would have to stink. I slipped into the warm bed and it was as my leg touched Jane's that she started. She turned, her eyes wide with fear and then when she saw it was me the fear turned to joy. "James, you are home," she whispered.

I kissed her, "Aye, and you have a fine homecoming present for me."

She nodded, "You were not here and we wished him christened for he was ill when he was born. We named him Roger, after my father. You do not mind, do you?"

"Mind? Of course not. He looks well now."

She smiled and laid him in the cot next to her side of the bed, "He is but he came early and was thin. Once he began to eat, he was transformed. I think he was eager to see you. He was born when you fought in Scotland."

I touched the cross the cardinal had given me. I would always remember that month-long campaign, "Then it will be easy to remember that the birth came when England and his father were fighting for their lives."

I lifted my arm and she snuggled beneath it. "And you are now home?"

"I am home."

"Good and I pray that this time it will be for good." She kissed me and then wrinkled her nose, "You stink of horses."

"I can wash if you wish."

I made to leave and she pulled me back, "I will endure it...Sir James."

I laughed, "It will take some time to become accustomed to the title, Lady Jane."

"You should see my mother. She thinks the title is hers. She insists on visitors calling her Lady Mary. She is humoured for it is good to see her smile once more. The raid by the Scots hurt her more than we knew." She suddenly sat up, "James? John? They are well? You have not mentioned them."

"They are well and I am sorry I did not speak of them. James has grown. He is almost a man now."

"But he is so young still."

"A man is not measured by the years he has lived on this earth but by his actions." I almost blurted out that he had killed a man but knew that this was not the time. Daylight would be needed and the presence of my son.

"You saw the king?"

"I dined with him and the cardinal." I held up the crucifix, "The cardinal gave me this. It was a gift from the pope and the king gave me a purse. The time I was away was well rewarded. We have more coins and I can pay for the hall at Clifton to be rebuilt."

She laughed, "My father is comfortable here. He often walks to the inn to drink with the old codgers, your father's friends and plays nine men's morris. He did it at first to get away from my mother but now he likes the ritual. He loves the grandchildren and knows that his estate is well-managed. Now that he has a grandson named after him then it will be hard to prise him from within these walls."

"And I have no need of that. The more who live within the walls of my hall the merrier." A thought struck me, "Elizabeth?"

"She is not ready yet but it will not be long. They have chosen names already. James if it is a boy and Betty if it is a girl for that is her mother's name."

I laughed, "At least when I am old and folk shout my name, I can plead ignorance and pretend it is a younger James that they seek."

"You will never grow old." She looked up at me, "Are your days of war over?"

I could not lie to my wife, "If I have any choice in the matter then, aye, I can hang up my billhook and sword. They can be there for baby Roger to admire when he is older but England is not yet at peace." I was thinking of the nest of conspirators we had unearthed. Until the king had a male heir then he was not secure. I would be needed to fight again but not yet, and not this year. We would celebrate Christmas and enjoy the short days of the winter months safe and secure within the walls of Ecclestone Hall. It was now the home of a knight. Jane and her mother would add to it so that it looked like one. I looked up at the ceiling as my wife drifted into sleep. "Mother, father, I hope that you are proud of me. The prodigal son is now a knight."

The End

Glossary

Broom – a yellow flowering and tall shrug

Carole - a song sung at Christmas and normally accompanied by a dance or a procession

Carter's Bread – dark brown or black bread eaten by the poorest people

Claidheamh-mòr – Claymore: a long sword that required two hands to wield

Cockpit - the place where cockfighting took place

Costrel - A wooden beaker with a hook to hang from a belt; used on a campaign to drink

Falchion - a short sword with a curved end. A single-edged weapon

Fauld - plate armour protecting the lower body

Gardyvyan - a sheet containing all the equipment that an archer needed

Gong scourer - a man hired to empty human dung and dispose of it.

Goose/geese - slang for whores

Goose bite - a euphemism for Venereal Disease

Hackney - a good riding horse, superior to a rouncy

Hogbog – a small enclosure close to the house for pigs and fowl, mainly chickens.

Jack – called a jakke as well, a padded vest sometimes made of leather and strengthened by metal. Often called a brigandine

Manchet – the best bread made with wheat flour and a little added bran

Marchpane- marzipan

Mesne- an old-fashioned word for the men who serve a knight

Nice- trivial (the original meaning as used by Shakespeare)

Raveled or yeoman's bread – coarse bread made with wholemeal flour with bran

Reivers - men on both sides of the Anglo-Scottish border who raid

Rondel dagger - the most common type of dagger with a short crosspiece and two blades

Rouncy - a good riding horse
Sallet - the most popular type of helmet at the time having a
flared back to protect the neck.
Terces - the third hour of the day
Twesilhaugh - Twizell Castle in Northumberland

Canonical Hours

Matins (nighttime)
Lauds (early morning)
Prime (first hour of daylight)
Terce (third hour)
Sext (noon)
Nones (ninth hour)
Vespers (sunset evening)
Compline (end of the day)

Historical Background

I have made up all the incidents involving James of Ecclestone.

This whole series evolved from a visit I made to Flodden with two of my grandsons. I have been to Waterloo and Gettysburg as well as Hastings but Flodden is the only battlefield I have visited where you can really see how the battle was almost won and then lost by the Scottish king. It is a very atmospheric place and well worth a visit.

I made up the kidnapping of James' in-laws but there were many provocative acts at that time. King James wanted a war. He had never won a major battle and he wished to go down in history as one who had reclaimed Northumberland for Scotland. His army was huge and it marked the first appearance of the gun now at Edinburgh, called Mons Meg. The Ill Raid really did happen and the numbers were accurate. Seven thousand Scots raided the Wooler plain and Sir William of Brancepath took border horsemen and two hundred mounted longbowmen. With the local levy, the eight hundred men ambushed the Scots and drove them home empty handed. The loss of Lord Home's banner was particularly embarrassing. Sir John, Bastard, of Ford was a real character and I have not made up his name or his actions. He was the real Border Reiver.

I have tried to be as accurate as I could about the battle and I hope the maps help. It was a battle won by two families: the Howards and the Stanleys. The Scottish army had an impregnable position and the earl knew that he would lose if he assaulted Flodden Edge. The long march around Watch Law could have ended in disaster but King James had fixed himself to the ridge and was reluctant to leave it. The English column was so long that Sir Edward, with the Stanley contingent, almost failed to make it, having become lost along the way. The actual battle started in the middle of the afternoon and ended in darkness.

Thanks to the drier ground on the Scottish left, Lord Home and Lord Huntley initially had great success and drove the men led by Sir Edmund Howard from the field.

The earl's son did not leave the field until the Bastard Ford rescued him. Baron Dacre and his horsemen, ably backed by the men of Whitby held the flank and Lord Home refused to attack any more telling the king that he had done his part. It was a crucial moment in this most important of Scottish losses. The lighter English ordinance was better managed and more accurate. The Scottish artillery was defeated before it could do any harm.

I am not sure if the attempt to make the Scots fight in the Swiss style contributed to their defeat but it cannot have helped. The pikemen had a very short time to become accustomed to the new tactics. Allied to the incredibly boggy ground at Flodden it destroyed their cohesion. Once disordered then the billhook came into its own. The English longbows compounded the defeat. While those in the front were plated and immune from an arrow attack, the ones at the rear were not. It was a bloody battle. Few shields were used and many men were simply battered to death. King James died almost unseen although the archer who sent an arrow into his jaw and the billman who half severed his hand must have known. Perhaps, in the real battle, they died. King James' body, naked and stripped of all signs of kingship, was found the next day. The Scots died bravely but in great numbers. According to most sources between 10,000 and 12,000 Scotsmen died at Flodden. Those dead included the king, a bishop, an archbishop and two abbots as well as the Dean of Glasgow. 21 earls died, 14 out of 29 lords of Parliament and 300 lesser gentry. The Pringle family died leaving the infant son to become the new lord. Sir John Maxwell died but not his son. The English admitted to 400 dead which is clearly too small a number and many historians put the figure closer to 1500. Whatever the figures, it was a great victory to rank alongside Falkirk, Neville's Cross and the Battle of the Standards.

The king had just won the siege of Tournai when he heard the news but the story of the Growler is pure fiction. I tell stories and I hope you liked this one.

One interesting element I could not put in was the death of Sir Marmaduke Constable who died in 1518. His death had nothing to do with the battle but is an interesting one. He was drinking a beaker of water when he swallowed a frog and choked. As one of the dog walking wags on the field said when I told him, "He croaked". I am not sure if this was the origin of having a frog in the throat but it amused me.

Books used in the research
- Tudors- Terry Breverton
- Tudor - Leanda de Lisle
- The Tower of London - A L Rowse
- British Kings and Queens - Mike Ashley
- Northumbria at War - Derek Dodds
- Flodden 1513 - Sadler and Walsh
- The Strongholds of the Border Reivers - Durham and Turner
- Scottish Renaissance Armies 1513-1550 - Cooper and Turner
- Henry VIIIth's army - Cornish and McBride

Griff Hosker January 2023

Other books by Griff Hosker

If you enjoyed reading this book, then why not read
another one by the author?

Ancient History

The Sword of Cartimandua Series
(Germania and Britannia 50 A.D. – 128 A.D.)
Ulpius Felix- Roman Warrior (prequel)
The Sword of Cartimandua
The Horse Warriors
Invasion Caledonia
Roman Retreat
Revolt of the Red Witch
Druid's Gold
Trajan's Hunters
The Last Frontier
Hero of Rome
Roman Hawk
Roman Treachery
Roman Wall
Roman Courage

The Wolf Warrior series
(Britain in the late 6th Century)
Saxon Dawn
Saxon Revenge
Saxon England
Saxon Blood
Saxon Slayer
Saxon Slaughter
Saxon Bane
Saxon Fall: Rise of the Warlord
Saxon Throne
Saxon Sword

Medieval History

The Dragon Heart Series
Viking Slave
Viking Warrior
Viking Jarl
Viking Kingdom
Viking Wolf
Viking War
Viking Sword
Viking Wrath
Viking Raid
Viking Legend
Viking Vengeance
Viking Dragon
Viking Treasure
Viking Enemy
Viking Witch
Viking Blood
Viking Weregeld
Viking Storm
Viking Warband
Viking Shadow
Viking Legacy
Viking Clan
Viking Bravery

The Norman Genesis Series
Hrolf the Viking
Horseman
The Battle for a Home
Revenge of the Franks
The Land of the Northmen
Ragnvald Hrolfsson
Brothers in Blood
Lord of Rouen
Drekar in the Seine
Duke of Normandy
The Duke and the King

Flodden

Danelaw
(England and Denmark in the 11ᵗʰ Century)
Dragon Sword
Oathsword
Bloodsword
Danish Sword

New World Series
Blood on the Blade
Across the Seas
The Savage Wilderness
The Bear and the Wolf
Erik The Navigator
Erik's Clan

The Vengeance Trail

The Reconquista Chronicles
Castilian Knight
El Campeador
The Lord of Valencia

The Aelfraed Series
(Britain and Byzantium 1050 A.D. - 1085 A.D.)
Housecarl
Outlaw
Varangian

**The Anarchy Series England
1120-1180**
English Knight
Knight of the Empress
Northern Knight
Baron of the North
Earl
King Henry's Champion
The King is Dead
Warlord of the North

Enemy at the Gate
The Fallen Crown
Warlord's War
Kingmaker
Henry II
Crusader
The Welsh Marches
Irish War
Poisonous Plots
The Princes' Revolt
Earl Marshal
The Perfect Knight

**Border Knight
1182-1300**
Sword for Hire
Return of the Knight
Baron's War
Magna Carta
Welsh Wars
Henry III
The Bloody Border
Baron's Crusade
Sentinel of the North
War in the West
Debt of Honour
The Blood of the Warlord
The Fettered King

**Sir John Hawkwood Series
France and Italy 1339- 1387**
Crécy: The Age of the Archer
Man At Arms
The White Company
Leader of Men
Tuscan Warlord

Lord Edward's Archer
Lord Edward's Archer

Flodden

King in Waiting
An Archer's Crusade
Targets of Treachery
The Great Cause

**Struggle for a Crown
1360- 1485**
Blood on the Crown
To Murder a King
The Throne
King Henry IV
The Road to Agincourt
St Crispin's Day
The Battle for France
The Last Knight
Queen's Knight

Tales from the Sword I
(Short stories from the Medieval period)

**Tudor Warrior series
England and Scotland in the late 14th and early 15th
century**
Tudor Warrior
Tudor Spy
Flodden

**Conquistador
England and America in the 16th Century**
Conquistador
The English Adventurer

Modern History

The Napoleonic Horseman Series
Chasseur à Cheval
Napoleon's Guard
British Light Dragoon
Soldier Spy

Flodden

1808: The Road to Coruña
Talavera
The Lines of Torres Vedras
Bloody Badajoz
The Road to France
Waterloo

The Lucky Jack American Civil War series
Rebel Raiders
Confederate Rangers
The Road to Gettysburg

Soldier of the Queen series
Soldier of the Queen
Redcoat's Rifle

The British Ace Series
1914
1915 Fokker Scourge
1916 Angels over the Somme
1917 Eagles Fall
1918 We will remember them
From Arctic Snow to Desert Sand
Wings over Persia

Combined Operations series
1940-1945
Commando
Raider
Behind Enemy Lines
Dieppe
Toehold in Europe
Sword Beach
Breakout
The Battle for Antwerp
King Tiger
Beyond the Rhine
Korea
Korean Winter

Tales from the Sword II
(Short stories from the Modern period)

Other Books
Great Granny's Ghost (Aimed at 9-14-year-old young
people)

For more information on all of the books then please visit the
author's website at www.griffhosker.com where there is a
link to contact him or visit his Facebook page: GriffHosker
at Sword Books

Printed in Dunstable, United Kingdom

75340003R00138